ALWAYS MY GIRL

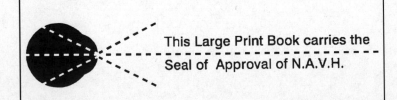

This Large Print Book carries the
Seal of Approval of N.A.V.H.

THE SHAUGHNESSY BROTHERS

Always My Girl

Samantha Chase

THORNDIKE PRESS
A part of Gale, Cengage Learning

GALE
CENGAGE Learning®

Farmington Hills, Mich • San Francisco • New York • Waterville, Maine
Meriden, Conn • Mason, Ohio • Chicago

GALE
CENGAGE Learning·

Copyright © 2016 by Samantha Chase.
The Shaughnessy Brothers.
Thorndike Press, a part of Gale, Cengage Learning.

LIBRARY OF CONGRESS CATALOGING-IN-PUBLICATION DATA

Names: Chase, Samantha, author.
Title: Always my girl / by Samantha Chase.
Description: Large print edition. | Waterville, Maine : Thorndike Press, 2016. |
  Series: Thorndike Press large print romance | Series: The Shaughnessy brothers
Identifiers: LCCN 2016037321| ISBN 9781410492821 (hardcover) | ISBN 1410492826
  (hardcover)
Subjects: LCSH: Large type books. | GSAFD: Love stories.
Classification: LCC PS3603.H37953 A78 2016 | DDC 813/.6—dc23
LC record available at https://lccn.loc.gov/2016037321

Published in 2017 by arrangement with Sourcebooks, Inc.

Printed in Mexico
1 2 3 4 5 6 7 21 20 19 18 17

Always My Girl

PROLOGUE

Twenty-four years ago . . .

Faster. I need to go Faster. The words were a simple chant in six-year-old Quinn Shaughnessy's mind. Whether it was running, swimming, or riding his bike, nothing felt good unless it was done really fast.

"Quinn Darragh Shaughnessy! You slow that bike down right this minute!" Lillian Shaughnessy watched with a hand over her heart as her young son raced down the block in front of their house. Why couldn't the boy simply do anything at a normal pace?

A minute later, Quinn skidded to a halt in front of his mother. He saw the look on her face and had the good sense to look ashamed. "Sorry, Mom," he said quietly.

"What have I told you about riding so fast?" she prodded gently.

Quinn sighed. He hated when she made him repeat the rules to her. "It's not safe and you won't stand for it."

"And?"

He looked up at her, his blue eyes wide and on the verge of filling with tears. This wasn't a new discussion, and he knew he had been warned that if she caught him riding recklessly again, he'd lose his biking privileges. "But . . . it wasn't that fast, Mom. Honest."

Looking down at him, she smiled sadly. "You know the rules, Quinn. You were told to slow it down and you didn't. Now go and put your bike away."

She was about to say more, he noticed, but her focus was on something behind him. Turning around, he saw some people walking toward them from the house next door. They had just moved in and he guessed they were coming over to say hello.

"Hi!" the woman of the family said as she approached Lillian with her hand held out. "I'm Mary Hannigan." They shook hands and then Mary turned to introduce her children. "This is my son, Bobby, and my daughter, Anna."

"It's a pleasure to meet you," Lillian said and then introduced herself. "This is my son Quinn."

"Is he your only one?" Mary asked.

"Oh, heavens no. I have a ten-year-old

son, Aidan, and an eight-year-old, Hugh. Quinn here is six, and then I have four-year-old twin boys — Riley and Owen."

"My! That's quite impressive!" Mary said. "Bobby is eight and Anna is six." She smiled at Quinn. "She's the same age as you!"

Quinn had no idea what the lady was smiling about. What difference did it make that some girl was his age? He looked over at Anna and saw she was staring at him with as much disinterest as he was showing her. Whatever. There was no way he was going to play with a girl anyway. Maybe Bobby would want to play.

"Why don't you come inside?" Lillian asked. "I'll introduce Bobby to the older boys. The twins are napping, but they're going to be up soon and I need to get back inside." She started to take a step away before turning back to her young son. "Why don't you put your bike away, Quinn, and show Anna the jungle gym? I bet she'd like to see it."

And with that, he was stuck alone with Anna. She wasn't really dressed like a girly-girl. Her blond hair was in pigtails and she wore a pair of jeans and a T-shirt. Most girls he knew wore dresses and bows in their hair. What was wrong with her? Without a word, he pushed his bike along the driveway

9

and walked toward the house.

"Where are you going?" she asked.

He sighed loudly. "Didn't you hear my mom? I have to put my bike away."

"Oh," she said. "Where's the jungle gym?"

"In the backyard, dummy. Where else?" Girls were dumb. No boy would ever ask such a stupid question.

"Why can't we ride our bikes? My bike is over in our garage. I saw you riding yours up and down the street. You were going really fast."

Quinn stopped in his tracks. "That's why I can't ride my bike. My mom got mad because she says I was riding too fast. But I wasn't."

"Yes you were," Anna corrected. "Really, really fast."

Yeah, girls were dumb. "Look, do you want to see the jungle gym or not?" he snapped.

"I guess." She quietly followed him up the driveway and watched as he put the bike away in the garage and then as he dragged his feet on the way out. "Are you sad 'cause you can't ride your bike anymore?"

"Well . . . yeah," he said sarcastically. "What's the point in riding a bike if you can't go fast? Now I'm in trouble and I can't ride my bike and my mom will probably stay mad and not let me have any of the cookies she baked today. That's gonna be my punishment."

"What kind of cookies?" Anna asked, her head tilting slightly as she studied him.

"Oatmeal raisin. They're my favorite."

"Oh. We made chocolate chip cookies today. We were going to bring some over but my mom said she wanted to bake a cake for you guys instead."

Quinn's head popped up. "Chocolate chip is my second favorite cookie."

A small smile played across Anna's lips. She looked around as if making sure they were alone before stepping in close and whispering, "We could sneak over to my house and you can have some. You know, since you're going to be punished and not get to have any from your mom."

Maybe girls weren't so dumb. "Really? Won't your mom get mad you went home without her?"

Anna shook her head. "It's only right next door, and we'll be superfast. She won't even know I'm gone. If you want, we can even grab some juice boxes. Then we'll eat out on the jungle gym, okay?"

"But . . ." Why was he arguing this? Free cookies! "Won't she notice some cookies are missing?"

"Nah, she made, like, a hundred of them. We'll just take a couple each."

For a moment, Quinn wasn't so sure it was a good idea. His mom was already mad at him for racing his bike up and down the street. She'd probably be even madder if she caught him sneaking a snack when he wasn't supposed to.

"C'mon," Anna said excitedly. "I'll race you!"

And in that moment, Quinn Shaughnessy decided girls weren't dumb at all. Especially Anna Hannigan.

CHAPTER 1

One look at the massive beach house had Quinn Shaughnessy shaking his head. Why this wedding couldn't just be a normal event — at a hotel — he couldn't understand. It would be easier. It would be more practical.

And it would mean there was a bar on the premises for him to go to and get away from his family for a little while and maybe pick up an attractive woman.

Not that he didn't love his family — he did. But three days with everyone back under one roof was a little more togetherness than he was in the mood for. No matter what the occasion.

Ever since moving out of the family home at eighteen and going to college, Quinn had never looked back. There were the occasional trips home for school breaks, when he was forced to go home and share a room with one of his brothers, but for the most part, he found excuses to stay other places.

He enjoyed his space, his freedom, and he'd never felt the need to make excuses about it.

Being one of six kids in a four-bedroom house growing up had been less than a dream. When he went to college — even though he shared a room there with one other guy — living in the dorm felt different. No one was looking over his shoulder or trying to get him into trouble or trying to tell him what to do.

It was like nirvana.

After graduation, he'd lived on his own while on the race-car circuit. When his career came to an end — sooner than he'd anticipated — Quinn still managed to land on his feet. And with a place of his own . . . rather than having to move back home.

The large house loomed in front of him.

Aidan and Zoe were getting married this weekend, and because Zoe didn't have any family left and Aidan was a private kind of guy, they'd opted for a small, intimate wedding. On the beach. With only the family and a few friends in attendance.

All under one roof.

He cursed under his breath and sighed. It was only one weekend. It was the chant he kept repeating in his brain as he climbed from the car and stretched. Why they had to choose a beach four hours from home when they lived at the beach in North Carolina was beyond him. And to make it worse, they'd chosen a location that wasn't all that far from Hugh's Hilton Head Island resort! They could all have their own rooms at a luxury resort right now, having drinks served to them by the pool instead of . . . this.

"Clearly, being in love makes you an idiot," he muttered and opened the trunk to grab his luggage.

"You've been here less than five minutes and you're already calling people idiots?" a voice said from behind him. Turning, he saw his brother — the groom — walking toward him with a big, sappy grin on his face.

Quinn straightened. "Not people, just you," he teased.

"Aww . . . you say the sweetest things," Aidan teased right back before grabbing Quinn in a bear hug. "Glad you made it."

"Like I had a choice."

Aidan sighed good-naturedly. "This makes Zoe happy. So I'm happy."

"You could have picked a place closer to home. Or Hugh's place."

Aidan shook his head. "The resort was beautiful and everything would have been taken care of, but Zoe and I aren't like that.

15

We wanted a place where —"

"You can be in control?" Quinn interjected with a laugh.

Aidan couldn't help but laugh with him. "Something like that. Either way, the house is great — six bedrooms — and we snagged the place next door for the rest of the guests."

"How many people are coming? I thought it was just us."

"No, we couldn't do that. We do have friends we wanted to have here, you know. Some of them had to travel a lot farther than you, so we wanted to have them close by and give them a place to stay."

"Makes sense. So who's on the guest list? Any single friends of Zoe's?" he asked with a lecherous eyebrow waggle.

"Keep your hands to yourself," Aidan chided. "Three of her friends from Arizona are flying in for the weekend. They'll get one of the bedrooms next door. Then Aunt Rose and Uncle Ryan will have one, Uncle John and Aunt JoAnn will have one, the Hannigans will be over there, and Bobby snagged the last bedroom. It's a kiddie space and we've all gotten a good laugh at that one. Can't wait for him to get here and see his reaction."

"Man, that's going to be good," Quinn

laughed. "So everyone else is over here? In this house?"

"Yup. It will be like old times."

Quinn groaned. "Oh . . . good."

"What? What's wrong with that?"

"I'm sure it's not a big deal for you — you get to share a room with Zoe. But I'm going to have to share a room with Riley and Owen. It's like I'm twelve again."

"Actually, you're sharing a room with Dad."

His eyes went wide. "Why?"

"Riley's people didn't want him traveling alone — he's made the news lately with his plans to take an extended break from singing and the press is hounding him. They're sending a bodyguard with him."

"So the bodyguard gets my space in the room?"

Aidan nodded. "So you'll be spooning with Dad."

Quinn groaned even louder. "Oh man, come on! Why me?"

"Because you've always bitched about sharing a room with the twins. Your entire life! So I figured you and Dad would be a better fit. It's only for a couple of nights. You can handle it."

"Dad snores."

"Trust me, bro, so do you. It's like a

17

match made in heaven."

Turning, Quinn picked up his suitcase and slammed the trunk shut. "Screw you. This sucks. Please tell me there's at least some beer in the fridge."

Aidan nodded. "Go around back. Zoe's out by the pool, and she'll give you the grand tour and show you your room — and where the beer is."

"Where are you going?"

"I'm picking up Riley, Owen, and the bodyguard from the airport. They're landing at one of the smaller ones to try and avoid some of the drama and bypass the press."

"Well, just give me a few and I'll go with you."

Aidan shook his head. "It's going to be tight in my car as it is and I have no idea what kind of luggage any of them are bringing. You hang out here and get settled in. Hugh and Aubrey should be arriving in about an hour, and Dad and Darcy shouldn't be too far behind."

"Fine," Quinn grumbled. "I'll stay and be the welcoming committee. Thanks."

"It's that sparkling personality of yours that helped me make the decision." He gave Quinn a friendly pat on the back. "Keep on smiling, sunshine."

Quinn cursed a little more colorfully this time and gave his brother the one-finger salute before turning and heading for the house.

"If this whole situation didn't suck before, it certainly does now." He made his way toward the gate at the side of the house. Aidan said he'd find Zoe back there. Maybe he could convince her to give him a sofa to sleep on rather than sharing a room with his dad.

That held little to no appeal.

Okay, fine, he'd share the room with his father and smile when he was supposed to and be nice to people. It was only three days and there were going to be three single, out-of-town girls here for him to entertain.

Maybe it wasn't going to be such a bad weekend after all.

"This is how life was meant to be lived."

"You got that right."

"Why don't we live this way?"

"Because we're poor and have to work."

"Oh yeah. I temporarily forgot about that. Thanks for the reality check." Anna Hannigan stretched out on her belly on the chaise lounge by the pool and sighed with happiness. Her best friend was getting married, she had the weekend off, and the sun was shining. Life didn't get much better than this.

"It's what I do," Zoe said from her chaise beside her. "Although, all this sun is going to give me a very freckly look soon."

Anna raised her head and looked at her friend. "You've got on a hat with a brim as wide as a UFO, and we've coated you with enough SPF one million to keep you safe. And, might I add, you're practically in the shade thanks to that giant umbrella."

Zoe sighed. "You have no idea what it's like to be a fair-skinned redhead. I just want to look perfect for tomorrow."

"Zoe, you could be freckly, blotchy, and have no makeup on, and you'd still be stunning."

"Ha! Clearly you have not seen that look on me before. Trust me. It's not pretty. And honestly, neither has Aidan. I'm saving it until after the wedding, when it's too late for him to turn tail and run."

"Good plan." They sat in companionable silence for a few minutes. "I love this."

"The beach?"

"The peace. It's so quiet and relaxing. I just feel all of the tension of the workweek rolling away."

"I thought things would be a little less intense for you since quitting the pub. Real estate isn't quite the same frantic pace."

"No, but it's a different kind of tension. It's all on me now, you know? Before, I collected a paycheck whether the pub was busy or dead. Now, I have to earn a commission and that means getting sales. I'm still settling in to the whole thing."

"Yeah, I know the feeling. Working essentially for yourself is never easy. But you had saved up enough to carry you through all this in the beginning, right? We went over your budget."

"I know and I appreciate you helping me with it." She paused and then looked at Zoe. "Can you keep a secret?"

Zoe nodded.

"Part of me really misses the pub. Maybe . . . maybe I made a mistake."

"Why would you say that? You just got started. It could just be nerves."

Anna shook her head. "No, it's more than that. You see . . . I didn't really make the career change for the right reasons."

"Uh-oh . . ."

"Yeah," Anna sighed. "I . . . I wasn't getting anywhere. I was meeting the same people and doing the same thing day in and day out. I want what you and Aidan have — to be in a relationship, to be in love, to know that the rest of my life is just getting started and there's a future to it that includes a husband and kids and a happily ever after."

Zoe was quiet for a moment. "Why didn't you tell me any of this before? And you think leaving the pub and going into real estate is going to help you achieve that dream?"

"I don't know." Anna shrugged. "But at least I'm getting out and meeting new people. Everyone who came into the pub has pretty much known me my entire life. I was never going to find my future husband there."

"Maybe you already know him and you just haven't realized it yet."

Anna made a face. "Please. I think I would know by now. It's the same old crowd in there, and they all still look at me like I'm the tomboy they knew in high school. They come in and talk sports with me and want to relive a little of their glory days. It's kind of sad."

"Quinn doesn't do that."

"Yeah, well . . . maybe not to all of it. Quinn likes to talk about himself, mostly. But at the end of the day, he still sees me as Anna, the girl he grew up with and played baseball with and who kicks his ass at basketball. I'm one of the guys to him."

"Maybe because it's all you let him see."

Anna put her head back down and sighed. "There isn't much more to see. This is who I am."

Zoe started to say something but cut herself off. "I'm going to get something to drink. You want something?"

"Some water would be great."

Standing, Zoe took her oversized hat off and placed it on the back of Anna's head. "Watch this for me, will you?"

Anna laughed. "Sure. Whatever." She wasn't sure why Zoe tossed the hat on her, but it didn't matter — she was too relaxed. Wiggling slightly, she got more comfortable and sighed. This was good.

"Hey, you made it," Zoe said quietly to Quinn as she approached him. "I didn't expect you here so early. I figured we'd have to send out the search party to get you."

"Yeah, well . . . I decided to skip work today and head down here and see if you needed help with anything." He looked past Zoe's shoulder and spotted someone lying on one of the chaises.

Zoe followed his gaze. "Well, why don't you come inside? I was just about to grab a couple of bottles of water and then I can show you your room."

Quinn shrugged. "Sure, yeah. Um . . . is that one of your friends from Arizona?

Aidan didn't mention anyone being here yet." He took a couple of steps past Zoe, a grin slowly appearing on his face as he appreciated the curvy, half-naked woman on the chaise. She was wearing a tiny blue bikini and was all tanned limbs.

"Uh . . . Quinn?" Zoe began.

"You go and grab the drinks. I'll go and introduce myself." He continued to walk.

Rather than do as he suggested, Zoe followed slowly behind him, anxious to watch what was about to unfold.

Quinn sat down on the chaise Zoe had vacated and cleared his throat. "Hey," he said smoothly. "I'm Quinn, Aidan's brother. Zoe's going inside to grab some drinks and I thought I'd come over and —"

Anna turned over, the large, floppy hat falling behind her.

Quinn quickly stood and stumbled and fell backward over Zoe's chaise. "Holy shit! *Anna?*" He slowly came to his feet. "What the hell?"

She shaded her eyes and gave him a sour look before looking over at Zoe. When Zoe started to come forward, Anna held up a hand to stop her. "I got this." Once her friend was gone, she returned her focus to Quinn. "Is there a problem?"

Quinn helplessly looked around and

grabbed the towel from Zoe's chaise and threw it at Anna. "For crying out loud, what are you doing?"

"Um . . . sunbathing? Lying out? Getting a tan? Really, take your pick."

He straightened the chaise and sat down, but his eyes stayed focused on the ground. "Well, maybe you've had enough sun for today and should . . . you know . . . put some clothes on."

A small laugh escaped before she could help it. It would seem she had finally managed to get Quinn Shaughnessy to notice she was a girl. Well . . . a woman. Great. It only took her being practically naked for it to happen.

When she stayed silent, Quinn lifted his head but kept his eyes firmly on hers. "I'm serious, Anna. You need to go and get dressed."

It was the tone that did it. Anna was used to him being bossy and condescending most of the time — it was who he was — but right now, all of her good humor and thoughts of teasing him went right out the window. "No," she said firmly and made herself more comfortable by rolling over onto her back.

He said her name again. This time it was nearly a growl.

She turned her head and looked at him. "If you have a problem, maybe *you* should go inside. I'm staying right here."

A stream of curses was his immediate response. "Any minute, my brothers are going to be showing up here. Is this how you want them to see you?"

Now she reached for her sunglasses that were tucked away under the chaise and put them on. "They've all seen me in a bathing suit before, Quinn. Why is this such a big deal?"

He stood angrily. "Because it is! This . . . this isn't a bathing suit," he stammered, waving his arms over her. "This is indecent!"

Zoe came sauntering back over with a huge grin on her face. "I know, isn't it fantastic? Who knew Anna was hiding such a rocking figure under those T-shirts and jeans?" She handed Anna a bottle of water and then a beer to Quinn. "I figured you might appreciate one of these."

Quinn took it from her and opened it, muttering the whole time under his breath about people being stubborn. He took a long pull of his beer before turning to Zoe. "Would you please tell her to go and put something on before everyone gets here? I mean, she's being stubborn."

"Aidan was here with her earlier and

everything was fine. I don't think anyone's going to have a problem with her," Zoe said evenly and gently moved Quinn out of her way so she could resume her position on her own chaise. "Can you hand me my hat, Anna?"

"No problem," Anna said sweetly and smiled at Quinn as she picked up the hat and handed it over to Zoe.

Quinn rolled his eyes and looked around for a place to sit. "At least roll back over. Or put on more sunscreen or . . . something!"

"I just got comfortable, Quinn. Now either be quiet, or go away. Go unpack or watch TV or just . . . stop being annoying."

"*I'm* annoying?" he asked sarcastically. "I ask for one simple request and I'm the one being annoying." He huffed. "When does your brother get here? I bet he'll back me up on this."

Anna lifted her sunglasses and glared at him. "I wore this exact bathing suit to the beach with Bobby last week. No issues. So why don't you unclench and . . . again . . . go away." Putting her sunglasses back in place, she wiggled a little — unnecessarily — and got comfortable. Was that a groan she heard coming from Quinn? She smiled to herself.

"You know, Anna," Zoe began, "it really has been a while since you've put on some sunscreen. You're probably due." Then she picked up her phone and began to furiously type something.

Anna looked at her quizzically.

Zoe nodded while Quinn wasn't looking and then nudged her head in his direction with a thumbs-up. "Yeah. I definitely think it's time. Especially on your back. Your shoulders are getting a little red." More typing.

Anna still wasn't sure what Zoe was up to. "Oh . . . um. Okay. Can you help me?"

"Sure, let me just grab . . ." And then her phone rang. "I really need to get this. Quinn? Can you help Anna? I need to take this inside. Wedding stuff." And then she was on her feet and walking away.

If Anna wasn't mistaken, Quinn was actually blushing. "You don't have to help me," she said quickly.

"No, no," he grumbled. "It was my suggestion, so . . ." He came and stood beside her. "I don't know . . . roll over or something."

She rolled her eyes and did as he requested. Why was he being such a jerk? And why did it only seem to make him more appealing? Clearly she needed to get her head

28

examined. Or get a boyfriend. Or just get some relief from the sexual frustration that was dominating her life right now.

She'd always been in love with Quinn. Ever since they were kids. She just . . . *knew.* He was the one for her. Her soul mate. The only problem was Quinn didn't feel the same way. She was his pal. His buddy. There'd never once been anything romantic between them, and if he even suspected how she felt, he'd never let on.

With a sigh, she relaxed back on her belly with her arms folded under her head. And now, even if he did suddenly notice she was a woman, it still didn't make a difference. He was still surly and difficult and not impressed. Rather than making him act a little more charming like he always was with other girls — her lying there in next to nothing was making him angry, and he tried to clover her up.

Quite the ego boost. *Not.*

And then his hands were on her and . . . *oh.* Slowly, those big, work-roughened hands started at her ankles and began a journey upward. *Oh my . . .*

She almost wanted to turn and watch him work. With his sandy-blond hair, blue eyes, and rough hands, he was her every dream. All the Shaughnessys had dark hair except for Quinn. It used to bother him, and by the way he normally wore some sort of hat or beanie, Anna could tell it still did. But he wasn't wearing one now, and with all the sensations he was creating in her, she wanted to roll over and rake her hands through his hair and pull him down toward her.

It was never going to happen, but the imagery kept her smiling while he touched her.

Quinn was completely silent and Anna seemed unable to breathe. She couldn't move, couldn't breathe . . . she could only feel. And, boy oh boy, was Quinn making her feel. His hands skimmed the backs of her knees, and when they hit her thighs and one finger came close to her bottom, she had to stifle a moan of pleasure.

His hands stopped for a moment as if he realized what he was doing. Anna almost lifted her head to look at him but thought better of it. And then his hands were on her again — this time on the small of her back. And then upward — circling, rubbing, massaging. She wanted to purr.

When they hit her shoulders, his motions seemed to slow as he went into what could only be described as a deep tissue massage. All of the tension from a few minutes ago completely faded away as his hands — those magnificent hands — worked on her. On any given day, Anna was all for a good massage, but this was beyond good. It was almost a religious experience. And this time she couldn't stop herself from purring.

His hands instantly were gone.

She didn't bother to look up. Didn't bother to question it. No good would come of turning around and seeing the look of horror on his face at her reacting the way she just had to him.

Idiot.

Beside her, Quinn cleared his throat and stood, the bottle of sunscreen hitting the ground. "Um . . . yeah, so . . . that should do it," he croaked. "You should be good for now. I'm going to go and find Zoe and get settled in. I'll see you later."

Again, Anna didn't bother to respond. The man was clearly running away because she had been foolish enough to let her guard down for a minute. She waited until she heard the sliding doors to the house open and then close before she allowed herself to lift her head and look around.

Out of the corner of her eye, she saw Zoe stepping back outside shaking her head. When she got closer, she said, "What did you do to him?"

31

"*Me?* Nothing! I just laid here and let him put sunscreen on me. Why?"

Zoe laughed as she sat back down. "He ran in the house as if he were on fire and demanded to know which room was his. I offered to show him, but he was already halfway up the stairs yelling for me to just tell him which one!"

"So weird."

"Tell me about it." Zoe relaxed back in her spot. "So . . . he didn't say anything to you? Not even while he had his hands all over you?"

Anna glared at her. "Yeah, thanks for that. The only time Quinn ever touches me is to give me a high-five or to punch me in the arm when I beat him at something."

"Ah . . . so this was the first time he, like . . . *really* touched you."

"What are you doing, Zoe?" Anna asked wearily. "Why are you stirring up trouble?"

"Because it's so obvious you're into him."

"Well, duh! It's no surprise. We've talked about this. A lot."

"Yeah, we have, but you never do anything about it. I was merely . . . prodding things along."

"Yeah, well, keep your prodding to yourself. In case you didn't notice, your little attempt failed. Big time. Now I know what it feels like to have his hands all over me, and while I'm sitting here in a puddle of my own drool, he's running and hiding in his room to escape. He couldn't get away fast enough."

"Oh, I don't think I'd count this as a fail, my friend," Zoe said sweetly. "I think you made him nervous. I think we prodded him just enough for the blinders to finally come off."

"What are you talking about? He was horrified. He was massaging my shoulders and I . . ." Anna paused and cringed. "I moaned."

"Like a sex noise?"

Anna shot her a look. "Yes, like a sex noise. Like a big, loud 'I'm on the verge of an orgasm' sex noise. There. Are you happy?"

Zoe threw he head back and laughed. "Oh my gosh! That's awesome!"

This time Anna twisted and sat up. "How is it awesome? He's going to avoid me like the plague from now on! It's bad enough he only sees me as a friend and now I'll lose that! Dammit, Zoe."

"Okay, hold on. You're freaking out over nothing. I'm telling you, that man just got the shock of his life. When he spotted you over here, he didn't realize it was you, and he was practically salivating."

"Yeah, and it all stopped as soon as he got a look at my face and saw it was me."

"Anna —"

"Forget it," she said and got to her feet. "I can't talk about this anymore. I'm going for a quick dip and then I'm going inside. Maybe *I* need to hide out in my room for a while." And then she took the few steps to the side of the pool and swiftly dived in.

Quinn slammed the door behind him, threw his suitcase on the bed, and then cursed a blue streak. Raking his hands through his hair, he paced the room from one side to the other, unable to see anything except Anna in her tiny bikini. Where did she get off having a body like that?

He cursed again.

Why had he never noticed that about her? He saw her almost every day. Okay, maybe not *every* day, but he'd seen her enough over the course of his life that he should have noticed she had . . . curves. Lots of them. Stopping, he racked his brain for what he normally saw when he looked at her.

Short blond hair. Brown eyes.

Jeans. T-shirts.

No curves.

"Man, was I way off base there," he muttered. Even now, he could close his eyes and see them, feel them.

Finally taking a moment to look at the room, he groaned. Twin beds, dresser, nightstands, closet. Small. The walls were closing in on him already. At least the beds were long twins. There was no way he and his father would be able to fit in anything smaller and even that was going to be pushing it.

Eyeing his suitcase, he contemplated unpacking but couldn't summon the will to do it. Instead he flopped down on the mattress and closed his eyes.

Big mistake because there she was again. Except now he was horrified to find his hands twitched with the need to touch her again. Her legs had been firm and soft at the same time. He knew Anna had always been athletic — hell, she competed with him in almost every activity and most of the time could kick his ass.

But the things he normally loved on a woman — the small of her back, her grabable ass — now he noticed on Anna, and it felt . . . different. Not wrong, exactly, but definitely different. Thank God Zoe was going to have her single friends here this weekend. Quinn had a feeling he was going to need a distraction or he'd end up pouncing on Anna, and he couldn't allow himself to do that. They were friends — *best* friends — and there was no way he was going to ruin that over a great ass.

Or long, tanned legs.

Or . . . He groaned. The list was now endless. How the hell was he supposed to survive the weekend like this? They were going to be together the entire time and Quinn had no doubt Anna was going to be in his face if he ignored her. No doubt she'd call him out on being a jackass and tell him to grow up. And in any other situation, he'd gladly take it and admit she was right. But now? He had no idea how he was going to look her in the eye without letting his eyes wander and wondering what she was wearing underneath her jeans and T-shirts.

Damn wedding.

Why couldn't he be at work right now? If he were working on a classic car, everything would be right with his world. When he was working on a project, it held his attention from start to finish — no distractions. Sure, he went out and socialized. Hell, he even dated. He was a guy, after all. But it was all superficial — a quick stop at the pub, a quick bite to eat, and some hot sex. But for the next three days, there was nothing but family and . . . Anna.

He seriously hoped Zoe's friends were hot. It would be a welcome distraction. It would quite possibly be the only thing that would save him from any awkward interactions with Anna. Then at night, he'd have to deal with the other awkward situation — sharing a room with his dad.

A shudder wracked through his body. He knew it was only for three nights, but the only person Quinn wanted to share a room with was Anna. *NO!* Wait . . . Oh hell. A woman. He only wanted to share a room with a *woman*! Damn Anna and her bikini. Now he was going to have to be even more careful for the rest of the weekend, or it wouldn't only be Anna getting in his face about his behavior. Soon his brothers would be in on it and eventually . . . Bobby.

Crap. It was no secret there was no love lost between Quinn and Bobby. He wasn't even sure when it started. They were all friends when they were kids, but somewhere along the way — probably around high school or maybe even as early as middle school — Bobby had taken a disliking to Quinn, and that, in turn, had made Quinn dislike Bobby. They'd had more than their share of brawls, but whenever Quinn would come out and say, "What is your problem?"

Bobby would just throw his hands up in disgust and walk away.

And it got worse when Bobby became a cop. Not to say he was harassing Quinn, but Quinn knew he got more tickets than the average citizen and it was usually over nothing. You'd think Quinn would just pack it in and set up his business's home base someplace else. But no. Not only did he set up one of his shops in his hometown, but he'd seriously expanded and made it his crowning location.

Idiot.

Okay, so now he was up to three awkward situations on tap for the weekend. Maybe he should just stay in his room and fake being sick or something. Luckily there weren't any medical professionals in the bunch. Riley wouldn't come near him for fear of getting sick and missing out on being with the public. Owen was a bit of a germophobe and would definitely stay away. Darcy would poke her head in just to be nosy, while Hugh wouldn't want to risk getting Aubrey sick. And Aidan . . . well, it was his wedding, there was no way he'd risk getting sick for his wedding day.

But could he really do it? Just to get a room to himself and not have to face Anna or Bobby? Was he really so completely selfish that he'd risk ruining Aidan and Zoe's weekend?

Maybe.

"No," he growled and sat up. He wasn't a coward. And hiding out implied he was. "I can face all of them and tell them each to go to hell if they have a problem with me." Well, except his dad. There was no way he'd say that to his dad. Ian Shaughnessy was the best dad a guy could ever ask for, and even though Quinn wasn't looking forward to bunking with him, it wasn't an attack on his father.

Just his snoring.

Outside, he heard a couple of car doors slamming. Walking over to the window, he saw Hugh and Aubrey had arrived. Another car pulled in behind them but Quinn didn't recognize it. It wasn't particularly unusual — there were guests coming that he didn't see on a regular basis. For all he knew, it was one of his aunts or uncles, the Hannigans, or even Zoe's friends. It could be . . .

Wait a minute . . .

Squinting a little, Quinn leaned closer to the glass and felt an impending sense of doom. Rising from the driver's side door of the second car was Martha Tate. Nothing wrong with that; she was Zoe's boss. She was laughing and smiling, and she waved at

Hugh and Aubrey like they were old friends. But she wasn't alone. Stepping out from the passenger side was . . . Oh dear Lord.

Ian Shaughnessy.

CHAPTER 2

"No, no, no, no, no, no," Quinn grumbled as he stalked across the room. This was the icing on the cake of a really crappy day. His father didn't drive anywhere with anyone. Hell, only recently had he started socializing with his old friends again, and the only people Quinn ever saw him driving around with were his own kids. Mainly Darcy. But Martha Tate? What the hell?

He took off down the stairs and nearly collided with Anna at the bottom. She had a towel wrapped around her, thankfully. "Whoa, where's the fire?" she said with a nervous laugh.

Quinn was sorely tempted just to step around her and keep going, but he figured Anna might be a little more in the know on this situation than he was because she was so close with Zoe. "Why is my father arriving here in Martha Tate's car?" he asked suspiciously.

Anna instantly looked uncomfortable. "Are they here already? I didn't think —"

"So you knew about this? And you didn't tell me?"

"There really isn't anything to tell. They've had dinner a couple of times, and I knew Martha was coming for the wedding. I guess —"

"When did they have dinner?" he snapped and then took a step away and raked a hand through his already-disheveled hair. "This is crazy!"

"It's really not that big a deal, Quinn," she said evenly. When he finally went to move around her, she placed a firm hand on his arm and stopped him. "What are you doing? You can't go out there like this."

"And why the hell not?"

"Because you're freaking out over nothing. So they drove here together. You're going to look like a crazy person going out there like this."

He seemed to consider what she said. "He was supposed to drive here with Darcy. So . . . where the hell is Darcy? And why is Martha here now instead?"

At that moment, Zoe walked down the hallway toward them. "Everything okay?"

Anna looked at Quinn and then back to Zoe. "Ian just pulled up with Martha," she

42

said and silently motioned to the look on Quinn's face from behind him. "Quinn wasn't aware of the situation."

"So there is a situation," Quinn interrupted, turning toward Anna.

She rolled her eyes. "Fine. Quinn wasn't aware they were arriving together."

"Oh no," Zoe said. "Neither was I. Martha said she couldn't make it here today. I don't have a room for her. All the bedrooms are taken."

"Maybe Hugh can get her a room at the resort. It's only thirty minutes away and —"

"No. I can't do that to her. We'll have to reconsider everything. Damn it. I hate when people don't follow the plan." And then she was gone, walking away and talking to herself about bedroom assignments.

Anna glared at Quinn. "There. Happy now?"

"Me? What did I do?"

"You upset the bride! Like she doesn't have enough to worry about without you freaking her out!"

"Hey!" he snapped. "In case you haven't noticed, I'm the one who's upset here! Why aren't you going out there and yelling at my dad and Martha for making me upset?"

The laugh came out before she could stop it. "Oh my God. Do you even hear yourself?

You're a grown man, Quinn. This isn't a big deal. Now take a deep breath and maybe go out back for a few minutes until everyone comes in. And for the love of it, keep your mouth shut for as long as possible."

"Why — ?"

Anna held up a hand to silence him as everyone started to file in. She could feel him bristling beside her and finally leaned back and elbowed him in the ribs. His muffled *"oof"* almost made her smile. Before she could do more than blink, everyone was talking and saying hello and she went from person to person hugging and greeting them.

"I can't believe you beat us here, bro," Hugh said as he shook Quinn's hand. "I thought for sure you'd be one of the last to arrive."

Quinn took the good-natured ribbing with a smile. Hopefully Anna was the only one to notice it was forced and that his eyes kept darting over to his father and Martha.

Deciding to keep things light for a little bit longer, Anna said, "Quinn? Why don't you take Hugh and Aubrey out back and show them the pool and get them a drink?"

He eyed her suspiciously. "I'm sure they can —"

"And see if Zoe needs anything," she

quickly added to cut him off. "You know she's feeling a little *frazzled* right now." Anna gave him a stern glare that warned him not to argue, and breathed a sigh of relief when he just nodded and led his brother and his brother's wife through the house.

When she heard the sliding glass doors open and close, she turned to Ian and Martha, who were looking at her oddly. "Okay, here's the thing," she began, her heart racing a little at having to have an awkward discussion with the man who had always been like a second father to her. "Quinn is a little freaked out that the two of you are here together."

Ian's brows rose. "Why?"

"Well . . . he was expecting you to arrive with Darcy." And then she looked apologetically at Martha. "And I'm afraid Zoe didn't know you were coming today. So she's panicking about where to put you. Roomwise."

The older couple looked at one another nervously and then back at Anna and her stomach sank. *Oh. My. God.* She said a silent prayer she was not going to be forced to stand here and listen to them talk about the new turn in their relationship and how they were hoping to share a room.

So not the discussion she ever wanted to have.

"Actually —" Ian began, unable to look Anna in the eye.

She cut him off before he could go any further. "It's okay. Really. You were supposed to room with Quinn, but I'm sure Zoe can find another spot for him."

"Why was I rooming with Quinn?"

Anna gave him the short version of Riley's situation with the bodyguard and how all of the rooms were filled. "I'm sure Quinn can sleep on one of the sofas or the floor somewhere or maybe with Bobby."

Ian laughed. "Let's hope it doesn't come to that. Those two will probably try to kill each other by the end of the first night."

The laugh came automatically, but Anna wasn't really feeling it. No doubt she was now going to have to be the bearer of this awkward news.

"Maybe I should find a hotel," Martha said after a long silence.

Ian looked at her apologetically. "I hate to see you do that. Why don't we wait and see how things unfold here?"

"Tell you what," Anna said, interrupting them again, "let me go and talk to Zoe and then we'll deal with Quinn. I'm not sure which room you're in, so just leave your luggage here and go on out back and grab a drink."

"Anna," Ian said, "I appreciate what you're doing, but maybe it would be better if I was the one to deal with Quinn."

It would have been easy to agree, but she had a feeling things would go a lot easier this weekend if she was the one dealing with Quinn's wrath rather than his father. "Let me at least try first. If I need to, I'll let you take over." She walked away before he could stop her.

When Anna was out of sight, Martha turned to Ian. "How long has she been in love with him?"

Ian sighed. "Since forever."

"Any chance of him feeling the same way?"

"I wish I knew."

Quinn's eyes kept darting toward the sliding doors to see if his father was coming outside. He had no idea what he was going to say to him, but he knew he had to say something. What the hell was he doing here with Martha Tate? Like a couple! And why hadn't he given any of them a heads-up? A warning? Something? Anything?

Beside him, Hugh and Aubrey were talking about how their neighbor was dog-sitting for them. Crap. Who cares? Didn't they realize there were bigger issues to be dealt with than making sure the dogs didn't shit in the house? It was on the tip of his tongue to say something when a movement caught his attention.

Anna.

She stepped out onto the patio — alone — and Quinn knew immediately she was gunning for him. Great. As if he needed her in his face any more today. And why wasn't she dressed yet? The towel was replaced with some sort of white, gauzy cover-up kind of thing and if anything, it was sexier than her just being in the damn bikini.

Closing his eyes, he shook his head. When he opened them, Anna was standing in front of him. "Are you okay?"

All he could do was nod. Quinn was certain if he opened his mouth to speak, he wouldn't be able to control himself and he'd end up not only ranting — loudly — about his father and Martha, but also about Anna and her current wardrobe. Or lack thereof.

"Everything okay?" Hugh asked. He looked at his brother and then at Anna and then back again. Aubrey stepped in close to them as well.

"Quinn's a little upset about your dad and Martha," Anna said quietly.

Hugh sighed. "Yeah. I have to admit it was a bit of a shock, but . . ." He stopped and shrugged. "He's entitled to have a life too."

"Does he have to have one now?" Quinn hissed. "I mean . . . this is a family event! He couldn't find a better time to break the news to us all?"

Hugh looked at him oddly. "Dude, where have you been? They've been dating for a while now. This is hardly news."

Quinn shot an accusing look at Anna. "So everybody knew except me?"

"Well," Hugh began, "I can't say with any great certainty, but —"

"What about Darcy? Does she know? Is she okay with it?" he snapped.

Anna looked between the brothers and stepped in. "Hugh, can you take Aubrey and check out the area we have set up for the dinner tonight and make sure it's all right? I know Zoe would appreciate it."

The couple took their cue and excused themselves, leaving Quinn alone with Anna. She glared at him before taking his hand and dragging him down to the beach. The sand was hot and he was all but fuming by the time they stopped.

"Okay look," she began, "I know you're upset —"

"You don't know the half of it," he countered.

"But," she continued, "you need to understand several things."

"Anna, please don't pretend you understand or that you've got it all figured out, because you don't. This was a crappy time for him to bring Martha around."

"Honestly, it wasn't," she argued. "If you had been paying attention lately —"

"I've been busy!" he yelled. "I've got a new phase of the business going on and that's where my time has been spent. Had I known I was supposed to be sitting around like a gossipy teenager watching my dad, someone should have told me. *You* should have told me," he accused.

"Oh, for crying out loud," she huffed and took several steps away before coming back to him. "It's not my job to keep you up-to-date on your family, Quinn!"

"And yet here you are doing just that."

She gasped and moved away again. It took a moment for Anna to find her voice. "Look, I'm not going to stand here and argue with you. All I'm saying is you need to calm down. This is your brother's wedding. Zoe's stressed out enough, and she and Aidan don't need you starting a fight."

"Oh, I'm not the one who's going to start

the fight. I can guarantee when Darcy gets here, she'll —"

"She won't do anything," Anna said bluntly.

Quinn could only stare.

"Who do you think encouraged him to start dating? Who do you think orchestrated their first date? Who do you think is the most excited about maybe having more women in her life?"

"But . . . no," he said adamantly. "Darcy wouldn't do that. She and my mom . . ."

Anna's shoulders sagged, her expression growing sad. "Quinn, Darcy doesn't remember your mom," she said softly. "I know we all like to think differently, but the reality is she was a baby when Lillian died. She has no memory of her and it's hard for her to pretend otherwise. It's hard for her to have a connection to someone she doesn't remember." She paused. "It doesn't mean she doesn't love your mom — she does. But it's not the same as the connection you and your brothers had to your mother."

It had been a long time since Quinn had felt overwhelmed with memories of his mother, but right now that was exactly how he felt. He swallowed hard and walked toward the water, not wanting Anna — or anyone — to see him like this.

Sometimes it was easy just to pretend everything was okay, that there wasn't this massive void in his life. And other times — like now — it was hard to ignore. With the scent and sound of the surf all around him, it was as if he were a kid again, on vacation with his family. It had always been their thing — they'd go to Myrtle Beach and spend the week just playing in the sand and the water.

Anna came to stand beside him, and suddenly he was back in the present. His mother wasn't here; they weren't on vacation. And the reality hit him like a punch in the gut.

"I wish Darcy remembered her," he said quietly. "I know Mom loved us all, but she was just over the moon when she had Darcy — finally had a little girl." He took a steadying breath. "I wish Darcy remembered some of Mom's joy."

"So does she," Anna replied before she turned and faced him. "It's not easy for her, Quinn, but you have to know that just because she encourages your father to date, it doesn't lessen her feelings for Lillian."

"I know."

"And you need to realize that just because he is dating, it doesn't mean he doesn't still love your mom. Or that he's forgotten her."

Quinn swallowed hard, his eyes still focused on the waves crashing over the sand. He felt Anna's hand slip into his and he grasped it hard. It was reassuring, soft, comforting. Everything he needed in that moment. They stood like that for several silent minutes before Anna simply leaned in and hugged him.

"You going to be okay?" she asked.

"I don't really have a choice, do I?" The anger from earlier was gone and in its place was quiet acceptance. It wasn't unusual for him to hug Anna, but it was normally in a playful manner. This quiet, intimate embrace was new. Different.

And yet not in a bad way.

"Come on. We should get back up to the house. The rehearsal for the ceremony is in a couple of hours, and then we have the dinner with everyone."

He sighed and released her reluctantly. "I guess I'm going to be relegated to sleeping on the couch now, aren't I?"

Anna chuckled. "I'm sure you can share a room with Bobby."

His laughter matched hers. "Thanks, but I think I'll take my chances with the couch. Your brother would probably smother me in my sleep."

"He's not quite that bad."

Quinn knew a token defense when he heard one. "You have to say that. He's your brother."

"It's only for a couple of nights. It won't be so bad."

"Yeah, yeah, yeah," he said and took her hand in his and together they walked back up to the house.

The sun was setting, and everyone was milling about, laughing and smiling. The rehearsal had gone smoothly, and now everyone was enjoying an amazing seafood buffet Hugh's resort had catered. Anna couldn't remember the last time she had seen such an incredible display of food.

As she mingled with everyone, her eyes kept straying to Quinn. At that moment, he was standing and talking with Zoe's friend Kathy. Anna had met all the girls earlier, and Kathy had shared that she was three months pregnant. Her husband hadn't come with her, though, due to a work conflict. Pausing, she discreetly watched as Quinn's smile faltered slightly; no doubt he was now finding out all his flirting was for nothing — married woman, baby on the way. He said something and smiled before walking away.

"If you don't watch where you're walking,

you'll end up in the pool."

She looked up and found her brother frowning at her. "I was watching where I was going," she said pleasantly even though she was annoyed Bobby had clearly caught her watching Quinn.

"Seriously, Anna, move on. The guy is not worth it."

"I don't know what you're talking about."

Bobby sighed loudly. "Okay, you're far too intelligent to pretend you're not. You were staring at Shaughnessy, and if I noticed it, I'm sure everyone else did too. You need to stop."

Anna felt tension and anger begin to rise in her but she managed to hold her tongue.

"Look, I'm not saying this to be a jerk or anything. I'm saying it because I love you and I don't like seeing you get hurt. Quinn's not the kind of guy you want to get involved with, and trust me when I say he's not the right guy for you."

"And you know this how?" she asked, hoping she sounded bored rather than defensive.

"You've known him almost your entire life. Has he ever even hinted he's interested in you?" He paused but didn't let her answer. "He's a serial dater, Anna. He goes out with a girl once or twice, sleeps with her, and then moves on. You wouldn't be any different. You'd just be one of many. I don't want to see that happen to you. You deserve better."

She rolled her eyes. "Look, let's not go there tonight, okay? It's Aidan and Zoe's party and I don't want to ruin it. Stop hovering and go socialize a little bit."

"Yeah, well . . . if any of Zoe's friends were single, it would be a lot more fun to socialize. This is basically just a family event." He sighed dramatically. "So my options were either come over here and play the big-brother card or go and kick Quinn's ass."

"Bobby —"

"I know, I know. Hugh already talked to me."

"About what?"

"It's nothing." He grabbed Anna and pulled her into his embrace and gave her a loud, smacking kiss on her head. "Behave yourself and go find someone else to get all moon-eyed over."

"Yikes," she chuckled. "Leave me alone."

"No can do. You're my baby sister and this is my job."

"You're killing me."

"Like I said . . . my job."

"You need to find something else to do, or I'll tell Mom you're bothering me."

He laughed a little harder. "Eventually you'll have to stop using that as your go-to defense. You're getting too old for it."

"And yet it works like a charm," she teased and gave him a wink before walking away.

Bobby was right — about all of it. She was getting too old to play the tattletale card, and she really did need to get over her stupid crush on Quinn. It wasn't healthy and it wasn't getting her anywhere. Looking around the yard, she saw everything she wanted: love, happiness, and a family. She envied what Aidan and Zoe had — more than she cared to admit. And if she kept on pining away for a man who was never going to be anything more than a friend to her, she was never going to have this for herself.

"A girl can dream," she said softly before walking over and joining her parents who were sitting with Ian and Martha.

"It's been very entertaining watching you," Riley Shaughnessy said with a cocky grin.

Quinn glared at him over his beer. "And why is that?"

"Well, it was impressive watching you strike out with all the bridesmaids. Really. I think it has to be some sort of Shaughnessy record. Epic, really."

"Shut up."

"I guess you missed the memo saying they were all married," Riley said with a wicked grin.

"Oh, and you knew this ahead of time?" Quinn snapped.

Riley nodded. "Oh yeah. I got the low-down from Aidan weeks ago. I'm surprised you didn't bother to inquire about it."

"Yeah, well . . . some of us genuinely have real work to do and don't have time to think about asking in advance if there are any potential hookups."

Riley's smile faltered a little. "So now I don't work?"

"Shit, Ry, don't start this again."

"No, come on. Tell me how it is I don't have a real job. Please," he said sarcastically.

Quinn sighed loudly. "I'm not doing this here, okay? I don't know what your deal's been for the last six months or so, but trust me when I say we all wish you'd get over it. No one's doubting you or your job or your career, talent, or whatever."

"Your comment a minute ago says otherwise."

"Look, you come over here and start mocking me and I'm not supposed to mock back? Seriously? What the hell?"

"Okay, fine. Let's just drop it." Riley

looked around the yard and then gave a low wolf whistle. "Look at little Anna Hannigan. She's grown up all kinds of nice, hasn't she?" he said with a grin. "Hard to believe she's the same tomboy who used to come around and play ball with you."

If Quinn had thought he was angry with his brother a minute ago, it was nothing compared to now.

"I know I saw her at Dad's birthday party, but I don't remember her looking so . . . hot," Riley said. "And when did she get so curvy?"

It wasn't until Riley went to step toward Anna that Quinn reached out and grabbed him. "Stay away from Anna," he said, his tone so low it was a near growl.

Riley arched a brow at him. "Is there a problem?"

"Right now? Specifically? You."

Riley chuckled. "I don't think so. I find it interesting how you've spent a large portion of the night hitting on married women —"

"I didn't know they were married!"

"Whatever. But you spent a large portion of the night hitting on them when you've clearly got a thing for our little Anna."

Quinn released him immediately. "I don't have a thing for her . . . or anyone. You don't know what the hell you're talking about."

"Um, I think I do," Riley teased. "Wow, I can't believe I didn't put it together sooner. Dad's birthday party, tonight . . . It all makes sense now."

"Ry," Quinn warned.

"So what's the problem? Why are you wasting your time hitting on married bridesmaids?"

"I already told you, I didn't know —"

"No one cares," Riley interrupted. "Why waste your time when you've got a thing for Anna? She's had a crush on you since forever."

"What? What the hell are you talking about?"

"Oh, dude, come on! How could you not know?"

"Anna and I are friends. That's it," Quinn said defensively.

Riley shook his head. "So delusional. Seriously, we all know it. She's been crushing hard on you for years. How could you not have noticed? You can't possibly be that oblivious."

Quinn didn't know what to say. Hadn't Anna accused him of the same thing a few hours ago where his father and his family were concerned? Was it possible he had missed out on the fact that Anna had feelings for him too?

He shook his head. No. It was impossible. If Anna had feelings for him that were beyond friendship, he would have known. They spent too much time together and he knew everything about her; he knew what she was thinking even before she did. There was no way Anna saw him as anything more than a friend.

Looking across the yard, he spotted her. She was wearing a nearly nude-colored dress that hugged her like a second skin. He couldn't help but frown. For years, Anna had favored jeans and T-shirts. Ever since she left the pub and started working in real estate, she was changing. And he didn't like it. Her clothes . . . her hair . . . Clearly he hadn't been paying attention because the woman walking around the yard right now bore little resemblance to the girl he'd grown up with.

In some ways she was the same, but he was beginning to feel like he was losing her — like she was slipping away. And he wouldn't be able to tolerate that.

Anna Hannigan was beginning to make him crazy in ways he'd never fully imagined, and if he didn't get a grip on it soon, Quinn wasn't sure what would happen.

"From the look on your face, I can see this may be brand-new information to you,"

Riley said from beside him, humor lacing his tone. He clapped a hand on Quinn's shoulder. "Just remember this, big brother — she's a beautiful woman and she's only going to sit around and wait for your dumb ass for so long."

Quinn wanted to argue, but he didn't know what to say. Up until today, he had never even imagined the possibility of him and Anna being anything more than friends. But after the whole bikini incident and now seeing her in that dress . . . well, he wasn't so sure he'd be able to think of anything but.

But the thought of losing her as his best friend? He wasn't sure he could handle it.

"Fine, stay there and think, Romeo," Riley said with a smile. "I'm going to go over and get reacquainted with the lovely Anna."

It would have been easy to grab his brother by the scruff of his neck and haul him back, but what was the use? There was no way he was going to make a scene in the middle of the party. And knowing Riley, his bodyguard would be all over Quinn in the blink of an eye and that would really ruin the party.

With nothing else to do, Quinn walked over and got himself another beer and sat in the corner.

■ ■ ■ ■

Anna couldn't sleep. The whole night had been a bit weird. Everything suddenly felt different, and for the life of her, she couldn't figure out why. Well, that wasn't completely true — Quinn's behavior was the real reason why. She just wasn't sure what to do about it.

Watching him flirt with Zoe's friends bothered her. But then again, it always bothered her to watch him hit on anything in a skirt. It was almost comical when he realized none of them were single. It seemed like he didn't know what to do with himself — other than glare at Anna.

She was getting pretty tired of Quinn's glare. Like it wasn't bad enough he didn't want her, was never going to see her as anything other than a friend . . . did he have to give her the kind of look that was pretty much killing her self-confidence too?

It was late and everyone had already gone to bed, but Anna knew she would only make herself crazy if she tried to force herself to go to sleep. Kicking the blankets off, she stood and decided to go and get some fresh air. Deciding to forgo a change of clothes, she quietly padded out of her room in her oversized T-shirt, down the stairs, and out to the back patio and the pool.

It was so peaceful and the sky was full of stars. There were a couple of small lights on around the pool to help her keep from tripping. At the water's edge, Anna crouched down until she was sitting on the concrete and then lowered her feet into the water. The pool was heated and the water felt good and she let out a small hum of delight. With her palms flat on the ground and her feet slowly swaying in the water, Anna threw her head back and sighed, finally feeling the tension leaving her body.

"It's a little late for a swim, isn't it?"

Dammit. Refusing to move or open her eyes, Anna forced herself to stay put. "I don't plan on swimming. I'm just dunking my feet." Even without looking, she could feel Quinn lowering himself down beside her. The slight splash as his own feet hit the water confirmed it.

"Fine. It's a little late for dunking your feet, isn't it?" he asked and then added, "Why aren't you asleep? It's late."

Anna shrugged, her head still thrown back, eyes closed. "Just couldn't sleep."

Quinn made a noncommittal sound beside her.

"What about you? What are you still doing up?"

"The couch isn't very comfortable," he said, and Anna could tell without even looking that he was pouting.

This time, she did open her eyes to look at him. "So that really happened, huh? I thought maybe you were still going to be sharing the room with your dad."

Now it was his turn to shrug. "Somehow, Zoe managed to move people around, and now Martha's sharing a room with Darcy," he muttered.

"I didn't think . . . I mean . . . I just thought . . ."

"Yeah, yeah, yeah, we all did. Shit." He raked a hand through his hair. "It sort of took us all by surprise. I can't believe he chose this weekend of all times to throw that bit of news at us."

"Maybe he thought it was safer this way."

"What do you mean?" he asked, brows furrowed.

"You know, less chance of anyone arguing with him about it. No one's going to pick a fight if Aidan and Zoe's wedding is tomorrow." She tilted her head back and sighed. "Although it might have been a whole lot less awkward if he and Martha had just stayed at Hugh's resort or something."

"It would be awkward no matter what. I

sure as hell don't want to think about my father and Martha sleeping together. Even now it makes me want to stab pointy things into my brain."

Anna chuckled. "Don't be such a baby."

"I'm not," he snapped. "All I'm saying is maybe he could have waited for another time to drop his bombshell. You know, maybe have a little respect for the rest of us."

With a slight turn of her head, Anna gave him a stare. "Do you even hear yourself when you talk?"

Quinn looked at her with utter confusion. "Of course I do. Why?"

She rolled her eyes. "Quinn, your father is a grown man. He has the right to do what he wants — with whomever he wants. He's been alone for a long time. Cut him some slack."

"Slack? *Slack?* What about me? Maybe if he had talked to me — or Aidan or Hugh or . . . anyone — things wouldn't have been so weird earlier! We had to try and maneuver everyone around, and now I'm sleeping on the damn couch without a room of my own! Everyone else here has a bed to sleep in but me!"

"But you . . . Wait. I'm confused. If your dad and Martha aren't sharing a room, why are you sleeping on the couch?"

"He pulled me aside earlier and wanted to talk to me about how I reacted when he and Martha arrived," he said with a huff. "I'm pretty sure it would have ended with a birds-and-bees talk and I just couldn't handle it. Plus, he snores." He shook his head slowly. "And now I'm stuck in the living room, with no privacy, sleeping on a couch."

"I thought the couch pulled out into a sofa bed."

"Yeah, it does. And the mattress is about two inches thick and painful as hell to sleep on!"

It was on the tip of her tongue to offer to switch places with him — it was the sort of thing she normally did — but she quickly opted not to. So she shrugged. "It's only for the weekend. Maybe you should just sleep on the floor. You know, grab a sleeping bag and camp out sort of thing."

"What am I? Twelve?"

"Sometimes."

"Ha-ha," he deadpanned and then sighed loudly. "Seriously, Anna, the whole thing is just . . . I don't know. It feels weird."

And right then and there, the old sympathy was back. Unable to help herself, she reached out and put a hand on his shoulder

67

and gave a small, reassuring squeeze. "Of course it does. And you're not wrong for the way you feel. It was always going to feel weird, Quinn. No matter when Ian started dating again, you and your siblings were always going to feel strange about it. It's been a long time. You've only ever seen your father with your mom. But he's finally getting out and socializing and having a life again. Don't make him feel bad about it."

Quinn was silent for several minutes. "I know you're right," he said quietly. "I just don't know how I'm supposed to act. I'm just . . . I feel . . ." He turned and looked at her. "Restless."

Boy oh boy, did she know that feeling well. It was exactly how she'd felt just thirty minutes earlier. A slight breeze blew and she shivered. Quinn moved closer and put his arm around her, and everything inside of Anna melted. If only he were hugging her as a lover rather than a friend. But that wasn't going to change and she had to accept it. Maybe she even needed a reminder of it. So she did the one thing that would certainly do the trick.

"Come on," she said, pulling away and rising to her feet. "I think I saw that *The Fast and the Furious* is on. We can watch it together if you want."

Quinn jumped to his feet. He towered over Anna by a good six to eight inches and he gave her a lopsided grin. "You'd stay up and watch a racing movie with me?"

God, what his grin did to her insides. Her stomach was doing little flips and her pulse kicked up. She willed them both to calm down. "I'm not tired," she said. "And if I get tired, I'll go to bed."

"Yeah, but . . . you don't really like the whole franchise. You say it all the time," he reminded her.

"I'm figuring it will put me to sleep."

Quinn laughed out loud and pulled her into his arms and gave her a quick hug. "Oh, the sacrifices you're willing to make for a friend," he teased.

Anna held in the sigh that longed to get out. If only he knew the sacrifices she was genuinely making on a daily basis where he was concerned. "And don't you forget it," she said and moved out of his embrace. Stepping around him, she straightened her nightshirt and made sure it was covering her completely before she made her way back toward the house.

"Jesus, Anna . . ."

She stopped and turned around and noticed Quinn hadn't moved. "What? What's the matter?"

He swallowed hard, his expression unreadable in the dim light.

Anna waited a full minute, and when Quinn didn't answer, she turned and walked into the house, suddenly unsure if staying up and watching a movie with him was really the smartest thing to do.

It normally took a lot to throw Quinn, but today he had hit his limit. As much as he wanted to keep blaming it on his father and Martha, the fact was that Anna and her curves were wreaking far more havoc on him than anything else.

Just thinking about it made him feel like a colossal jerk. If he'd caught other guys ogling her, he would have kicked their asses. But if he was being honest, he had ogled her a time or two himself. Great, now he was going to have to kick his own ass.

"Quinn? You coming?" Anna called from the doorway.

Shit. With the light from the house shining behind her, he could practically see through the white T-shirt she was wearing. Was she trying to kill him? She probably would if she knew he was checking her out.

It didn't matter what Riley had said earlier. She couldn't think of him as anything more. And really, he couldn't think of her as more either.

Or could he?

Anna called his name again and snapped him out of his wayward thoughts, and Quinn knew he'd have to keep his eyes above her shoulders if he was going to survive watching a movie with her. Like a man walking to his execution, he made his way into the house, locking the sliding doors behind him and shutting off the outside lights.

"Oh no," Anna muttered from the living room.

"What's up?"

"This has got to be the smallest television in the house, and you were right about the bed."

He almost swallowed his own tongue. "Bed?" he croaked.

"Well, yeah. You've got it opened up, so I just figured we were going to sit on it to watch TV, but it really is uncomfortable." She stopped and chewed on her full bottom lip for a minute. "Maybe I can find an extra blankct or two to pad it with." And before he could stop her and say maybe they should just skip the movie, she was on the move and out of sight.

"Damn it," he mumbled. He had completely forgotten about the open bed. It was one thing to sit on the couch and watch a movie; it was another to be on the bed. Looking around, Quinn made a snap decision and quickly folded up the bed and put the sofa back together.

"Hey," Anna said, confusion written all over her face, an extra blanket in her hands as she looked at the now-closed sofa. "Why'd you close it up? I just went to get stuff to make it more comfortable."

Heat crept up his cheeks. "Oh, um . . . well, I don't think there's enough extra blankets to make this thing even remotely comfortable. At least this way we can sit with the cushions and have real padding."

"Oh. Okay." She looked at the sofa and then at the blanket in her hands. "I'll just leave this out here for you to use later, I guess."

"Yeah. Thanks." Damn. When were things ever this awkward? Oh, that's right. A lot. Especially lately.

They'd missed the first thirty minutes of the movie but it didn't matter; they'd seen it several times already. Quinn did his best to focus on the film, but out of the corner of his eye, he saw Anna slowly slouching down. Her legs — those gloriously bare, silky looking legs — were curled on the couch, her feet almost touching his thighs.

He had to fight the urge to reach out and touch her.

"You don't have to stay up, Anna," he said softly.

With her head resting on the armrest, she kept her eyes on the TV. "It's okay. I'm good."

But Quinn knew her. Anna liked to have her head on a pillow. She was a bit fanatical about feeling comfortable, really. Reaching over to the chair beside him, he grabbed a throw pillow and put it on his lap before reaching for her hand.

"What? What's the matter?" she asked, raising her head.

"Come on. I know you're not comfortable." With a little tug, he had her sitting up. Why he didn't just give her the pillow, he couldn't say for certain. It would have been easier — on him at least — if she kept her distance, but right now it was the last thing he wanted.

"It's not a big deal," she protested and then yawned. "I can just —"

He didn't let her finish. He tugged again until she was leaning against him. "Just, you know, get comfortable. We're missing the movie," he added lamely.

Anna's look was hesitant, but she finally shifted and lay down — stretching out

73

beside him with her head on the pillow in his lap. One hand rested on his knee. It felt . . . right, Quinn thought. Forcing himself to go back to watching the movie, it wasn't until sometime later that he realized Anna was asleep and he was gently playing with her hair.

"I'm totally losing it," he muttered but didn't pull his hand away. The movie was almost over, and once it ended, he'd wake her up. But for now he was going to enjoy how soft her hair was. She was growing it longer — something she hadn't done in a long time. He wasn't sure how he felt about it, but for right now he liked it.

Fifteen minutes later, the movie was over. It was after two in the morning, and he finally felt like he could sleep. His hand drifted from Anna's hair to her shoulder. It felt small under his palm. He gave her a gentle shake. "Anna?" he whispered.

"Mmm," she hummed.

"The movie's over," he said softly. "Come on. You need to go up to bed."

She snuggled up closer, her hand on his knee gently squeezing. "Too comfortable."

He couldn't help but chuckle. It never occurred to him how by making her comfortable, he wouldn't be able to wake her up. Shifting slightly, he maneuvered himself until he could stand up. Anna didn't stir. The first order of business was to stretch. He had been sitting for so long he felt a little stiff and achy. Gazing down at Anna, Quinn forced himself to really look at her.

Her dark blond hair was getting longer and he realized now he preferred it short. The sun had given her skin a golden glow today, and she had a band of freckles across her nose. He knew her face as well as his own. He couldn't remember a time when she hadn't been there with him, for him. Just the thought of her not being his friend caused a tightening in his chest he'd never felt. He'd never had to consider it before.

She was the one constant in his life. Sure, he had his brothers and Darcy, but it was different with Anna. They had simply clicked as kids, and she was the only person he felt truly comfortable around. She didn't judge him — at least not that he was aware of. If she did, she kept it to herself.

Unlike his siblings.

In all honesty, she was his safe spot. His home.

And it killed him how even looking at her now had him thinking about sex rather than getting the comfort he normally did.

"Okay, that's enough," he mumbled and leaned forward to gently shake Anna again.

She still didn't stir, so Quinn cursed and then reached for her to pick her up.

Bad idea, he immediately thought. Now he could feel the silky skin of her legs, and as the T-shirt rode up her body, he saw her plain white cotton panties. And damn if they didn't look sexy as hell too. Images of Anna in her bikini immediately came to mind, and Quinn knew he was going to have to practically sprint to the bedroom and drop her on her bed and run if he was going to survive.

And that's pretty much what he did. Walking quickly up the stairs to Anna's bedroom, he simply deposited her on the bed and pulled the blankets over her before he walked from the room, quietly closing the door behind him.

And then breathed a sigh of relief.

It was going to be a long weekend.

Anna woke up slowly and for a moment forgot where she was or how she'd gotten there. The last thing she remembered was Quinn getting a pillow for her and then tugging her down beside him. They'd never done that before — the whole closeness on the couch thing. So many changes in the last twenty-four hours. It made her head hurt and made her want to pull the blankets over her head and go back to sleep.

The knock on her door was the only thing stopping her.

"Are you awake?" Zoe asked, peeking her head in the doorway.

"Barely."

Stepping inside, Zoe closed the door behind her and sat down on the corner of the bed. "Well, you need to work on it because we have a lot to do and not a lot of time to do it in."

Anna looked at the clock and then back at Zoe. "You realize it's only seven a.m., right?"

Zoe nodded. "Exactly. We should have been up an hour ago. We have the hair and makeup girls coming soon." Then she paused and grinned broadly. "It's my wedding day! Can you believe it?"

Forcing herself to sit up, Anna couldn't help but smile back. "I can totally believe it. What I can't believe is how bad you are at math."

Zoe frowned at her.

"The girls aren't coming until eleven. That's four hours from now. We have plenty of time. What you need is to relax."

"Oh, I'm relaxed. Completely and utterly relaxed," she said, still grinning.

"Yeah, yeah, yeah. You had sex this morning and you're all glowy. Good for you," Anna said as she slumped back against her pillows. "There's no need to brag about it and make the rest of us jealous."

"Rest of you?"

"Okay, fine. Me. No need to make *me* jealous. There. Happy?"

"You're awful grumpy this morning. Didn't you sleep well?"

Anna wanted to argue that she had slept fine — and it was probably because she had fallen asleep against Quinn — but she decided to keep quiet. "It's seven in the morning, Zoe. No one's cheery at this hour."

"I am."

"Yeah, well, it's because you're getting married today. You should be cheery."

And then Zoe's smile fell a little.

"What? What's the matter?" Sitting back up, she reached up and placed a hand on Zoe's arm.

"I just . . . I wish . . ."

"Your mom was here," Anna finished for her, and Zoe nodded. "I know, sweetie. And I'm sorry. You know we're all here and we're all your family, but I know it's not quite the same."

"I know I'm so lucky," Zoe began, "and so blessed to have gained such a big family between you and the Shaughnessys, but I can't help but feel a little outnumbered here today."

"You know she's watching over you and smiling down on you today, right?"

Zoe nodded again. "I think she would have loved everyone. I know she would have loved Aidan."

Anna squeezed her arm reassuringly. "Of course she would. He's an easy man to love. You're very lucky."

And then her smile was back. "I am, aren't I?"

It was Anna's turn to nod. "And you're going to make a beautiful bride."

Zoe leaned over and hugged her. "And you're going to make a beautiful maid of honor. Thank you for being here for me."

"I wouldn't have missed it for the world."

They slowly moved apart and got comfortable again. "So," Zoe began, "last night was interesting, don't you think?"

"You mean the whole Ian and Martha thing? Yeah, it was kind of funny watching everyone's reaction."

"Um, no, clueless one," Zoe teased. "I'm talking about Quinn."

"Oh no," Anna mumbled under her breath.

"Come on. You know what I'm talking

about. He was trying so hard to stay away from you and make it seem like he was interested in my friends, but he didn't take his eyes off you all night. Hugh had to keep Bobby from going over and punching him!"

"Not again . . ."

"We were starting to take bets on how long it would take before Bobby snapped, but Hugh put a stop to it. He said it wasn't the time or place for a fight."

"Thank God someone was thinking clearly. I know my brother can be a bit of a hothead where Quinn is concerned."

"Again, clueless." Zoe sighed. "Anna, your brother isn't a hothead simply where Quinn is concerned. He's a hothead where Quinn and *you* are concerned. He doesn't like the way Quinn treats you."

This wasn't new information. Anna just didn't like to think about it. "Well, it really doesn't matter. I'm just glad someone had the good sense to keep things from getting out of hand."

"I know it was a good thing, but still, it's going to happen eventually. You know that, right?"

Unfortunately, she did. No matter how much she tried to pretend it wouldn't, Anna knew her brother too well. He'd always been protective of her — particularly where guys were concerned — but his feelings toward Quinn were completely different. There was rage there, and it really was only a matter of time before he let loose.

With a nod, Anna sighed. "As long as it's not today, I'll be happy."

"You and me both, girl. You and me both."

CHAPTER 3

"You know this is a happy occasion, right?"

Anna's reaction was a simple look of annoyance.

Quinn and Anna were dancing together along with the rest of the family at the reception, and Quinn noticed the teary look on Anna's face. "Look around," he said cheerfully. "Nothing but smiles and happy people. What gives?"

"It was all just so beautiful, and I know Zoe was feeling a bit overwhelmed earlier — missing her mom and all — but watching her now, you'd never know it. She's positively glowing."

"So then why do you look like . . . ?"

"Like what?" she asked defensively.

He shrugged. "I don't know — like you're ready to cry." And then he silently prayed she wasn't going to.

"People cry at weddings all the time."

"Um . . . yeah. And they also cry at funerals."

Anna rolled her eyes. "Oh, shut up," she sniffed.

This was another new layer — Anna acting all . . . feminine. She used to laugh and make fun of the kind of girls who cried at movies or just in general. She was tough. She was edgy. The woman in his arms was softer, and it was freaking him out. It was suddenly too much. He had to say something or the dialogue in his head was going to make him crazy.

"You're acting weird lately. What's going on?"

Her gaze immediately snapped to his. "Weird? What are you talking about?"

Great. Why couldn't she just agree with him and read his mind like she normally did? "I don't know . . . the job, the wardrobe, and now you're all crying and acting like, all girlish."

"In case you haven't noticed, Einstein, I am a girl."

Yeah, he'd noticed. "I get it, Anna, but all these changes, it isn't you. So again, what's going on?"

She sighed, and he knew the sound well. Her posture relaxed slightly as she looked away. "It was just time for a change. I didn't want to work at the pub for the rest of my life, and believe it or not, this is how most women dress and look. I can't sell houses wearing jeans and sneakers, you know," she said.

"Okay, okay, no need to get all snippy. It's just . . . you're making a lot of changes and I'm not used to it."

"Yeah, well . . . *get* used to it," she said, but there was little strength behind it.

"Hey," he said softly and waited until she looked at him. "If this is what you want to do with your life, then I'm right there with you. I'll get used to the changes and what-not. And I'll support whatever it is you want to take on next. You've always been there for me. It's what friends do, right?"

Maybe he was testing her. Maybe he wanted to see if she would react in some way to his reminding her of their status as friends.

Anna smiled. "Yes. It's what friends do."

And dammit, he couldn't read anything in her reaction. It was all just . . . Anna.

"I'm serious, Anna. I mean, I don't understand why you feel the need to make all these changes. There wasn't anything wrong with you. But if quitting the pub and selling real estate makes you happy, then . . . I'm happy."

Was it his imagination, or did she just blush? Or maybe it was wishful thinking.

The music ended, then they were getting corralled for pictures and the moment was gone. And Quinn was left possibly more confused than he already was.

They posed for pictures and everyone ate and danced and celebrated. When the time came for Quinn to give his best man toast, he found, for the first time, he was possibly at a loss for words. He had a basic outline written down for what he wanted to say, but when it was his turn to stand, suddenly none of it seemed right.

"I didn't meet Zoe under the best of circumstances," he began. "She and Aidan weren't speaking. I had to get Darcy home from a job site, and then I needed to get back to work. It was one of those times when there was just way too much going on." There were smiles and nods all around the room. "Anyway, I was kind of proud of myself that I threw the poor girl back into Aidan's path. You see . . . my brother can be a bit difficult, and he was off pouting, so I threw Zoe right into the lion's den with him." Quinn chuckled. "So I guess you can say they owe their reconciliation and now their marriage to me!"

Everyone laughed and Quinn looked at

his brother with a big grin before winking at Zoe. When everyone quieted down, he continued. "When he brought her home for one of our traditional Friday night pizza nights, it was amazing how she instantly fit in. Considering we never really invite anyone to join us for that kind of thing, it was really cool how it just seemed as if Zoe was meant to be there." He paused. "And she was. I'm a firm believer that things happen for a reason, and knowing what I know now about Zoe, there isn't a doubt in my mind that our mom chose her specifically for Aidan and sent her our way."

There was the familiar pang in his heart at thinking of his mom. When he looked over at his brother and his brother's bride, he couldn't help but feel a little bit envious. Maybe someday he'd have what they did. But not right now. He wasn't looking for the whole love, marriage, and all that went with it. There were still so many things Quinn wanted to accomplish with his life and his business, and he didn't want a serious relationship getting in his way.

It was why he had to stop thinking about what Riley had said last night. Anna was his friend and that was the way it should be. Quinn knew he needed Anna to keep his life on an even keel. It wasn't worth losing their friendship — no matter how attractive he suddenly found her or what his family thought about her feelings for him.

The room was fairly silent, and that's when he realized he needed to finish his toast.

Zoe was resting her head on Aidan's shoulder, tears glistening in her eyes. "I wish the two of you a lifetime of happiness." He raised his glass and everyone joined in. Quinn took a long drink of his champagne before setting it back down.

Music started up again and after several songs, he found himself paired back up with Anna. Funny how it kept happening.

"What happened to you up there?" she asked.

"When?"

"During your toast. You sort of zoned out for a minute."

Crap. He wondered if anyone else had noticed. It would be easy to pretend he didn't know what she was talking about, but knowing Anna, she would call bullshit on it. Might as well be honest. Or . . . almost honest.

"I was thinking about the sudden change in my family."

"What? You mean with Aidan and Hugh both married? And having more women as part of your family?"

He nodded. "Yeah. I mean, I get it with Aidan. He's the homebody type. If ever there was a guy who was the poster child for marriage and kids and the white picket fence, it's him. But Hugh? That one still stumps me."

"Why?"

"He travels all over the world. He was a major player. He had all kinds of beautiful women at his beck and call. The fact that he chose to settle down with just one? It just boggles my mind."

She stiffened in his arms. "Jeez . . . what in the world, Quinn?"

"What? What did I say?"

"You're a pig, you realize that, right?"

"Me? Why am I a pig?"

"Did it ever occur to you that not everyone wants to just sleep around? That maybe the thought of random hookups isn't appealing?"

"No, actually, it didn't." He smirked.

She made a sound of disgust and almost pulled out of his embrace.

"Anna," he said with just a hint of a whine as he pulled her back in close, "you know me. I never saw the appeal of marriage and kids and mortgages and all that crap. Especially when there are so many options out there."

For a minute, all she could do was stare at him. "So you subscribe to the theory of plenty of fish in the sea, life is like a smorgasbord, blah, blah, blah. Is that what you're saying?"

He nodded. "Sure am. How can you possibly know you've picked the right person to settle down with when there are so many to choose from? I just don't think Hugh should have given up so quickly."

"He didn't give up, you moron! He fell in love! People do it all the time, you know!" She was clearly pissed off and was pulling away again. Quinn knew he needed to calm her down before she started talking any louder and drew attention to them.

He tugged her in close. "Okay, okay, calm down. No need to get all huffy."

"Huffy!" she cried. "What is wrong with you? You can't possibly stand here and tell me you don't see how Hugh and Aubrey are completely in love. You just can't!"

"Sure . . . for now. What's gonna happen when Hugh goes back to traveling and Aubrey's left behind and some hot chick hits on him, huh? You don't think he's going to wonder about all he's missing?"

"No, I don't! When did you become so

cynical? When you fall in love, you don't sit around thinking about what you're missing!"

"Says you."

"Says anyone who's ever been in love! You mean to tell me that in all of the relationships you've had, you've never been in love?" Then she stopped and shook her head. "What am I saying? Of course you haven't."

"No, I haven't, and it's not a crime."

She studied him for a long moment before a small smile played across her face. Quinn knew that look and it kind of freaked him out.

"What are you thinking?" he forced himself to ask.

"I think it would be kind of fun to watch all of those things happen to you."

"All of what?"

The song ended and Anna stepped away from him and started walking back toward her table. Quinn was hot on her heels, and just as she was about to sit down, he placed a hand on her arm and gently spun her around. "All of what? What the hell are you talking about?" he demanded.

"Tell me something . . . describe your perfect woman."

He swallowed hard because right now the

only woman he could picture was her. Needing a moment, he tried to come off as being bored. "Why?"

"Just humor me. Please." She crossed her arms over her coral bridesmaid gown.

With a sigh, he mimicked her pose. "Okay, the perfect woman . . . She'd be tall, skinny but curvy." He stopped and thought a little more. "Big boobs, the kind of ass that —"

"Okay, stop describing the latest *Playboy* centerfold, perv," she interrupted. "Personality. Let's focus on the kind of personality you look for in a woman."

"I don't look at personality," he said, his tone challenging.

"Fine," she said with a huff. "Here's the thing, Quinn, sooner or later you're going to find a woman who is your ideal — in looks and personality. She'll be someone you're going to want to stick around for more than a night or two, and when it happens, you'll have to eat those words."

"What words?"

"You're such a douche sometimes," she said, shaking her head. "You're going to realize you're no different from your brothers. They found the perfect woman for them."

"Not gonna happen, Anna. There is no perfect woman out there — for me or otherwise."

"So cynical."

"I'm a realist. There is no such thing as perfect," he said with a shrug.

"So if you met a woman who . . . let's just say . . . enjoyed racing. It wouldn't mean anything to you?"

He shook his head. "Not particularly."

"What if she enjoyed other sports too — particularly baseball. Then what?"

He thought about it for a minute. "Well, it would be cool, sure. But it wouldn't make her perfect."

"And she could cook."

"Lots of women can cook."

"And she knew how to fix cars."

"Keep talking . . ."

"And she was independent — not clingy — and preferred burgers and pizza to steak and lobster."

"Does she have a nice ass?" he asked, a smirk on his face.

"Naturally."

"And is she good in bed?"

"Like a goddess," Anna instantly replied.

Quinn took a moment to process it all. "Okay, you find me *that* woman, and I'll eat my words about Hugh and Aidan and let you do the 'I told you so' dance."

Anna's smile grew. "You're on."

■ ■ ■ ■

For the remainder of the weekend, Anna had to wonder what in the world had gotten into her. Why had she even made that bet with Quinn? She didn't want him to find the perfect woman; she wanted him to find . . . *her*!

It wasn't until she was driving home that the idea came to her — she was already in the process of making herself over. Why not make herself over into the woman she described to Quinn? She almost squealed with joy. It wouldn't take much. Most of the things she described already fit her to a T. Well, except the car fixing and goddess in bed things, but hey, a girl could learn, right?

For the first time in . . . forever . . . Anna honestly felt hope for her and Quinn.

The key to it was not making it too obvious or too easy. No. She needed to become a little less accessible and make him come to her. But how? There were the obvious methods — simply not being available for him like she normally was. That made her laugh. She'd need a backup for the plan. It didn't seem to matter when he called or what he wanted, she usually went running. She was going to need someone who was in on her plan to make sure she stayed strong and in control.

The obvious choice was Zoe. Although she had just left on her honeymoon, Anna made a mental note to get together with her for lunch as soon as she got back. That would give her time to really formulate her plan of action.

"Operation Get Quinn." She chuckled to herself as she drove through town, thankful to almost be home. "Oh, it's going to be perfect!"

Zoe would be the only one who could know what she was doing. To the rest of her friends and family, it would look like she was finally moving on — she'd go on dates that would hopefully make Quinn jealous, and take some classes to make it look as if she was just broadening her horizons. She thought of her brother and their conversation back at the wedding and knew he'd probably be the most excited at her new pastimes.

Then he'd be pissed when he found out she was doing it all to get Quinn.

"Then he won't find out why I'm doing it," she quipped with another laugh and felt as if everything was already falling into place.

When she pulled into her driveway and

got out of the car, Anna had a little spring in her step that hadn't been there before.

And it felt pretty damn good.

For the next week, Anna did her research. Community college courses, YouTube videos — you name it, she was using it. Of course, there were some things you couldn't take a class for. Like the sex goddess thing.

I draw the line at taking a class on how to be like that in bed, she told herself. More than once.

The Internet was really quite handy, and she hadn't appreciated all you could learn on it up until now. Over the last several days, Anna had learned to change a flat tire and to do minor maintenance on her car, like changing out windshield wipers and several filters.

It was Saturday, and today's project was learning how to change a spark plug. The first thing she was trying it on was her lawn mower. It was an old one — her father had given it to her when he'd upgraded — and she figured it was a good place to start. Five minutes later, she was done.

"Well, that was a little anticlimactic," she muttered, sitting on the floor of her garage.

The car was a different matter. Unwilling to spend a fortune on a set of tools, Anna had had no choice but to call Bobby and ask to borrow some of his. Luckily, his timing was perfect, and when she looked over her shoulder, he was already pulling into the driveway.

"What's going on, squirt?" he asked as he strolled her way.

"I told you," she began, rising to her feet, "this old car is starting to show its age, and in order for me to be responsible, I need to learn how to do some basic stuff to it."

Bobby rolled his eyes. "That's what you pay a mechanic for."

She rolled her eyes right back at him. "And that's not being very responsible. Come on, Bobby, you know I'm trying to be financially responsible. Some of the stuff this car needs I can probably do myself." Then she showed him the new wiper blades. "And . . ." she said, popping the hood, "new air filters! Look at me! I'm practically a mechanic!"

Bobby leaned over the engine and looked around. "Not bad. Not bad at all." Then he straightened. "Why the sudden interest in car repair? I mean, I know what you just told me, but this car's been a bit of a nightmare for a while."

She shrugged. "With the new career and all, my schedule isn't what it used to be.

I've got student loans to pay off and I'm just trying to save money where I can."

"Dammit, Anna, do you need money? I knew when I moved out things were going to be harder on you and . . . shit . . . I should have offered to keep helping you out with some of the bills."

"Oh, for crying out loud," she huffed. "No, I don't need money. Why is it so wrong for me to just want to learn something new that will help me? I can't keep running to you or Quinn whenever I have car trouble."

"You certainly can keep running to Shaughnessy. With everything you do for him, he should be putting a whole new engine in this thing for you! With all the food and the running around for him and —"

"I'm not doing this with you!" she cried in exasperation. "Seriously, I am so tired of having this conversation with you over and over. Quinn is my friend! You have got to get over this . . . thing you have where he's concerned! I don't get on you about your friends!"

"That's because my friends don't take advantage of me like he does you!" Bobby fired back. "You keep chasing after him, hoping he'll fall in love with you or something. You can stand here all day long and play the 'he's just my friend' card, but you're not only lying to me, you're lying to yourself!'"

It really sucked when she was so transparent.

"Look, are you going to help me or not?" Anna said, crossing her arms over her chest.

"Anna, all I'm saying is —"

"Enough with the lectures, Bobby! I'm a grown woman! Jeez, I just need a little help from my brother, so I can be a little more independent. I didn't think it was a bad thing!"

Bobby had the good sense to know when to quit arguing. "You're right. I'm sorry. I really do think it's a good thing for you to know how to take care of yourself and your car. I'd hate to think of you broken down someplace and not knowing what to do."

"Believe me, if I'm broken down someplace, I'll definitely call for help. But the maintenance stuff just seems like a smart place to start."

He stepped closer and wrapped her in a brotherly embrace, kissing her on the forehead. "I'm proud of you, Anna. I know I don't say it enough, but I really am proud of all you're doing with yourself."

She beamed at his praise. "Thank you," she said. "Now, show me what kind of thingamajig helps me get a spark plug out of a fifteen-year-old Honda."

Business was booming for Quinn. The new auto shop had a waiting list of people wanting their cars looked at, and the custom restoration part of the shop was finally coming together. Standing back and looking at the two cars currently sitting in the bays was almost enough to make him giggle like a schoolgirl.

Cars had always been his passion — he loved to drive them; he loved to take them apart and put them back together. His years on the racing circuit with NASCAR had been like a damn dream come true — the cars, the speed, the women. When one of his best friends was killed in a crash, Quinn had walked away from the circuit. Watching Todd's family in the days and weeks following the accident had been a real eye-opener. There was no way he wanted his family to go through something like that — and watching footage of the crash every time they turned on the TV.

Crashes had been an everyday occurrence for so long that Quinn had thought himself desensitized to it. That had changed in the blink of an eye.

Once he retired, he was thankful for having the business sense to have invested his money during his career. True, he'd thought he'd have at least another ten years to keep putting money into it, but it was still enough for him to move on to the next phase of his life in automotive repair and restoration.

His brothers had thought he was crazy. His father had simply asked if he needed a hand getting started. And Anna? Well, she had brought him food at all hours of the day and night because he had refused to stop working in those first few months, and she had always made sure he was taken care of.

Shit. He hadn't allowed himself to think about her much since the wedding. The entire weekend had pretty much messed with him on multiple levels. The whole thing with his dad and Martha still made Quinn want to shudder, but he knew it wasn't something that was going to go away. His father deserved to be happy, and if right now that meant dating Martha Tate, then who was Quinn to try and stop it?

But the whole revelation thing with Anna? It was something that was going to stick for a while. Besides the whole crazy bikini body thing, having his brother tell him Anna had been crushing on him for years? Hell, he still couldn't wrap his brain around it.

The sound of approaching footprints had Quinn looking over his shoulder. A smile soon followed. "Hey! Wasn't expecting to see you around so soon," he said as Aidan walked up and gave him a hug.

"We got back last night, and I was driving through town and saw your car outside and figured I'd stop by and see the new shop. I haven't been in here since before you opened."

"Yeah, I know, and it was really starting to piss me off," Quinn teased.

Aidan looked around the shop and then spotted the two cars, his eyes going wide. "Holy crap," he said with a hint of awe. "Is that . . . ? Are those . . . ?"

Quinn stepped up beside him and placed an arm around his brother's shoulder with a friendly pat. "Yup. You are looking at a 1969 Chevy Camaro and an amazing 1960 Corvette."

Aidan simply stared at the cars for a long moment before turning toward Quinn. "Am I allowed to touch them?"

A loud laugh escaped before Quinn could help himself. "Dude, you can even sit in them."

"Seriously? That's allowed?" he asked even as he walked toward the Corvette. "I don't think I've ever seen one of these up close.

How'd you get your hands on one?"

"They belong to a buddy of mine I used to race with. He's a collector, and he's had these two cars in storage for a while and finally decided he wanted to go ahead and restore them."

Aidan gingerly opened the car door and sat down. And sighed. "Oh man . . . this is incredible. It almost seems a shame to do anything to it."

Quinn chuckled. "Yeah, I used to think of it like that too, but Jake wants to be able to take them out once in a while. Personally, I'm all for it. Cars are meant to be driven and enjoyed — not just looked at."

"So what are you going to do to them?"

Walking around each of the cars, Quinn allowed himself to get a little lost in the details. "Both of their engines are in fair condition, so we're going to take them out, clean them, and replace whatever needs replacing. The Camaro has a fair amount of rust, so we're going to be sanding the body down and setting it right and then repainting. New tires for each of them. Replacing the vinyl on the interior of the Corvette and the entire backseat in the Camaro."

"Damn. That's a lot of work, Quinn."

"And that's only the half of it."

"No!" Aidan cried, climbing from the car

and walking over to the other.

Quinn nodded. "There's a lot to it. Each car will almost be completely pulled apart then and put back together to make sure everything is pristine — the wiring, the fuel system, the exhaust . . . everything."

"What's your timeline on something like this?"

"It's not a quick turnaround if that's what you're thinking."

Aidan shook his head. "No, I'm serious. You've never done the restoration around here, close to home, so I have no idea."

"At minimum? You're looking at a thousand hours per car at least. And that's if there aren't any surprises, complications, or mishaps. The average car collector — if he was doing it on his own — could take up to two years to complete a job like this on one car."

"Holy crap."

Quinn nodded again. "Exactly. I'm going to go a little in between and figure about fifteen hundred man hours per car."

Aidan chuckled. "Good thing your friend isn't in a rush."

"That's the beauty of working with a fellow car enthusiast. They know the importance of doing things right. If he gives me the time now, he'll get all the time he wants out of the car when I'm done."

Aidan stopped and thought for a moment. "You said this guy's name is Jake?"

"Yeah."

"You mean Jake Tanner? *The* Jake Tanner?"

Quinn rolled his eyes. "Yes, Jake Tanner. Why? Got a man crush on him?"

Aidan let out a bark of laughter. "Cute, but no. I just remember he was an amazing driver. I used to follow him when you were racing."

"Oh yeah? Then you know that I ranked higher," Quinn said a bit defensively.

"Easy there, baby girl. No one's saying he was better than you. I was merely pointing out that I was a fan."

"Yeah, well . . . you were supposed to be cheering for me. Not following and cheering other racers."

Aidan ran a hand gently over the Camaro's hood. "Insecure much? What's going on in this family? First Riley, now you?"

"I'm not insecure. I just didn't realize you followed anyone else in racing other than me. And as for Riley, who knows? I'm sure it's hard for him. There are new bands coming out every day. There's constant competition and he's having to prove himself on a daily basis. Anyone would get freaked out from time to time if they had to live like that."

"I guess." Stepping away from the car, Aidan sighed. "Where were cars like this when we were kids?"

"Out of our price range."

"Oh yeah. That's right." Aidan laughed and then straightened and looked at his brother. "So things are going well?"

"Absolutely. I didn't think I'd enjoy sticking around town for so long, but it's really not so bad."

"I never understood your need to move around so much."

"Yeah, well, you're a homebody. No one else in the family is, other than Dad."

A small shrug was Aidan's only reply.

"And now that I've got these babies here, I'll be around even longer," Quinn continued. "I promised Jake I'd be the one to do the bulk of the work."

"Is that smart for you? I mean, you have other shops to manage."

"It's not a big deal. I have a great team of mechanics and managers. I'll still go and spend some time at each of them, just not the extended amount I was doing before."

"You've done other restorations before. Why is this one such a big deal?"

"The other cars weren't nearly as impressive as these — at least not to me. I've done cars from the thirties and onward, but the muscle cars? Those are my favorites. And to have two of them here?" He sighed dramatically. "It's almost enough to give me a hard-on."

"Grow up."

Then Quinn's teasing grin faded. "If I get these cars right, besides making a boatload of money on them, it will go a long way in cementing my name in the industry. There are still a lot of people who think this is just a hobby for me and that I don't take it seriously. I really need to get everyone to see how I love what I do and I'm good at it."

Aidan nodded. "I get it. And you'll get there, Quinn. You do great work and it's going to speak volumes."

"I don't know. So many things have come easily to me, and this is the first time in my life I'm having to really prove myself. Car restoration isn't a quick turnaround. It's not like racing or baseball, where I could have a good season and make the news. I just . . . I didn't think it would be so hard."

"It's not a bad thing, you know. Having to work a little harder. Makes you appreciate it all the more."

"Yeah, well, I'm not getting any younger."

Aidan laughed. "Or prettier."

"Shut up," Quinn said and walked over to the cooler he kept in the corner and grabbed a couple bottles of soda, handing one to Aidan. "Anyway . . . what about you? How's married life?"

Aidan broke out in a sappy grin. "Loving it."

"Figures." He was about to say more when his cell phone rang. He motioned to his brother to give him a minute before answering it. He listened intently and then said, "Sounds good. See you in a few minutes."

"Everything okay?" Aidan asked.

"Yeah, but you may want to take a minute and prepare yourself."

"Oh, really? Why is that?"

"Because that was Jake and he's on his way here."

"What?" Aidan cried. "Now?"

Quinn rolled his eyes. "Yup, so you better go fix your hair and make yourself pretty."

"Screw you."

But as Aidan walked off, all Quinn could do was laugh.

Clearly, Anna was a glutton for punishment. She had just finished showing a house and was on her way home. This particular route took her past Quinn's shop. She hadn't seen or talked to him since the wedding and . . .

well . . . she missed him. It wasn't unusual for them to go a week without seeing or talking to one another, but right now she just really wanted to see him.

Pulling into the parking lot, she noticed Aidan's car and smiled. It was on her mind to give Zoe a call and now she knew for certain they were back from their honeymoon.

Waving to one of the mechanics, she was immediately told — without asking — that Quinn was over in the restoration building. It was separate from the main shop, out back with its own office and setup. She knew why Quinn set it up that way, and she was excited because if he was back there, it meant he had some new cars to restore. She was almost giddy at the thought of what kind they might be.

Letting herself in, she immediately heard the loud male laughter and knew both Quinn and Aidan were there. A minute later, she heard a voice she'd never heard before. As she stepped into the bay area, Aidan spotted her first.

"Anna!" He walked toward her, his arms open wide. "How are you?" He hugged her and kissed her on the cheek. "Have you spoken to Zoe yet? I know she was dying to tell you all about the trip."

She hugged him back. "As soon as I saw your car, I made a mental note to give her a call when I get home." She stepped back and smiled. "Was it wonderful?"

His grin was the only answer she needed.

"So what brings you here?" he asked.

"I was driving by and thought I'd stop in and say hello." Aidan was looking at her a little funny until Anna started to squirm. "What? What's wrong?" She looked down at her outfit and wondered if she'd spilled something on herself.

"I still can't get used to seeing you in career-woman mode. I miss the girl in the blue jeans who makes the world's greatest burgers."

Anna blushed. "I'm still the same girl, Aidan," she said shyly. "But sometimes a girl has to grow up." She was saved from saying anything else when Quinn walked over with a guy she didn't recognize.

"Hey, Anna," Quinn said with a smile that didn't quite reach his eyes.

"Hey," she said, forcing her own smile while checking out the attractive guy standing beside him. Without waiting for an introduction, she held her hand out. "Hi, I'm Anna. I'm a friend of Aidan and Quinn's."

Mr. Tall, Dark, and Muscular gave her a

sexy smile and took her hand in his. "Nice to meet you. I'm Jake. Also a friend of Quinn's."

"Really?" she said, her smile growing until her cheeks hurt. "Then how come we haven't met before?"

Jake stepped in closer, shouldering Quinn out of the way. "I have no idea. I used to race cars with Quinn. We met on the circuit." He still hadn't let go of her hand. "Do you follow racing, Anna?"

For a minute she almost wanted to pinch herself. Here was an incredibly attractive man — almost too good-looking for his own good — practically flirting with her, and she hadn't had to lift a finger. Aidan was grinning and Quinn looked ready to spit nails. It was almost as if she had scripted the moment herself!

"Oh, I follow all kinds of sports, Jake." She quickly racked her brain for racing stats until she remembered something about Jake's. "You used to drive a Chevy, right? Number thirty-four?"

His smile grew and his grip on her hand tightened before his thumb began to stroke her wrist. "That's right, darlin'," he drawled. "I had a lot of good luck with that car." Then he leaned in close. "And in Quinn's last season, I beat him by twenty points."

"It was *two,* Jake," Quinn corrected. "Two. Not twenty. Every time you tell that story, you embellish."

Jake stepped back and finally released Anna's hand. "So what is a lovely woman like you doing in a dirty garage like this?" he asked.

Before she could answer, Quinn spoke. "Dude, what the hell? It's a brand-new shop and it's just Anna. She's been in my shops before."

Anna shot him an annoyed look. "Oh, I don't mind coming to the shop. It's not a big deal. A little engine grease and some exhaust fumes don't bother me. I actually do some work on my own car."

"Since when?" Quinn demanded.

She ignored him and focused on Jake. "Of course, I don't drive anything like these cars." Looking over at the classic cars, she sighed. "Those are real beauties. Whoever owns them is really lucky."

Quinn groaned, Aidan chuckled, and Jake stepped forward and wrapped his arm around Anna's shoulders. "It just so happens I own them."

"No!" she cried.

He nodded. "I sure do." Then he led her over to them, leaving Quinn and Aidan behind.

It took a full minute before Quinn could find his voice. "What the hell just happened here?"

Aidan was practically wiping tears from his eyes from laughter. "I think your friend just swooped in here and swept Anna off her feet."

"No," Quinn said firmly, defiantly. "No way. Anna doesn't go for that type."

"What? The tall, dark, good-looking, and successful type?" Aidan teased.

Quinn glared at him. "Are we talking her type or yours?" He shook his head in disgust. "Anna is not impressed with that kind of stuff. She's been around drivers before and it never made a difference."

"I'm sure there's a big difference between the way they treat someone they meet while on the track and off." He nodded in Jake and Anna's direction. "There's no distractions here, and if you ask me, she definitely seemed . . . impressed."

Quinn shook his head. "Uh-uh. No way. She's just being nice. There's no way Anna would go out with a guy like Jake."

"How much you wanna bet?"

Just then, Anna let out a very feminine giggle that echoed off the shop's walls. And suddenly, Quinn wasn't so sure about anything.

CHAPTER 4

"Look at you . . . all glowy."

"I know."

"How were the Mayan ruins?"

"I have no idea."

"How were the beaches?"

"Not a clue."

Anna sighed and threw her head back in disgust. "You know, it's as if this were the first time you and Aidan had sex! You went to Mexico for a week, and you're telling me you didn't leave the room?"

Zoe giggled. "I know it sounds crazy, but . . . we had our own little villa and just enjoyed staying in our cocoon."

"Unbelievable."

"Don't be hatin'," Zoe said, standing and going to the kitchen to get them each another drink. "The thought of playing tourist just wasn't appealing."

"Okay, let's just leave it at that. I don't need to know all the details of what the two of you were doing in your cocoon."

"Don't worry. I wasn't going to share."

"Thank you."

Sitting back down on the sofa, Zoe curled her legs up under her. "So what about you? What's been going on this last week? Aidan said he saw you yesterday at Quinn's shop."

"Yeah, I was just driving by and decided to stop and say hello."

"Uh-huh. Right."

"What? I did!"

Zoe gave an exaggerated wink. "Okay. I also heard there was a very good-looking race-car driver there who seemed a little smitten with you."

"Did Aidan honestly describe Jake as good-looking and use the word *smitten*?"

"Okay, maybe I'm putting my own spin on it but the results are the same. So? Spill it! Did he ask you out?"

Anna nodded. "Well, he wanted to take me to dinner last night but I turned him down."

"But . . . why? Did you already have plans?"

"No . . . not exactly."

"Okay, now you really have to spill it. I know that look on your face. You're up to something."

Anna explained her plan to get Quinn to

notice her. "So you see, it's perfect. Here's this amazing guy and I didn't have to do a thing!"

"Um, I hate to point out the obvious, but the only way to make Quinn jealous because you're out with some guy is to actually go *out* with said guy. You just said you didn't."

"No, but I will. He called me last night just to talk, and then again today."

Zoe let out a little squeal. "Anna, that's great! So when are you going out? Tonight? Where is he taking you?"

"Yeah . . . um . . . no. We're not going out tonight either."

Zoe sagged in her seat. "Okay, you've lost me. Why aren't you going out with him?"

"I don't know. I can't seem to get excited about saying yes. I figure with a guy like him, it's all about the ego. He's going to keep calling until I say yes. So maybe by next weekend, I'll finally be able to make myself go."

"Maybe this isn't such a good idea. Why would you want to go out with someone you clearly don't have any interest in?"

"No one else is asking me out!" she cried. "Do you think I like this? Do you think I like sitting around pining for a guy who has zero interest in me?"

"Oh, sweetie," Zoe began, "I know it's

hard and I'm sorry. I just don't want to see you do something you really don't want to just because you think it *might* make Quinn sit up and take notice. You know there's no guarantee of that, right?"

Unfortunately, Anna refused to think that way. At least she had until just that minute. "I guess I thought if I made myself into his perfect woman . . ."

Reaching out, Zoe put her hand on top of Anna's and squeezed. "If he doesn't love you for who you are, then you need to move on. It will never work if you're trying to be someone you're not."

"I have to admit, I started doing the online stuff and researching car repairs as a way to impress Quinn, but as it turns out, it's not so bad." She shrugged. "It's a lot like cooking — with the right tools, you can do almost anything."

Zoe gave her a small smile. "You need to be doing these things for you. You should be choosing classes and hobbies based on your interests, not Quinn's."

"I have another two weeks of the auto-mechanic thing, so —"

"Anna."

The reality of the whole situation was finally starting to sink in. Zoe wasn't saying anything Anna hadn't heard before — from her parents, her brother, and, if she were honest, herself. Looking up at Zoe, tears filled her eyes. "I just don't know how to move on. He's been such a huge part of my life for so damn long and I've been in love with him almost since the beginning. How do I just stop?"

"I wish I knew, Anna. I really do. Maybe you need to, you know, step away from the situation for a while and try dating."

"I guess I can still go out with Jake."

Zoe shook her head. "I don't think it's a good idea."

"Why not?"

"It's still too close. No doubt Quinn's name will come up in conversation, and that's just going to keep you in this place. That's the last thing you need."

"I don't know. Maybe. But I have a feeling I'm not going to quit hearing from him until I at least meet him for a drink or dinner."

Zoe frowned. "Okay. So go for something short, like a drink, and then tell him you're not interested. Hopefully he'll take you at your word and move on."

Now Anna sagged down on the sofa. "Why does this have to be so damn hard? Why can't I just meet someone and fall in love and be happy?"

Once again, Zoe squeezed her hand. "Because you keep putting yourself in Quinn's path. You need to make a clean break — no stopping by the shop, no baking cookies or bringing him food . . . none of it."

"Damn. How am I supposed to do that?"

"Cold turkey. Trust me. I think it's the only way."

"But —"

"Go on the date with Jake. Maybe go out with your new coworkers and see if you like anyone there. Just . . . no Shaughnessys."

"But you're a Shaughnessy," Anna said with a slight pout.

"Okay, let me clarify — no *Quinn* Shaughnessy. Deal?"

It pained her to do it, but she agreed. "Deal."

Ten minutes into her date with Jake, Anna was already regretting it. On the surface, Jake Tanner was the complete package. After a little while, however, she began to realize he was also a complete tool.

The man talked about nothing but himself. His career. His cars. His conquests — yes, the man even talked about all the women who threw themselves at him. Anna knew she certainly wasn't going to be one of them. Jake had pursued her. Relentlessly. Since she'd talked to Zoe, he'd continued to call every day until she said yes.

It wasn't as if Anna was a stranger to dating. She had an okay dating life, even with her stupid crush on Quinn, but this date was definitely one of her worst. Looking around the bar he had suggested they meet at, Anna wondered if the bathroom window was big enough for her to climb out of.

Jake had gone to the bar to get their drinks, and when Anna saw him heading back toward her, she thought she was going to be sick.

Placing the drink down in front of her, Jake sat down and smiled. "So tell me, Anna, how do you like selling real estate?"

Wow. A question about her. Color her surprised. "You know, it's not so bad. I've only been doing it for about six months."

"And what did you do before that?"

"I managed a pub in town," she said and noticed the bored look on Jake's face. "I started out waitressing and tending bar every now and again, but then took over managing it and even did most of the cooking."

"Great," he said, but his eyes didn't meet hers. He nodded toward her drink. "You should try it. See if you like it."

She looked at him oddly. "It's just a Malibu and pineapple. They're pretty hard to screw up."

He gave her a weak smile. "Is there a big housing market here? I mean, it's a pretty small town. Do you have to travel a lot to get listings?"

And we're back to me. Impressive. "I do have several listings in surrounding towns, but there are plenty of vacation rentals here that keep me busy, and I'm branching out into the commercial sector."

"Really? Like what? Shopping centers?"

She shook her head. "Right now I'm working on a project for a large resort. The property was originally zoned for a subdivision, but it fell through — before I started working in the industry — and now we're looking to build a luxury resort on the land."

"Very nice."

They were quiet for a minute and Anna realized she should probably ask something about his life. Again. Not that she really wanted to know, but clearly he didn't engage in conversation unless it was about him.

"So . . . what have you been doing since you retired from racing?" Clearly it was the right thing to ask because he immediately started talking. Taking a sip of her drink,

Anna looked around the bar and wished someone she knew would come in and save her. It would be rude of her to just get up and say she wanted to leave and that she had no interest in seeing him again. One drink. She'd have this one drink and then tell him.

". . . I have a vacation home in Maui I love to visit . . ."

Her head felt funny. She looked at Jake and could see his lips moving but couldn't quite focus on what he was saying. The music and voices around her suddenly seemed like one long hum.

". . . my private jet can get us there in a couple of hours if you'd like . . ."

"Excuse me," Anna forced herself to say, and before Jake could say another word, she ran for the ladies' room, certain she was going to be sick.

Once she was safely ensconced in a stall, she fished in her purse for her phone. The screen was blurry, and she did her best to get her eyes to focus and find Bobby's number. She hit "call," and it went directly to voice mail. "Damn," she muttered and scrolled again, hitting "call" and praying someone would answer.

"I'm telling you, Zoe, if my brother hadn't

found you first, I would have married you."

Zoe laughed out loud. "Good one, Quinn, but I highly doubt it."

"It's true!" he said, slapping his hand on the dining room table for emphasis. "Your cooking is amazing. Can I have dinner with you guys every night?"

"See?" Aidan said. "The way to a man's heart truly is through his stomach."

"Leave my brother," Quinn said, his blue eyes big and pleading. "We can run away together. I'll get us a house with the world's biggest kitchen."

Tears of laughter streamed down Zoe's cheeks. "As flattering as it is that you only want me for my mastery of Irish cuisine, I'm afraid I'll have to pass" — she walked over and kissed Aidan soundly on the lips — "because your brother here owns my heart."

"Well damn," Quinn said with a pout. "All of the good ones are taken."

Zoe was just about to speak when her cell phone rang. "Excuse me," she said with a smile as she picked up the phone.

"Uh-oh, this can't be good if you're calling me already," she said as a greeting. "Are you home or on your way there?"

"Z . . . Zoe?" Anna's voice was small and weak.

"Anna? Sweetie, what's the matter? Are you all right?" Both Aidan and Quinn stopped talking and turned toward Zoe.

"I . . . I don't feel right."

"Did you eat something bad? Are you sick?"

"Drink," she said. "Only one sip."

"Did you watch the bartender? Do you think something's wrong with the drink?"

"Jake . . . gone for a while. He got the drinks."

"Okay, okay. Tell me where you are, Anna. Tell me and I'll be right there to get you."

"I'm in the bathroom. Don't want to go back out there."

"Good. That's good. Stay in there until I get there. But I need to know the name of the restaurant you're at."

"Tavern . . . something tavern."

Zoe placed her hand over the phone and looked at Aidan frantically. "Where is the tavern? Some place around here with the word *tavern* in it."

Both brothers jumped up. Quinn demanded, "What's going on?"

"Something's wrong with Anna. I need to go pick her up."

"No," Anna mumbled. "Don't send Aidan. Don't tell anyone. Just you. You come and get me. I'm so embarrassed, Zoe. Please."

"Okay, don't worry. I'm on my way. Stay on the phone with me, Anna."

"Can't," she said. "I . . . I think I'm going to be sick." And then the phone went dead.

"Damn it," Zoe said as she ran across the room and grabbed her purse.

"What's going on?" Aidan asked.

"Anna . . ." she began and then looked at Quinn and hesitated. And then it didn't matter. "She's out with Jake Tanner and . . . I don't know. She said she took a sip of her drink and now she doesn't feel right. She's in a bathroom stall at this tavern place and I need to go get her."

"Son of a *bitch,*" Quinn cursed as he kicked his chair out from behind him. "Not again."

"What?" Zoe asked. "What do you mean by that?" She grabbed Quinn's arm as he walked out of the kitchen but he didn't stop.

"We're going with you," Aidan said, opening the front door.

"She's scared and sick and embarrassed, Aidan. She doesn't want an audience."

Quinn called over his shoulder as he went right out to his car, "Well, that's too damn bad."

His car was out of the driveway by the time Aidan and Zoe got into theirs.

■ ■ ■ ■

Anna's head was spinning. Someone knocked on the stall door and asked if she was okay, and she merely mumbled her response. A few minutes later, someone else came and said her date was worried about her.

"I want to go home," she whispered and wished Zoe would get there and help her leave.

After a few minutes, she forced herself to do the one thing she hated more than anything — throw up. If there was something bad in her system, she wanted it gone. Once she was done, she slowly got to her feet, and when the room stopped spinning, she left the stall.

Her reflection nearly made her scream. She rinsed out her mouth and was about to leave the ladies' room when two women walked in.

"Don't go out there!" one of them cried. "There's a fight going on."

"Did you see him? I mean, he just came into the bar and walked right up to that guy and punched him in the face!"

"I think I recognized the guy in the booth. He's a race-car driver. You know . . . from

NASCAR."

Oh no. Anna quickly made her away around the two women and pulled the door open — and ran directly into Zoe.

"Oh thank God," Zoe cried, pulling Anna into her arms. "Are you okay?"

"I . . . I don't know. I think so," Anna said. The sound of a loud crash had her looking over Zoe's shoulder. "What's going on?"

"I'm sorry. I really tried to stop him, but —"

"Oh my God . . . is that Quinn?" Anna tried to step around Zoe, but she held her firm. "Zoe?"

"Sweetie, don't, okay?"

"Why is he here? And why is he beating up Jake?"

"We'll talk about it later. Let's get you home."

Anna's head was starting to clear. She managed to outmaneuver Zoe and headed toward where Jake and Quinn were pounding on one another.

"You son of a bitch!" Quinn snarled. "Is this the only way you can get women to go home with you?"

"Screw you," Jake spat.

"I will end you," Quinn said and got in one more punch before Aidan pulled him off.

"That's enough!" Aidan said, yanking his brother back. "The last thing you want is to make this worse."

Quinn broke free and turned on him. "*Worse?* This asshole drugged Anna!"

"You don't know that," Aidan said, trying to be the voice of reason.

"He's done it before," Quinn said, his breathing ragged. "Granted, it was years ago, but . . . it's why she's sick right now."

Neither of them noticed Anna's approach. "You knew he drugged girls?" she asked, her voice small and shaky as she came to stand in front of Quinn. "You knew and you didn't tell me?"

"Anna, that's not . . . I didn't think . . . I had no idea you would actually go out with him."

She slapped him hard across the face.

The room went silent.

She looked over to where Jake was sprawled out on the floor and felt her insides lurch again. Placing a hand on her stomach, she forced herself to breathe through it. Then she returned her focus to Quinn and almost smiled at the red hand-print on his cheek. "Honestly, the *one time* you don't warn me off a guy."

Quinn reached for her, but she stepped away. "Anna . . . I'm sorry. Please. Let me explain."

She turned and spotted Zoe, who was now standing next to Aidan. "I'd really like to go home now."

Without a word, Zoe took Anna's hand and together they walked out of the bar.

Five minutes later, Aidan and Quinn came out, their expressions grim. "You should have taken her home," Aidan said softly to Zoe when they got close enough.

"We needed to make sure the cops weren't coming and that you were okay," Zoe replied. "Everything okay in there?"

"We just wanted to talk to the manager and apologize for what happened. Sort of." Aidan turned and took Anna in his arms. "You okay, kiddo?"

She nodded and let out a shaky breath. "Yeah. I'm going to be okay. The fresh air is really helping."

"Come on, we'll take you home," Aidan said and turned them toward his car. "We'll pick up your car in the morning."

"No," Quinn said. "I'll take her home."

"Quinn," Aidan warned. "This isn't the time. Let it go for tonight."

"No," he repeated, more firmly this time. "Please."

Aidan looked at Zoe and then Anna. When she nodded silently, Aidan kissed her on the top of the head and stepped away. "Call us if you need anything," he said as he put his arm around Zoe, watching as Quinn stepped forward and put his own arm around Anna. She immediately moved away and Aidan and Zoe couldn't help but smile.

"I think she's going to be okay," Zoe said quietly.

"Are you kidding me? She's going to be great. I just wish we could be flies on the wall to watch her do to him what he just did to Jake."

The entire ride was spent in silence.

Anna couldn't wait to just get home, take a shower, and put the whole night behind her. It probably wasn't the smartest idea, letting Quinn be the one to take her home, but she knew him well enough to know that if she hadn't let him, he would have shown up eventually to check on her. Maybe now she could just get it out of the way and be done with him for tonight.

"Thanks for the ride," she said as soon as the car came to a stop in her driveway and reached to open the door. When Quinn shut the car off and she heard the jingle of keys, Anna turned and faced him with disbelief. "What are you doing?"

"I'm coming in with you," he said gruffly,

his expression tinged with anger.

"Um . . . no, you're not. It's been a bad night and I didn't invite you in." Quickly, she climbed from the car and walked up to her front door. Quinn was beside her in an instant.

"Seriously?" she said over her shoulder. He didn't budge or even react, so she opened the door and stepped inside.

Quinn shut the door behind him and watched her move around the house. "What's going on, Anna?"

Without looking at him, she nervously fluttered around, hoping he'd take the hint and just leave. "It's been a long night. I've got a headache and I just want to go to bed."

"Do you feel all right? I mean . . . do you still feel sick from — ?"

"From the drug your friend slipped me?" she asked sarcastically.

Quinn cursed. "Damn it, Anna, I swear it never occurred to me he'd do something like that again. It was years ago and it was never proven, but he'd been accused of it."

"You should have told me," she said defensively. "You heard him ask me out in your shop that day and you didn't think to warn me? I mean, what the hell, Quinn? You warn me off guys all the damn time! You once told me not to go out with a guy because he liked to listen to jazz music, and you didn't think telling me Jake had a history of drugging women was important enough to mention?"

"Okay, I'll admit it, I screwed up! You can't possibly know how sorry I am, but . . . come on. I've apologized. What more do you want from me?"

She stared at him hard. "I want you to leave."

"No."

Her brown eyes widened with disbelief. "Excuse me?"

"I'm not leaving. I think it's time you and I sat down and talked."

"I don't want to sit and talk, Quinn. I'm fine. I just want to go to bed."

He stepped farther into the room. "Quit shoveling, Anna."

"Shoveling? What the heck does that even mean?" she asked, looking up at him from across the room.

"I know when you're lying and when you're just shoveling bullshit around. So spill it. I know you're dying to light into me about tonight. And normally you wouldn't have held back this long. You haven't been acting like yourself lately and you've been blowing me off and I want to know why."

Anna rolled her eyes. "Okay, for starters,

yes, I would like to light into you, but in case you haven't noticed, I'm not quite feeling like myself. I had to stick my finger down my throat to get whatever was in that drink out of me. Excuse me if my feeling like hammered shit hasn't allowed me to put all my attention on you."

"Anna —"

"And for the record, I haven't been blowing you off, Quinn. Sheesh. Has it ever occurred to you that I have a life and I have better things to do than wait on you?"

"You've been there for every move and every store opening I've done in the tri-state area. It's a whole new phase for me starting now and you've hardly come by. And the one time you do come by, you spend the entire time flirting with Jake. And look how that worked out for you."

"You bastard," she hissed, ready to smack him again. "You're seriously going to stand here and lecture me? Now? Do you have any idea how scared I was tonight?"

He immediately apologized. "I . . . I am so sorry. You're right. That was a low blow. I don't know what I was thinking." They stood in silence, facing one another. "You're just never around anymore."

A million retorts were on the tip of her tongue — most were childish — so she went for the basics. "I have a new job, a new career. I don't have time to play cheerleader for you and bake cookies. Besides, you have more than enough people around you helping out." Turning her back to him, she put her purse on the kitchen table and then walked in the direction of her bedroom. "Be sure to lock up on your way out."

Closing her bedroom door, she silently prayed she'd ticked him off enough to make him leave. Maybe something would go her way tonight. With a sigh, Anna kicked off her shoes, walked over to her dresser, and pulled out her pajamas. Without a thought to keeping her room neat, she stripped right there on the spot and walked to the en-suite shower, turned the hot water on full blast, and stepped in. It wasn't about relaxing or luxuriating; it was simply about washing the night off of her.

It would have been easy to just stand there and cry, but she didn't even have the energy for that. With swift efficiency, she shampooed her hair and soaped her body from head to toe. She stood under the spray until the water cooled.

Stepping out, she dried off and pulled on her flannel pajama pants and slipped the cami over her head. A quick glance in the mirror showed a very tired, very defeated woman. After taking a minute to towel-dry her hair and brush her teeth, she sighed.

"It figures the only kind of guy I'd attract with any ease is a psychopath," she muttered. Kicking her discarded towel aside, she shuffled back into the bedroom, and when she had nothing left to do, she contemplated going back out to the living room.

She no longer had a headache.

And she wasn't tired.

She could only hope Quinn was gone.

Off in the distance, she heard the ding of the microwave and sighed with defeat. Not only had the jerk not left, but he was clearly making himself at home. She pulled the door open and spotted Quinn walking across the room with a large bowl in his hands. "What do you think you're doing?"

"I made us some popcorn. I haven't had any time to just chill in a while, so I thought we'd watch a movie."

"Didn't you hear me? I'm tired. I want to be alone." She said the words, but there was little force behind them.

"I'm not going anywhere," he said defiantly. If it were anyone else, she would have thrown him out on the spot. But this was Quinn, the one guy she could talk to about anything.

"Quinn," she whined. "I think I've earned

the right to be alone after the night I've had. Can't you just for once deal with not getting your own way?"

"This isn't about getting my own way," he said quietly, his voice thick. "This is about making sure you're okay."

"Well, I'm not, okay?" she cried. "I went out on a date I really didn't want to go on and the guy was a freak! Even if it weren't for the fact that he slipped something into my drink, he was a complete ass! He only talked about himself!"

"Then why'd you go out with him?"

"Why not?" she said, self-loathing lacing her tone. "He was a good-looking, successful man and he wanted to go out with me. He called me every day for a week. I figured what harm could one date do?" She gave a mirthless laugh. "Well, now I know, don't I?"

"Anna —"

"No, it's the truth. Clearly, the only guys who want to go out with me are freaks. Banner day for Anna Hannigan!"

"That's not true and you know it." His expression softened. "I'm so sorry. I really don't even know what to say. It's not like Jake and I are really good friends. We're just doing business together. It wasn't until you called Zoe that I even remembered the incident when he . . . you know . . . years ago. Please tell me you forgive me, Anna. Please."

She was completely torn. It would have been so easy to just say yes and forgive him, but she also knew that if she did, it would just take her back to where she had been before.

It was a no-win situation no matter what she did.

"Come on, Anna. Just come and sit on the couch. You can have the sectional and relax." He put the bowl down on the coffee table and turned back toward the kitchen to grab some drinks. "And besides, *Monty Python and the Holy Grail* is on."

Dammit. That movie was one of her weaknesses and judging by the smirk on Quinn's face, he knew it.

Jerk.

"Fine. Whatever," she muttered and walked over and flopped down on the couch.

With a full-blown grin, Quinn sat down and picked up the bowl of popcorn and put it between them before reaching for the remote and turning to the movie.

As much as she wanted to be pissed, the scene was oddly comforting — probably because it was something they'd done since they were kids. It just sucked that she wanted more — wanted Quinn to see her as a woman instead of a buddy. A lover instead of a friend.

It didn't take long for them to settle into the movie and soon they were laughing and quoting lines right along with the actors. Anna snuggled with her favorite throw and found that the more comfortable she got, the heavier her eyelids felt. She thought she could hold out until the end of the movie, but the reality was she was practically asleep.

Quinn looked over at Anna and smiled. He didn't know what had been going on with her lately, but he missed her. There were a ton of questions he'd wanted to ask her tonight, but he had decided to just let them go and do what he could to get her to relax around him and to try and erase the thought of what could have happened to her.

Beside him, Anna sighed and began to lean toward him. If he didn't do something, she was going to fall face-first into the popcorn bowl. He quickly scooped it up and put it on the coffee table — and froze with shock when Anna shifted and lay down with her head in his lap. It took a moment for the shock to wear off, and then he slowly let himself relax. The last time they had been like this had been the night before Aidan and Zoe's wedding and at least he had had a pillow acting as a buffer then.

"Not a big deal," he muttered and shifted to get them both a little more comfortable. The movie was almost over, and it didn't take long for him to get pulled back into the plot while he mindlessly played with Anna's hair. When the movie ended and he realized what he'd been doing — again — he pulled back like he'd been burned. He cursed. "I have *got* to stop doing that!"

"Anna?" he whispered, but she didn't move. He muttered under his breath and tried to think of what he should do. He knew he needed to leave — it was late and he had a lot to do at the new shop early in the morning — but he didn't want to disturb her.

The scene was eerily familiar and was seemingly becoming a habit for them.

While he continued to study her face, he finally let the guilt wash over him. He'd heard Jake ask her out and it had pissed him the hell off. He knew Jake was a player, but when Anna had turned him down, he'd thought that was the end of it. Quinn had been so wrapped up in — *hell, just call it what it is* — jealousy that he hadn't really thought about all the reasons why Anna shouldn't go out with Jake.

Because she's mine.

Yeah, that was becoming more and more apparent, but for the life of him, he didn't know what to do about it. And now, because of his own stupid pride and childish behavior, Anna could have been seriously hurt.

It wasn't something he was likely to forget anytime soon — or be able to forgive himself for.

Carefully, he slid out from under her head. Standing, he walked into her bedroom and pulled the comforter and sheet back and then looked around and chuckled. The room was a bit of a mess, but then again, he knew Anna wasn't the prissy type who obsessed about everything needing to be in its place. If anything, it comforted him to see her room in slight disarray.

He walked around and really looked at the space. The light-colored furniture and the pastel-blue walls gave the room a beachy vibe he knew Anna tended to favor. On her shelves were books and knickknacks and pictures. He chuckled at how many different types of frames she had — another quirk of hers. But as he took a minute to look at the actual pictures, he noticed one thing — he was in most of them.

Pictures from her childhood, holidays,

parties, and just . . . life. And he was there for all of them. They were laughing and smiling, and in some of them, Quinn could actually remember what it was they were joking about. A soft chuckle slipped out as he found a picture from Anna's sixteenth birthday. Her parents had gotten her a car. It was a used Mustang, and they had parked it in the driveway with a big red bow on it. In the picture, she was smiling so brightly, and he was standing right beside her.

Quinn ran a finger over the picture. It was her special day, and she had begged him to be in the picture with her. She did that a lot. Hell, he didn't think his own father had as many pictures of him as the Hannigans did.

He put the picture back down on the shelf and moved over toward the lone framed picture on her nightstand. For some reason, his heart began to race as he reached for it. It was a fancy silver-and-crystal frame. In it was a picture taken about a year ago of the two of them. It wasn't a special occasion; it was just a family day at the beach. They were sitting side by side in the sand, and he remembered Darcy coming over and snapping the picture. Anna's head was on his shoulder and they were smiling and looking so happy and relaxed and . . . He swallowed a lump in his throat. Being with Anna was normally the only time he felt happy and relaxed.

At least until recently.

Or maybe some time after this picture was taken.

Could he have known even then that things were changing? Was he subconsciously already noticing Anna wasn't just his pal but a woman?

Carefully, he put the picture back down and sighed. Tonight wasn't the night to figure it all out. Too much had happened, and his mind was spinning with it all. It was late, and he needed to help Anna get to bed and then go home himself. He was suddenly very tired — exhausted, really — and knew it would be better for both of them if he just gave her a little space.

Once back in the living room, he stood over her and studied her for a minute. She was out cold. They were going to have to talk. Really talk. Soon. They'd been friends for too long to just . . . stop. He needed Anna in his life — couldn't imagine a life without her in it. Eventually he'd wear her down and get her to tell him how he'd screwed up and then they could move on. He was just impatient, and wished she'd tell him now.

"Problem for another day," he whispered. "Anna? Anna, come on. You need to go to bed."

"Too tired," she murmured as she shifted on the couch.

Quinn sighed and reached down to gently scoop her up into his arms. He straightened and stiffened when Anna snuggled closer and seemed to hum her approval. He took a step but instantly stopped when he felt her breath on his neck. And then her tongue. And then her lips. *What the . . . ?*

"What are you doing?" she whispered sleepily.

"Taking you to bed," he said gruffly.

"Mmm . . . finally," she purred.

This was Anna. *Anna,* for crying out loud! He chanted to himself to just keep walking, and almost made it to the bed when once again her breath was replaced by her lips. Quinn froze as Anna slowly kissed and licked her way up the column of his throat and then nipped at the line of his jaw. He jerked back and looked down at her face as he continued to hold her in his arms. Her eyes were closed, but there was a very sexy smile on her face. "Anna," he whispered.

In a flash, her hands raked up into his hair and pulled his face closer to hers, and then Quinn was lost. He closed the distance between them and tentatively touched his lips to hers.

And then all rational thought left him.

Her lips were softer than he'd ever let himself imagine, and when she purred into his mouth and opened for him, he felt a sense of completion he'd never felt before. Slowly, he lowered Anna to the bed as her arms wound around him, holding him close. Quinn stretched out on top of her and smiled at Anna's whispered yes.

It was instantaneous, the surge of arousal and excitement he felt. He kissed her, as ravenous as a starving man at a feast, as her legs came up and lazily wrapped around his waist. He wanted to touch her, taste her everywhere, while at the same time he was questioning his own actions and sanity.

This was Anna. His best friend.

And clearly she didn't know what she was doing.

Cursing, he forced himself to move away from her and rose from the bed. She moaned her disapproval and whispered his name again before her head rested to the side and she sighed.

"Don't go," she said softly, but her words sort of trailed off, and then she rolled over and didn't say another word.

Shit. She was dreaming.

And he felt like a complete jerk for giving in to the temptation. He knew she was tired — clearly more tired than he'd realized — and he should have just put her down and left.

If she didn't hate him before, she'd certainly hate him now. Forcing himself to look away, he slowly backed out of her room and shut the door before making a hasty retreat from her house.

Cursing himself and his lack of control the entire time.

CHAPTER 5

The next morning, Anna felt marginally better. Not great, but better. Other than being angry at Jake and what he had tried to do, she was embarrassed that she was so stupid and had so many witnesses to her rotten luck. After a cup of strong coffee, she reached for her phone and called Zoe.

"How are you feeling? Any better?"

"You mean other than like a giant idiot?" Anna asked, sitting on her sofa and putting her feet up on the coffee table.

"You're not an idiot, Anna. God, when I think about what could have happened to you, I'm so glad you had the good sense to get away from the table and call me!"

"I don't know how much of it was good sense. I never should have gone on the stupid date to begin with. I should have listened to you in the first place."

"Look, no one knew Jake was going to be such a freak."

"Quinn knew."

Zoe sighed. "Yeah, but . . . I don't know. I don't think he really expected something like that to happen. When he heard me on the phone with you, he really freaked out. I thought he was going to kill Jake."

"Right."

"No, I'm serious, Anna. I don't think I've ever seen Quinn so angry. The whole time we were driving over there and Aidan was trying to keep up, even he was saying how out of character it was for Quinn. We were seriously worried things were going to get a whole lot worse."

"Well, I do appreciate the fact that you all came down there to help me. I wasn't at the time — mainly because I was so out of it — but the more I thought about it, the more I realized how blessed I am to have such good friends. So . . . thank you."

"You never have to thank me. I'm just glad we were able to get there and help you."

"I guess it's a good thing Jake didn't press charges against Quinn."

Zoe snorted with disbelief. "Are you kidding? If he had tried to do it, the cops would have arrested him too for slipping something into your drink."

"We don't know that for sure —"

"Anna, stop!" Zoe cried. "Stop defending

people! Stop always making excuses for them! Bobby's going down to talk to the bartender —"

"*What?* How does Bobby know what happened?"

Zoe hesitated. "Well, you know . . . small town and all."

"Zoe . . ."

"All right, all right. Aidan called him. But don't be mad! He was seriously just looking out for you!"

"Great, now on top of everything else, I'll —"

As if on cue, her front door opened and her brother walked in.

"And here he is," Anna said. "I have to go. I'll call you later."

"Don't be mad at him, Anna. He's just doing his job."

Anna wasn't so sure, but she didn't mention it. Once she hung up the phone, she faced her brother. "What brings you here today, Officer Hannigan?"

Bobby was dressed in his full police uniform and had a murderous look on his face. "I had to find out from Aidan Shaughnessy that some guy slipped you a roofie? Are you kidding me, Anna? Why the hell didn't you call me?"

"I did!" she cried, jumping to her feet.

147

"You were the first person I called, but it went right to voice mail!"

"So call the station! They would have found me!"

"Bobby, I barely knew my own name at the time. After I couldn't get through to you, it was pure luck I managed to hit Zoe's number!"

He began to pace. "I'm going to the tavern as soon as it opens and looking at security footage and talking to the staff. I want you to press charges against this guy."

Without a word, Anna walked to the kitchen and poured Bobby a cup of coffee. He followed her and sat down at the breakfast nook. When she put the mug down in front of him, he looked up at her sadly. "Are you all right? I mean . . . do you feel okay?"

She shrugged. "I don't feel great. I forced myself to get sick to get it out of me, but . . . I'm more embarrassed than anything."

"Damn it, Anna, I can't believe something like this happened. Nothing like that has ever happened around here."

"Well, Jake isn't from around here."

Bobby frowned. "No, he's not. Leave it to Quinn to bring that sort of element into our lives."

"Oh, for the love of it . . . Please don't make this about Quinn."

"But it is!" Bobby yelled. "It was *his* friend who did this to you, and from what Aidan told me, the guy has a history of doing this! What the hell was Quinn thinking, letting you go out with a guy like that?"

"It wasn't his call to make!"

"Bullshit! Quinn Shaughnessy has had something to say about the guys you date for years! All of a sudden he chooses to keep his big mouth shut? When I get my hands on him —"

"That's enough!" she shouted, and Bobby instantly stilled. Anna never raised her voice to him, but she had hit her limit. "I am so sick and tired of this! If you are here as an officer or my brother, your rage should be on one person and one person only — Jake Tanner!"

Bobby stared at her with disbelief that quickly turned to shame. "You're right. I'm sorry, Anna. I just . . . I hate that I wasn't there for you."

"You can't be there all the time," she said softly, resting her elbows on the counter and facing him. "What happened last night was really scary, and like I was just telling Zoe on the phone, I feel incredibly blessed I have such good friends who were able to come and help me."

"Including Quinn," Bobby muttered and

then flinched when Anna slapped him upside the head. "Ow! What'd you do that for?"

"Because you're still being an idiot!"

He took a drink of his coffee and waited a minute before speaking again. "Okay, I'm going to stop being your brother for now and be here in official police capacity."

"Bobby?"

He looked up at her.

Anna's eyes suddenly filled with tears. "Don't ever stop being my brother." And then she walked around the counter and let him hold her while she cried.

Quinn couldn't focus on anything.

Standing in the shop that housed Jake Tanner's two classic cars, he wasn't sure what he was supposed to do. He'd beaten the crap out of Jake last night. There was no way the two were going to work together, and as much as he was fine with never seeing the smarmy bastard again, he kind of hated the idea of losing the cars.

Which pretty much made him an equally smarmy bastard.

The door to the shop opened, and his main shop manager, Troy, stepped in. "Hey, Quinn. Jake Tanner's here to see you."

Son of a —

Quinn couldn't believe the guy was stupid enough to come around, but since he himself had just been thinking about the situation with the cars, it wasn't really surprising Jake was too. "Show him in, but I want you to stay close by, okay?"

Troy didn't question it; he simply nodded and walked out.

When Jake walked in, Quinn felt a real sense of satisfaction at the amount of bruising on the guy's face. Even though Jake was wearing sunglasses, Quinn could see enough of the bruising to know he'd done some damage.

"You've got a hell of a nerve coming here," Quinn said, standing with his feet planted firmly and his arms crossed.

"We need to make arrangements for the cars," Jake said, his speech a little slow — no doubt thanks to his split lip.

"You could have had someone call."

Jake shrugged and then winced. "Look, you can tell me to go to hell, and after last night I wouldn't blame you, but . . ." He stopped and sighed. "I'd still like you to do the work on the cars."

Quinn was shocked. It was the last thing he'd expected to hear. His eyes narrowed. "Why? Why would you even trust me to work on them? Who's to say I won't mess them up on purpose?"

"You wouldn't do that. You're an arrogant pain in the ass and have a colossal ego. There's no way you'd damage your reputation by messing with cars of this magnitude."

Damn it, he was right.

"You've got a gift for this sort of thing, man. Like I said, you can throw me out of here and tell me to go to hell, but last night—"

Quinn moved before Jake could blink and had him by the throat, his back slammed against the wall. "You're just lucky you didn't get the chance to put a hand on her or you wouldn't be breathing right now." The hand on Jake's throat tightened just for good measure.

Jake squirmed and managed to shake Quinn off. He was gasping for air as he held up a hand to ward Quinn off. "Just . . . hear me out."

"I don't think so. You need to leave," Quinn said through clenched teeth.

"Think about it. It's all I'm asking. You won't have to deal with me personally. I'll have my manager take care of everything. I've already got several publications interested in doing stories on the cars. You'd be getting all kinds of free publicity for you and the business."

Bile rose in Quinn's throat. Was this bastard seriously trying to negotiate a business deal after what he'd done?

"You're out of your mind, Tanner. You picked the wrong girl to mess with. Anna is —"

"Yeah, yeah, I get it. I don't know why." He paused and cleared his throat before straightening. "Call it ego. It pissed me off how she kept turning me down. Now that I know about you and her . . ."

Quinn could only stare. "Be very careful what you say because I'm not afraid to finish what I started last night."

"That won't be necessary."

Quinn and Jake both turned to find Bobby Hannigan and another police officer standing in the doorway. For once, Quinn was genuinely relieved to see Bobby. Taking a step back, he simply motioned for the officers to come in and do their job.

Once Jake had been read his rights and was being led out, Bobby turned to Quinn, his expression fierce. "The only reason I'm not pounding on you the way you pounded on Tanner is because I promised Anna I wouldn't."

Quinn nodded.

Bobby nodded once and started to turn

away but stopped and faced Quinn again. "Thank you. For being there for her when I couldn't be."

"I'd die before I let anything happen to her," Quinn said solemnly.

Another nod and then Bobby strode out of the garage.

Two days later, Anna stared at her reflection in the mirror for a solid ten minutes before she finally decided it was the best she could do. This whole dressing-up thing was really starting to get old. While she knew it went with the job and the whole life-change thing, she couldn't help but let her gaze linger longingly on her old jeans and sneakers.

Checking herself from every angle, she knew she looked professional. The muted-mint-green sundress was simple, with wide shoulder straps, a gentle curve-hugging bodice, and skirt cut to the knee. Paired with a little white cardigan and a casual strand of pearls, she felt ready to go.

Her client today was an important one — Dan Michaels, an old high school classmate who had done very well for himself and now was looking for a beachfront home. When he had specifically asked for Anna, she had been excited to see him. When she found out how much he was looking to spend on a property, she was damn near ecstatic.

Real estate was challenging, and there were things Anna really wanted to accomplish with her life. She had dreams and goals, and her commissions weren't making them happen just yet. But if she could find Dan the perfect property, the commission would help her a lot. Student loans would start to get paid off and she might even be able to get a decent car.

Plastering a smile on her face, she checked her reflection one last time before grabbing her purse and heading out the door. The high wedges she was wearing were already annoying her, and she stopped and looked back at her house and wondered if she should grab a pair of flats just in case.

"No," she told herself as she unlocked her car door. "You're an adult. Act like one. Dress like one." Once inside, she started the car and kicked on the air conditioning and thought about how she wished her mom had warned her of how uncomfortable adults had to be in the real world.

Fifteen minutes later, she pulled up in front of the house she prayed would impress Dan. Beachfront, three-car garage, four stories. It had six bedrooms, eight bathrooms, a theater room, a game room, an elevator, plus an outdoor entertaining area that included a multilevel deck, a heated pool, outdoor kitchen as well as an outdoor shower. Hell, if it was missing anything, she'd be completely surprised.

Grabbing her purse, she got out of the car and went into the house. It was currently vacant but fully furnished. Walking through the main floor, Anna fluffed pillows and opened the sliding doors that led out to one of the decks before making sure everything looked dust free. By the time Dan pulled up, she was almost out of breath from going up and down the stairs.

"Anna Hannigan," he said with a smile when she opened the door. "You look amazing." Reaching for her hands, he squeezed them and leaned in to place a kiss on her cheek. "How are you doing?"

For a minute, Anna was speechless. Dan Michaels had been cute in high school. He was out-and-out gorgeous now. She had to stop and swallow before she could speak. "I'm good," she said and then cleared her throat. "I'm good. How about you?"

She motioned for him to come inside and managed to get one of her hands free of his. Dan held on to the other. Amazingly enough, she didn't mind.

"I'm doing well," he said. He was six feet

tall with dark brown hair and eyes. With an easy grin that showcased his dimples, she couldn't help but smile back. Stepping into the main living area, he let out a low whistle of approval. "Wow. When you said you knew of the perfect place, you weren't kidding."

This time when he moved, he did release Anna's hand. She read off the list of all the house had to offer as she followed behind him. "With a little over six thousand square feet, you won't have any privacy issues when you have your family here with you."

He chuckled. "That's definitely a good thing. I know my brother and sister and their families are going to want to come and visit for extended weekend trips. I love my family, but with all their kids, it's nice to know I can hide out if I want to."

So he isn't married, she thought to herself. *Interesting.*

They slowly toured the entire house from top to bottom, talking the entire time not only about the property, but also about high school and mutual acquaintances and just getting caught up on each other's lives. All in all, Anna found him to be incredibly charming. And if it hadn't been for her unfortunate incident with Jake, she would probably have been angling for a chance to go out with Dan for a drink.

Not yet. She wasn't ready to trust anyone just quite yet.

When they found themselves back on the main floor and looking out at the ocean, Anna looked down at her watch. Two hours! They had been walking around and talking for two hours already! Not that she had anything to do, but she just couldn't believe how fast the time had flown by.

"So . . . what do you think, Dan?" she finally asked. "Is this one a contender, or do you want to look at a few more properties?"

He took a deep breath and smiled. "I love the smell of the ocean, don't you?"

Anna smiled. "Absolutely. I can't imagine living anywhere else but near the coast. I would miss it too much."

He nodded. "I moved away when I left for college and stayed away all this time. Now that my life has calmed down a bit, I know what I want. If I'm going to invest in a home, I want it to be here. We never lived right on the beach, but I always dreamed of it." He looked at her with a lopsided grin. "And now I can do it."

"You're very lucky."

They stared at one another for a minute before Dan looked back at the ocean. "This one is definitely a contender, but I'd like to look at maybe a few more properties just to be sure. Do you have anything else available?"

Pulling her tablet out of her purse, Anna pulled up one of the other listings she had considered. "This one here is similar in square footage but has a few more updates. I can see if we can look at it now, if you have the time? It's only about a mile up the road."

"That sounds great," he said and stepped away while Anna made the call. When she was done and told him they were welcome to go and see the house, he added, "I'll follow in my car. I have a dinner appointment in town I'll need to get to."

"If you'd prefer to go another day . . . ?"

He shook his head. "No, today is fine. I'd really like to see it, but I probably won't linger as long as we did here, if that's okay."

It was said with a smile, but Anna made a mental note to stick to business and ease up on the personal chitchat. "Not a problem. I just need to close everything up here." She wrote down the address on the back of her business card and handed it to him. "Why don't you head down there and at least get a look at the outside? I'll be five minutes behind you."

"Sounds good, Anna. Thanks for understanding."

She watched him walk out the door and sighed. Here was a perfectly nice man, and if she were a normal woman, she'd be attracted to him and flirting with him. But between Quinn and the Jake incident, the idea of dating wasn't appealing at the moment.

Walking around and double-checking all the doors and windows, she quickly scooped up her purse and made her way out the front door.

In a perfect world, she would make this sale, get her finances in order, and find the man of her dreams.

Instead, she walked down the front steps, climbed into her old Honda, and faced the reality of having to put her dreams on hold for a little while longer.

It was another two hours before she watched Dan drive away. After another lengthy house tour, he told her he loved both houses but needed to think about it. Of course she understood — it was a pretty massive purchase.

Still . . . it would have been nice if he had wanted to sign a contract today.

With the house locked up, Anna climbed back into her car and headed toward home. It was dinnertime, and she was hungry but didn't feel like cooking. Takeout was looking more and more appealing. Maybe some Chinese food, or maybe she'd stop at the pub and grab a burger, or —

The check engine light came on.

Again.

"Dammit," she muttered. Quinn had been after her about it for a long time, and Anna had a feeling she couldn't ignore it much longer. The drive through town to her house would take her right by the new shop, and if she just didn't let herself worry about getting a lecture about car maintenance or about the incident with Jake, she could actually stop in and ask Quinn to look at her car without feeling like an idiot.

Or maybe she could wait another day.

As if on cue, the car started to sputter a bit, and Anna knew she had pushed her luck as far as she could. The car definitely needed to be looked at.

Another sputter.

There went her hopes of getting takeout.

At this point, she'd be lucky to make it to the shop without having to push the damn car.

Anna turned the corner and pulled into the parking lot of Shaughnessy Automotive and Restoration. The parking lot was empty, and Anna worried that it was after hours.

Quinn's car was there, however, so there was no avoiding him. Taking a deep breath, she climbed from the car and went in search of him.

It didn't take long — he walked out of the open garage bay as she was approaching. "Hey," he said and Anna thought his tone was a bit . . . cautious.

"Hi," she said, forcing a smile.

He looked her over and frowned. "What are you so dressed up for?"

Anna looked down at herself and then back at him. "Dressed up? Quinn, you've seen me in this dress about a dozen times before. I had a house to show."

He grunted and shrugged. "You never wore it with high heels before."

Rolling her eyes, she got to the purpose of her visit. "The, um . . . the engine light came on again. And it's sputtering."

Quinn's eyes never left hers. "And isn't it a little late in the day for a showing?"

"For crying out loud, can you please look at the car? I really think it's bad this time. I'm afraid to drive it home!" she said with exasperation.

"I thought you knew all about car maintenance now," he said with a hint of sarcasm. "Isn't that what you said the other day?"

Doing her best to remain calm, she met

his gaze. "I can change a tire, replace an air filter, change a spark plug, and even replace my windshield wipers. Whatever's going on this time is way beyond that. Can you please just not be a jerk for five minutes and cut me some slack?"

Without a word, Quinn walked over to the car and popped the hood. Anna couldn't help but stand back and admire his physique from behind. Faded blue jeans hugged him, and his gray T-shirt — even though it was stained — just accented how muscular he was. And then there was the cap. Today it was one of his old baseball caps worn backward. Somehow he managed to even make it look sexy. The man seemed to only get better with age. A small sigh escaped before she forced herself to walk over to the car.

"Jeez, Anna. I told you this piece of junk was gonna crap out on you. I mean, until I get it on the lift, I can't say for certain, but knowing its history, it could be about a half a dozen different things. You need a new car."

Her spine stiffened. She hated that superior tone he used. "Oh, really? Gee, Quinn, I didn't know that," she retorted. "Tell you what, let me go and rub my magic lamp and see if my genie will grant me a new car."

Quinn stood and wiped his hands on the rag he had hooked in his back pocket while giving her a sour look. "This isn't news, Anna. And you have a job. It's not like you can't get a new car."

They'd had this discussion before and it always ended like this — with an argument. "I told you I don't want a car payment right now. Getting my real estate license wasn't free, you know!" She huffed and paced away and then back again. "Can't you just . . . do something with it? You know, to tide me over?"

"What, again?" he asked, crossing his arms over his chest.

That was it. It was all too much, and she finally hit her limit. Tears were starting to build, and there was no way she was going to let Quinn see her cry. She'd take the risk and drive the damn hunk of junk home and find another mechanic tomorrow. Maybe Bobby could help her with getting around and to and from work for a little while.

Without looking at him, Anna stepped forward and slammed the hood closed before opening the car door.

"What are you doing?" he asked.

"Leaving."

"Why? Because I asked you an honest question?"

Anna threw her purse back into the car before facing him again. "No, because you're a jackass." She growled with frustration. "If I can convince Dan to buy the house I showed him today, I'll make enough commission to make a reasonable down payment on a used car. But for now, I just needed a little help, not a lecture. Obviously it was too much to ask!"

Quinn reached out and tugged her away from the car before she could sit. "Dan who?"

"Dan Michaels. From high school. Remember him?"

Quinn thought for a moment. "Pretty boy. Played baseball with me junior year. When did you see him?"

"Today. That's who I was with earlier. He's looking at the Stanleys' place on the beach. The house is like a damn showplace, like something out of a magazine, and if I can convince him to buy it, the commission will go a long way toward giving me some breathing space. With this car thing now, I need it more than ever."

"So you dressed up for him in hopes of enticing him to buy?"

"What?" she cried with disbelief. This time she shoved at his chest with both hands. "What is the matter with you? What

165

the hell have I ever done to you to make you be such a complete ass to me?" They were both breathing hard as they glared at one another.

Quinn cursed under his breath and stormed back into the shop through the garage. Anna quickly followed. It wasn't an easy task in the dress and heels — which she cursed the entire time. She found him in his office, throwing the rag down on the desk.

"Hey," she snapped, slamming the office door closed behind her. "I asked you a question." Quinn's blue eyes flashed with fire as he looked at her. Anna had seen that look before, normally directed at other people. It was the first time she had been on the receiving end of it, and she wasn't sure if it scared her or just served to make her madder.

"Oh yeah? Well, I asked *you* one earlier and you didn't answer. I guess we're even." Crossing his arms over his chest, he waited her out — a smug expression on his face.

"Seriously? Are we really going there? The whole 'I'm rubber, you're glue' thing? Aren't we getting too old for this crap?" And then the fight started to leave her. This wasn't getting her anywhere. The man clearly had an issue with her that he wasn't going to share and she was just tired of the whole thing. "You know what? Never mind. Just . . . never mind," she said wearily and turned to open the office door and leave.

"Did you kiss him?" he called after her and waited until she turned around and looked at him. "Did you kiss him too?"

Slowly Anna stepped back into the office and looked at Quinn as if he'd lost his mind. "Are you high or something? Kiss him? Kiss who? Could you please explain to me what the heck you're talking about?" She was completely confused by the turn in the conversation. Did he think she'd kissed Jake? Other than Jake, she hadn't even been out on a date in what felt like forever, so what was he even referring to?

He moved in close and kept going until Anna's back was against the wall. "Is that your new thing? Just kissing guys to pass the time?" Quinn's breathing was ragged as he looked down into Anna's wide eyes.

"I don't know what you're talking about. I haven't kissed anyone," she said shakily as her tongue came out to moisten her suddenly dry lips.

"You kissed me."

Those brown eyes got impossibly wider as she softly gasped. "No, I didn't."

Wait . . . did I? Was that not a dream the

other night?

"Yeah, you did," he said in a low voice. "You fell asleep on the couch, and then I carried you to bed and you kissed me."

She shook her head, unable to find her voice. But even as she tried to deny it, the image came to her mind that she would have sworn had just been a dream — not that she was going to share that bit of information with Quinn.

He continued to watch her, his eyes never leaving hers. "Yes. You. Did."

"I . . . I don't believe you," she stammered, wishing like hell she could just escape and die of embarrassment.

"Let me remind you," he growled fiercely as he closed the distance between them so they were pressed together from head to toe. His hand reached up and anchored itself around her nape as his mouth crashed down on hers.

Shock held Anna still for only a few seconds before she gave in and kissed him back. It was better than the dream! Well, clearly not a dream, but reality. Unable to help herself, she sighed and completely melted against him. His lips were softer than she'd imagined, and when his tongue reached out and teased hers, she thought she'd melt in a puddle at his feet.

Quinn changed the angle of his head and his lips gentled against hers. Suddenly, neither of them was quite so frantic. Now they were sipping at each other and getting acquainted with the feel, the taste of each other. Anna sighed into his mouth as her arms wrapped around him — knowing that she was really doing it and was allowed to touch him was a complete turn-on.

Quinn must have felt the same way because he suddenly crowded her in and then his hands started to wander — first to her shoulders, then slowly downward as he skimmed his hands along her sides to her waist, her hips. They gripped there as they gently kneaded and rocked her against him.

Yes, yes, yes! her brain cried, and then she got in on more of the touching too. For so many years, she'd thought about it — fantasized about it — about touching Quinn at her leisure and she was finally allowed! Her hands moved up and down his muscled arms first and gently squeezed his biceps.

They were hard and huge, and he flexed them beneath her hands.

Then they wandered up the column of his neck and up into his thick, silky hair — knocking his hat off — and gripped it. It made him growl, and she held on a moment longer just because she could.

Distantly, she realized his hands had continued downward and were now at the hem of her skirt and he was slowly raising it. Should she protest? Help? Hell if she knew. For now she'd go with enjoying it. When he had it up to an obscene height, Anna shamelessly hooked one leg up around Quinn to hold him even closer.

Another masculine growl.

"Damn, Anna," he panted, kissing and licking his way across her cheek, her throat, her collarbone.

It was on the tip of her tongue to beg him not to stop, to take her right there, but clearly he was one step ahead of her. His hand came up and firmly cupped her cheek, forcing her to look at him, his eyes glazed with desire.

"How . . . how did this happen?" he whispered, his eyes scanning her face.

"I don't know." She almost cursed her honesty. Now wasn't the time for her to come off as being unsure of anything! What if he pulled back? What if the fog of lust suddenly cleared and —

"I want you," he said thickly, hotly.

"I'm yours," she whispered, and then his lips were back on hers as he clasped her waist and lifted her until both her legs wrapped around his waist. The sensations

were glorious. The feeling of Quinn —
aroused Quinn — between her legs was
every fantasy come to life. Anna had never
found the appeal in wearing dresses before.

She did now.

One of Quinn's hands moved from her
waist to her hip and then to cup her bottom. Her panties were of the barely there
variety and clearly he approved. She felt him
wrap the fabric in his fist as he began to
tug.

And then the phone rang.

"Quinn," she whispered.

"Ignore it," he said and immediately went
back to kissing her and adjusting his grip
on her panties.

While the phone on his desk continued to
ring, his cell phone began to go off with
what sounded like a dozen text messages
arriving at once.

This time, she didn't have to say his name;
they were on the same page. Something was
up and needed his attention. As much as
Anna wanted to argue how much *she*
needed his attention, it was obvious something was wrong. Quinn gently lowered her
to the floor, and Anna silently fixed her
dress while he picked up his cell phone in
one hand and the office phone in the other.

"What?" he barked into the office phone.

He raked a hand through his hair as he listened then cursed. "I'm on my way." Then he slammed the phone back down and focused on his cell phone before shoving it into his pocket and turning toward Anna.

"What is it?" she asked nervously. "Is everything okay?"

He shook his head. "Aubrey's in the hospital."

Without a word, Quinn picked his hat up off the floor and searched for his car keys. Anna didn't ask; she simply followed him outside as he locked up before running to her car and grabbing her purse. When she turned around, Quinn had already pulled his truck up behind her and was waiting.

She found comfort in the fact that they were in sync. Climbing into the truck, all she said was, "Let's go," and Quinn immediately put the truck in drive and took off.

They had barely left the parking lot when Anna pulled her phone out. "Okay, what's going on? Who called? Who texted?"

"It was my dad on the office phone. Aidan texted."

"What do we know? What happened?"

"Hugh's away on business. Aubrey was supposed to go with him, but they didn't have anyone to watch the dogs," he said with exasperation. "Owen was driving through on his way to some seminar, and he stopped by, not knowing Hugh wasn't home, and found her passed out on the floor."

Anna gasped. "Oh no!" They all knew of Aubrey's history with cancer as a teen, so any mystery illness was cause for alarm. "Where is Hugh?"

"He's on a flight home right now from New York." Quinn cursed. "I'm sure he's freaking out."

"Of course he is," she said. "So is everyone on their way to the hospital?"

He nodded. "Aidan and Zoe probably got a thirty-minute start on us, and Dad's ahead of them. Owen called him first after he got Aubrey to the hospital."

"He didn't drive her himself, did he?"

"I don't even know. Once Dad said what was going on, I just sprang into action. Why don't you call Zoe and see if you can get more details and if she knows how Hugh is getting to the hospital from the airport? We can meet him if we need to."

Nodding, Anna dialed Zoe's phone and was relieved when she answered. "Hey, where are you guys?"

"We're about thirty miles out from the

hospital," Zoe said. "What about you?"

"I'm with Quinn and we just left the shop. Who's getting Hugh from the airport?"

"Ian is going to pick him up. So we'll all meet up at the hospital."

"What happened? Do you know?"

"All I know is Owen stopped by and found her on the floor. I can't . . . I don't even know what to think. I mean, did she fall? Was she sick? We don't know!"

Anna sighed. "Poor Hugh. Has anyone talked to him?"

"Just Ian. We didn't want to add to his stress — plus he's on a plane right now, so we probably wouldn't get through to him."

"Did Owen drive her to the hospital? Did she wake up?"

"No," Zoe said. "He called 9-1-1 and rode in the ambulance with her. He's a wreck."

"I'm sure. It had to be pretty scary finding her that way."

"I think he was more upset he couldn't help diagnose what was wrong. He told Aidan he'd never felt so helpless in his life."

It was exactly how Anna felt at that moment — it was good to know she wasn't alone. "Okay, so Ian's getting Hugh, Owen's with Aubrey . . . are we missing anything? What about the dogs? They're going to need someone to go in and let them out, I would imagine. Right?"

"I didn't even think of that. Damn it."

"Okay, you guys go on to the hospital, and Quinn and I will swing by the house and check on them. Aubrey's mentioned her next-door neighbors have helped her out with the dogs before, so we'll check in with them."

"Sounds good. If I hear anything, I'll let you know, okay?"

"Thanks, Zoe. We'll talk to you soon."

After she hung up, Anna looked over at Quinn. "I hope you don't mind. I volunteered us to check on the dogs."

He shook his head. "No, it was a good idea. Since Aubrey didn't go on this trip with Hugh because of the dogs, we may not be able to find anyone else. The more we can do to help, the better. Did she tell you anything different or have any updates?"

"Nothing yet. Your dad's going to pick up Hugh. Owen's at the hospital."

"He's a mess, isn't he?"

"Who? Owen?"

Quinn nodded.

"You know he's not good in situations like this," Anna said softly. "His bedside manner isn't exactly warm and fuzzy. He's going to get all clinical."

Quinn chuckled. "He can't help it. It's

175

how his brain works. But I'm sure he's also nervous because he's not comfortable with Aubrey yet."

"It's not like she's new to the family," Anna pointed out. "She and Hugh have been together for almost a year."

"Yeah, but he hasn't been around much, so he's only met her a handful of times. He was the same way with Zoe."

Anna nodded. "Hell, I grew up with you guys and it took Owen until I was almost fifteen before he would say more than two words to me."

"Yeah, well . . . you intimidated him."

"What? Me? How?" she asked, laughing a little.

"You held your own with all of us — you played ball and ran around and climbed trees. You didn't fit his perception of a typical girl."

Anna wasn't sure how to take that, so she let it be. "Well, he didn't fit my perception of a typical boy either, you know. I don't think I've ever met anyone as smart as Owen. He still has a way of intimidating me by making me feel like a moron."

"Join the club. He does it to all of us. The key is to just remind him he's talking Klingon and he'll stop." Chuckling, he shook his head. "Although he may take that as a compliment. Then we'd have to be the ones explaining to him how it's not."

That made Anna laugh. "I don't want him to get a complex. There's nothing wrong with how he speaks or the things he says. He just needs to . . ."

"Dumb it down?" Quinn suggested with a grin.

"Exactly!"

The drove without talking for a while, the radio playing softly in the background. For the first time possibly ever, Anna was grateful for Quinn's driving skills. She was certain they'd get pulled over due to the way he was speeding, but he drove with confidence into the night. She'd deal with the white-knuckle grip she had to take a time or two if it meant getting to Hugh and Aubrey faster.

"I hate to ask," Anna finally said, "but I was on my way to get some dinner when the car started doing its thing. Do you think we can go through a drive-through and grab something? I don't want to hold us up but I'm starving."

"Oh thank God," Quinn said with relief. "I was thinking the same thing but I figured you'd yell at me for stopping when we needed to get to the dogs and then to the hospital."

177

"You will never get yelled at by me where food is concerned."

A bark of laughter was his first response. "That is not true!" He looked over at Anna. "You yell at me all the time about food!"

"That's because you're normally calling me at some crazy hour wanting cookies or burgers or something ridiculous!" she replied with a laugh.

"Oh, I see. So as long as you're getting fed too, it's okay. Is that it?"

Anna pretended to think about it. "Hmm . . . maybe."

Quinn pulled in to the first burger place they came to and ordered enough food for six people.

"Are we bringing food to the hospital?" she asked.

"No. Why?"

"You cannot possibly be that hungry! The amount of food you just ordered is way too much for one person."

"You're eating too," he reminded her.

"Um . . . one burger, one order of fries, buddy. The rest is all you."

"So you're saying you don't want one of the milk shakes I ordered."

Dammit. She did enjoy a good milk shake. "Okay, fine. I'll take one of the milk shakes."

"And onion rings. You're not gonna have any?"

Anna sighed loudly. "You know I will. They're just so crispy and good!"

"And the freshly baked cookies," he said, shaking his head. "I guess I'll have to eat them all." He turned and winked at her. "And I do enjoy a good chocolate chip cookie."

"You're the devil, you know that, right?"

His smile grew and became just a bit wicked. "You know it, sweetheart."

By the time they reached the hospital, it was after nine. Quinn knew they weren't going to be able to get in and see Aubrey, but he wanted to be there for Hugh. The dogs had been let out and fed, and the neighbors had promised to go over again before midnight if no one had come home.

Sitting in the waiting room with his family, Quinn felt restless. Uneasy. The last time he had sat like this was after the crash that had taken his friend Todd's life. He had sat in the waiting room with Todd's family and what seemed like a hundred members of the NASCAR family. He could still see the look on the doctor's face when he came out to talk to Todd's wife. His stomach sank.

It was the same look they had all seen the

night his mother had died. Taking a shaky breath, Quinn wiped at his eyes, certain he felt tears welling there.

And then Anna's hand was on his arm, her head on his shoulder. He couldn't move, didn't want to draw attention to the fact that he was overwhelmed emotionally. That was the last thing anyone needed right now. So he sat and drew comfort from her until he could get himself under control.

Just think of something else. Anything. Just move on from all thoughts of doctors and hospitals and focus on something else.

He thought about what had happened earlier at the shop, and it brought up an entirely different emotion. Anna had been so hot in his arms, and he couldn't believe how incredible it had been.

Kissing her, touching her, was not part of the plan. Any plan. Especially after the other night at her house; but once he saw her in that dress, it reminded him of the curves she had beneath it. And then when she mentioned being with another guy? Well, something had simply snapped. He didn't want her with another guy — for business or otherwise — and now that he had experienced what it was like to kiss her when she was completely into it too?

"I'm yours."

Anna's words played in his head over and over. It was inevitable. She *was* his. It was still hard to wrap his brain around it, and they were going to have to talk about it. No doubt it would be awkward. He hated the thought of doing anything to jeopardize their friendship, but they'd crossed that line together and there was no way he could just forget it happened. Hell no. He'd been replaying the kiss they'd shared at her house almost nonstop since it had happened. Add tonight's escapade to it, and he had his own X-rated movie going on in his head.

Tilting his head, he rested it on Anna's. Quinn heard her sigh. It was weird how he kept thinking about Anna in this new light — this new sexy light — and it wasn't weird. He would have thought going from thinking of her as a buddy to thinking of her as a lover would have been difficult, but it wasn't. If anything, the thought of it was an incredible turn-on. His fingers almost twitched with the need to touch her and find out what she liked, what turned her on. He was almost desperate with his need to discover her.

"I'm yours."

Yeah. She was.

And it scared the shit out of him.

CHAPTER 6

"Well? Any news?"

Hugh Shaughnessy walked into the waiting room looking as if he hadn't slept in a week. It was after midnight, and he had been back with Aubrey and the doctors ever since he'd arrived. He sat down in a chair next to his father as the entire family leaned forward and waited for the update.

"She's awake," he said and then yawned broadly. "She didn't fall, so there's no injury or concussion from that." He shifted in the seat to get more comfortable. "They did find she was mildly dehydrated and right now we're just waiting for some test results. Because of the late hour, we'll probably have to wait until morning for them to do the more . . . you know . . . invasive tests."

Quinn silently cursed. It wasn't fair. Even though they all knew there was a possibility of Aubrey's cancer coming back, no one expected it to happen so soon. "What are they thinking?" he asked.

Hugh wiped a weary hand across his face. "Honestly, they're stumped. Aubrey goes for exams twice a year and hasn't presented any symptoms that raised red flags. When the doctor asked how she felt before she fainted, all she could say was she was hungry and was going to get something to eat and then she felt dizzy and . . ." He shrugged. "It could be something really simple or it could be —" He stopped and hung his head.

"How is she doing now?" Anna asked softly.

Lifting his head, it was easy to see the tears. Hugh didn't bother to wipe them away. "She feels fine. She's tired, so the doctors said the best thing was to let her sleep and they'll come in and see her first thing in the morning."

"Are you going to stay the night?" Ian asked, his hand firmly on his son's shoulder. "Or do you want me to take you home?"

"I honestly don't know. I hate the thought of leaving Aubrey alone here, but . . . there's nothing else I can do tonight. I'm not going to be any use to her tomorrow if I've been up all night watching her sleep."

They all nodded. "Then let's go back to your place," Ian suggested. "You may not get a lot of sleep, but it will be more than you'll get here sitting in a chair. We'll get up early so you can shower and change your clothes, and we'll have you back here first thing."

Wordlessly, Hugh nodded and then stood. He looked around at his family. "What about the rest of you? You'll all come back to the house for the night, won't you? It's too late to drive home."

"You sure you want us all camping out at the house?" Aidan asked. "We can go to a hotel if it would be easier on you."

Hugh shook his head. "We'll make it work. There's only three bedrooms including mine, so . . ."

"We'll make it work," Zoe said. "Don't worry."

But Hugh was a planner at heart. It was something that came naturally to him and helped relax him. "No . . . no . . . we'll put Dad and Owen in one room." He turned to his younger brother. "You're staying, right? Or do you need to get going to your seminar?"

Owen shook his head, his jet-black hair in disarray, his glasses slightly crooked. "I gave myself extra time so I could visit with you. I've got a couple of days."

Hugh smiled. "Good. You and Dad will

room together. Aidan and Zoe will take the other room and" — he looked over at Quinn and Anna — "you guys can camp out in the den. Will that be okay?"

"Absolutely," Anna said with a warm smile while Quinn nodded.

"Zoe, Anna, you guys can borrow something to sleep in. Aubrey's got a pretty extensive wardrobe, and I know she won't mind."

"Hugh?" Zoe interjected. "Stop talking. You're exhausted. It's late. Let's just go home," she said as she walked over and hugged him. "We'll worry about the little things when we get there, okay?"

He nodded and yawned. "Okay."

It was two in the morning and Anna was wide-awake. They were all back at Hugh and Aubrey's home, and it had taken a little while to get everyone situated and settled. She was standing in the doorway to the den looking at Quinn, who was shirtless in his well-worn jeans. Memories of what had happened between them earlier in the shop flooded her, and she wondered what was going to happen now that they were alone.

"This opens up into a bed," Quinn said when he saw her standing there. "Or we can use the blankets and pillows and camp out on the floor. What do you think?"

What did she think? Um . . . bed please! She searched for a way to say it without it sounding as if she was nervous — like it was the most natural thing in the world for them to be talking about sharing a bed or camping out on the floor together. Well, camping out on the floor kind of wasn't a big deal. They'd done it a ton of times while growing up.

"The bed should be fine — just as long as it's not like the one at the beach from Aidan and Zoe's wedding."

Quinn chuckled and began to pull the cushions from the couch. In minutes, he had it all unfolded and was sitting on the bed. "This is a pretty good mattress. You can't even feel the bars." He lay down and moved around a bit. "Nope. It's definitely better than the other one."

He jumped up and began making the bed. Anna walked over and helped him. It didn't take long to do, and once all the sheets and blankets were on and the pillows back in place, there didn't seem like there was much to do except . . . get in the bed.

Looking around, Anna saw a pile of blankets and some pillows still on the floor. She looked at them and then back at Quinn. He shrugged. "You take the bed. I'll camp on the floor."

Disappointment swamped her. So they weren't picking up where they left off earlier. Well . . . damn. Of course it made sense. The den in Hugh and Aubrey's house was certainly not the place she wanted to get intimate with Quinn for the first time. But still.

"Unless . . ." he began, and Anna's gaze instantly went to his.

"Unless?"

Quinn cleared his throat and looked at the floor — very insecure and very unlike the confident man she knew him to normally be.

"Unless you wouldn't mind . . . sharing." He looked up at her, his blue eyes uncertain as his gaze held hers.

This was it. This was her chance to finally live at least part of the fantasy. "I wouldn't mind," she said softly and smiled when she saw his shoulders relax, as if he was relieved.

Suddenly shy, Anna looked down at the oversized T-shirt she was wearing. She was comfortable in it, and knew Quinn had seen her in one just like it not too long ago, but suddenly she wished she were wearing something sexier. Her hand smoothed over the fabric, and when she looked up, Quinn was standing right beside her.

His hand came up and caressed her cheek. "You're beautiful," he murmured, but he didn't do anything else — didn't touch her anywhere else, didn't attempt to kiss her. Instead, he stepped back, pulled the blankets down, and motioned for Anna to lie down. Then he walked over and closed the door to the den and turned out the light.

Anna's heart was racing. All of her senses were on high alert. She heard him walking back over to the bed, where he stopped. The sound of the zipper on his jeans going down seemed unusually loud, and she found her breath coming in little gasps. Was he going to completely undress? She heard the jeans hit the floor and then felt him climbing into the bed beside her.

She went perfectly still — afraid to move, afraid to breathe. Quinn moved closer and she almost let out a loud *whoosh* of air when she realized he still had his boxers on. There was just a sliver of light shining into the room through the blinds, enough for her to see him lying on his side looking at her.

"Are you okay?" he asked quietly.

"Uh-huh."

He chuckled. "It's just me, Anna," he said, and then he did reach out and touch her — just on her arm, but even that light touch was enough to make her skin tingle.

"I know," she said, finally letting herself relax. "This is just . . . new."

"But it's not bad, right?"

Was it? Right then she'd have had to say no, but the timing was less than ideal. "No, it's not bad. A little confusing, but not bad."

Beside her, he shifted so his head was resting on his pillow, but his eyes never left hers. "This wasn't the way I pictured the night ending. What happened in my office . . . well . . . If the phone hadn't rung —"

"I know," she whispered.

"You're trembling. I can feel it."

She let out a low, nervous laugh. "It's just . . . I never thought . . . I mean, it's you and me. I always wanted —"

"You did?" he interrupted.

Uh-oh. It was too late to take it back. Thank God for the lack of real lighting. Maybe Quinn wouldn't be able to see how embarrassed she really was. She nodded and then realized he probably couldn't see that either. "Yes."

"Jesus, Anna. I never knew. How come you never said anything?"

"Seriously?"

"Yeah. We tell each other everything."

"Quinn, you never once looked at me as anything other than a friend. We've been hanging out together since we were kids. You tell me about the girls you date and the hookups you've had. I figured if I told you how I felt, you'd —" She stopped and tried to keep her voice steady even though her heart was ready to beat right out of her chest. "I figured you wouldn't want to be around me anymore."

"Anna . . ."

"I'd rather have you as my friend than lose you."

Quinn reached and took one of her hands in his. "You're never going to lose me."

"How can you be so sure? What if . . . what if we . . . change things and it doesn't work out? Are you honestly telling me things would go back to the way they were before? That it wouldn't be weird to hang out together?"

"I honestly don't know," he said, his voice calm and soothing. "But . . . I'm also not afraid to try." He raised her hand to his lips and kissed it. "All I know is that for a long time now, things have been . . . different between us. It bothers me to see you with other guys, and I miss you when you aren't there. I didn't understand what I was feeling. Or at least I didn't until the last couple of days."

"Oh," she said on a breathy sigh.

"Yeah," he said, his own voice sounding a bit breathless. "I want to kiss you again, Anna." He leaned closer until his lips touched her cheek, her jaw. "I know nothing is going to happen here tonight, but I'd really like to kiss you and hold you. Can I? Would that be all right?"

If she hadn't been in love with him before, she certainly was now. This was a side of Quinn she hadn't really thought existed. She knew the cocky and arrogant side of him. She knew the loud and boisterous side. Hell, she even knew the condescending and jackass side. But this considerate one? This was brand-new, and she really liked it.

"Yes. I'd like that a lot." And then she held her breath as one arm moved across her and his weight shifted so his body covered half of hers. It felt better than she'd fantasized. He was large and warm and so damn muscular she almost purred.

Then his lips were on hers — softly exploring, familiarizing himself. Anna was doing the same with him. They shared lazy kisses and sweet, slow caresses, and rather than being awkward, to Anna it felt like coming home. Like this was what had been missing from her life.

She lost track of time and let herself just get lost in Quinn and all he was doing to her — which was mild in terms of anything sexual but it was arousing nonetheless. When he finally lifted his head, he placed one last kiss on her forehead before wrapping an arm around her shoulder and tucking her in beside him.

"We need to be up early for Hugh. I think we should try and grab a couple of hours of sleep."

Anna nodded and couldn't help but place her hand on the middle of Quinn's chest and then place a kiss there as well. He hissed in a breath.

"Careful, Anna. I'm trying to behave here tonight."

She giggled. "Sorry. I just always wanted to do that."

He hugged her to him. "Well, when we're someplace other than my brother's den, I'll let you do that all you want."

"Promise?"

He chuckled. "Definitely."

Anna sighed beside him and fell asleep with a smile on her face.

It was almost lunchtime and they were all sitting in another waiting room. Hugh had gone to the hospital before the rest of the family that morning, but they weren't too far behind him. Now, as they sat silently drinking coffee, reading newspapers, and watching the muted television, they were anxious for an update.

Quinn took the last sip of his coffee and grimaced. It was cold and completely disgusting. Beside him, Anna sat flipping through a magazine.

Last night had been amazing. For the first time in his life, Quinn had simply enjoyed the act of kissing a woman. He hadn't done that since he was fifteen. He had been filled with awe every time he touched Anna. She was a mystery and yet still familiar to him, and it was an incredibly heady experience learning this side of her.

Being here for his brother and Aubrey was his first priority, but he couldn't help but feel a little impatient to get Anna home and be alone with her. He looked at his watch and sighed with frustration — not just for himself but for Hugh. It had been hours, and as far as he knew, there hadn't been any updates on Aubrey.

"Maybe we should go down to the cafeteria and get some lunch?" Anna said to him as she put the magazine down beside her.

"I don't know. What if the doctors come out and we're not here?"

She bit her lip while she thought about it. "Perhaps Hugh will want to stay here and we can bring something back for him. What do you think?"

Zoe looked over and smiled. "What's going on?"

"We're thinking about lunch," Anna said.

Aidan perked up and looked over at them. "I could eat."

They all stood and walked over to where Hugh, Ian, and Owen were sitting. Quinn told them what they were planning and asked if they wanted to join them. Hugh refused, not wanting to take the risk of missing the doctor. Ian opted to stay with Hugh. Owen stood and said he'd go along.

The five of them walked to the cafeteria in silence. They grabbed their food and found a table, and there was a collective sigh as they sat down. Quinn knew they were all worried about the same thing — what if the doctors came out and said Aubrey's cancer was back? How would Hugh survive, and how could they all be there to help? It was too much to think about, so Quinn did his best to find another topic.

"So, Owen, where were you heading to? Some big seminar or something?"

Owen slowly unwrapped his sandwich before answering. "I've been down in Atlanta for a couple of weeks and was heading up to Washington, DC, to the Albert Einstein Planetarium. I'm going there to teach a couple of classes."

"Well, that's exciting," Zoe said. "I've never been to that one. I've gone to the Moorehead Planetarium in Chapel Hill, but never thought to go to another one. Do you like the Albert Einstein? Have you been there before?"

This time Owen took a bite of his sandwich and chewed slowly and took a sip from his bottle of water before answering. "It's one of the top ten planetariums in the United States. Some people find it a bit intimidating, but it's really quite fascinating."

"Why is that?" Anna asked.

"Well, for starters, it's part of the Smithsonian Air and Space Museum and is the largest of the Smithsonian's nineteen museums. Its Center for Earth and Planetary studies is one of the institution's nine research centers."

There was a collective "wow" around the table before Owen continued. "The museum's collection encompasses some sixty thousand objects ranging in size from Saturn V rockets to jetliners to gliders to space helmets to microchips. Fully one-third of the museum's aircraft and spacecraft are one of a kind or associated with a major milestone." He paused and took another bite of his sandwich and another drink.

"Plus, more than twelve thousand cubic feet of documents recording the history, science, and technology of flight are housed in the museum's archives. The facility also holds the most complete collection of aviation and space images — more than 1.75 million photographs and fourteen thousand film and video titles. All of which I'll have access to. It will aid in teaching my classes."

Quinn couldn't help but smile. He may not have a bit of interest in what Owen was talking about — or understand it half the time — but it still gave him a sense of pride to see how his little brother was doing what he loved. "I'm sure you'll kick ass, Owen," he said and then noticed the look of horror and confusion on Owen's face. "It means you'll do great."

Everyone chuckled and eventually Owen joined in.

"You really need to brush up on these phrases, bro," Aidan said before reaching over and patting Owen on the back. "The younger generation is going to confuse the hell out of you if you don't keep up with the lingo."

"Scientists don't really use lingo. We use

scientific facts and phrases. You'd be surprised at how intense it can be. If you came and sat in on one of my classes or seminars, you'd find you'd be in the minority."

"Owen," Aidan began apologetically, "I wasn't judging. I just meant —"

"I know," Owen said quickly. "You're not the first person to mention it and you won't be the last." He sighed. "More times than not, I'm around other scientists and it's not an issue. But I know eventually that's not going to be the case. It's not easy to change the way I think and act and speak. Sometimes I wish I could."

It was probably the longest speech Owen had ever given that didn't include some sort of statistic or fact, and Quinn felt bad for him. Reaching over, Quinn put his arm around him and gave him a brotherly hug. "It's not all it's cracked up to be, Owen. Don't worry about it. You're fine just the way you are."

"Absolutely," Anna chimed in, and that made Owen blush before he ducked his head down and finished his lunch.

The rest of the meal was eaten in relative silence until Aidan's phone buzzed. He looked down at the screen and his shoulders sagged.

"What?" Zoe asked. "What is it?"

"The doctor just called Hugh back. Dad said he looked pretty grim."

"Shit," Quinn muttered, and they all stood and quickly began clearing the table. It didn't take long for them to head back up to the waiting area, Quinn and Anna bringing up the rear.

Anna gripped his hand. "I'm afraid to go back up there."

He nodded. "I know. Me too. But we have to be brave for Hugh. And for Aubrey. We can yell and scream and cry when we get home, but we have to make sure we hold it together up there."

They were all standing waiting for the elevator and nodded at Quinn's words.

"Do you really think it's going to be bad?" Zoe asked no one in particular.

"Unfortunately, it's hard to think otherwise. And the fact it wasn't something that was easily diagnosed makes me think it has to be something more serious than the flu or an ear infection," Aidan said solemnly.

They rode up to the fifth floor in silence and found Ian sitting by himself, praying. They each took a seat around him and bowed their heads and silently joined him. When Ian said "Amen," it wasn't long until each of them raised their heads too.

"Any word yet?" Quinn asked.

Ian shook his head. "This is the hardest part. The waiting. I'm sure Hugh is feeling some relief because they're finally telling him something. I just pray it's not as bad as we're all thinking."

There was another round of nods, and just when they were all settling back in and relaxing, Hugh came out, his face wet with tears.

Anna gripped Quinn's hand tightly in hers as he cursed under his breath again. He had really hoped the news would be good, that they'd be sending Aubrey home and it was all going to be all right.

The last time Quinn had seen his brother cry was when their mother had died, and in that instant, he felt as if he had traveled back in time and they were standing in the waiting room that cold October day hearing that she was gone. It was Anna's hand stroking his that brought him back to the present and kept him from staying locked in the memory.

"Well?" Ian said, standing up and going to his second oldest child.

Hugh didn't speak. He sat down and seemed to crumple into a chair as he openly wept. Ian, Aidan, and Quinn were instantly beside him, each with a hand on him. Owen got up and went to grab a cup of water.

Anna and Zoe clung to each other, tears welling up in their eyes.

"It's going to be all right, Son," Ian said. "Whatever it is, we're all here for you. Whatever you and Aubrey need, we're here, you understand?"

Hugh nodded but still didn't look up. Owen came back and knelt in front of Hugh, the cup of water in his hand. They all stayed like that — the four Shaughnessy men huddled together as if trying to give Hugh their strength. Anna and Zoe stood up and joined the huddle, where they stayed for another few minutes before Hugh cleared his throat and straightened.

Wiping his tears away, he took a minute to compose himself. "I'm sorry I fell apart like that," he finally said. "It's . . . I just never . . ."

"It's all right, Hugh," Aidan said. "Take your time."

Everyone stepped back and took a seat, giving Hugh the time he needed. Owen handed him the drink, and when Hugh drank it all, he looked at everyone and gave a weak smile.

"What did the doctor say?" Ian finally asked. "And how is Aubrey?"

"She's great," Hugh said and they all looked at one another with mild shock.

"She's feeling much better today. And surprisingly enough, she got a good night's sleep and that helped."

Everyone started to speak at once, but Ian held up a hand to stop them. "I don't understand. What did they find, Hugh? What caused her to faint in the first place?"

Hugh straightened in his seat and took a steadying breath. "She's pregnant."

And then everyone really was talking at once, but this time joyfully. They stood and took turns hugging Hugh and asking when they could see Aubrey.

"I don't understand," Quinn said when things calmed down. "I thought you said . . . you know . . . it wasn't possible."

Hugh shrugged. "That's what Aubrey had been told years ago and she never questioned it. And to be honest with you, as much as I was disappointed at the thought of never having kids of our own, in the end it didn't matter. I was in love with Aubrey and wanted to spend my life with her." Then he blushed. "So we haven't taken any precautions because we didn't think . . ."

"This is incredible news!" Ian cried. "A miracle, really!"

Hugh nodded enthusiastically. "I'm in shock! Aubrey's in shock! We were preparing ourselves for bad news. We never expected something like this."

"So when can she go home?" Anna asked.

"They're going to keep her one more night for observation. This is still going to be considered a high-risk pregnancy, and she'll probably spend a lot of time being poked and prodded by doctors, but we'll gladly deal with it."

"We're so happy for you," Aidan said as he pulled Hugh in for a hug. "Seriously, we're so happy and so relieved."

"You and me both," Hugh replied.

"Can we see her?" Zoe asked.

"Absolutely. Come on. She's in room five seventeen." Hugh motioned for everyone to follow him but held back and waited for Anna. "Can I talk to you alone for a minute?"

"Sure," she said. Quinn was beside her and he looked at his brother quizzically.

"You don't mind, do you?" Hugh asked with a knowing grin.

"I'll see you guys inside," Quinn said and walked away, giving Anna's hand one last squeeze.

Hugh led Anna back to the sofas and sat down. She sat down beside him. "What's going on?"

"I know this may seem like odd timing, but . . . remember the property you showed me a couple of months back?"

Anna nodded.

"Is it still available?"

Again, she nodded.

"You up to writing up some contracts?"

"Are you kidding?" she cried, a smile spreading across her face. "Why? How? When?"

"Exactly!" Hugh said with a laugh. "It's been on my mind for a while, and it was something I had planned on pursuing a little further down the road, but with this news about Aubrey and the baby, I don't want to be traveling. I want to stay close to home. Getting this property and starting the plan-and-design phase of it will keep me here and give me something to do other than hovering over my wife — something I'm sure she'll appreciate."

"Hugh, are you sure? It's a really big investment. I know we've done the research but —"

"Anna, one of the most important rules of business — don't talk the customer out of making a purchase, okay?" he said with a wink.

"I'm just so surprised!" she said. "I would have thought this would be the last thing on your mind right now."

"Like I said, I've been thinking about it

for a while, and Aubrey and I knew it was something we wanted to do. It's something we can work on together from start to finish, and I'm really excited about it. So what do you say? Are you ready to make some serious money?"

"Um . . . are you kidding? Hell yes!" she said with a laugh.

"All right then," he said and held a hand out for her to shake. Once she did, he pulled her in for a hug. "Come on, we can celebrate after we sign everything."

"You're on!"

They rose and he put an arm around her shoulders as they headed down the hall toward Aubrey's room. "So . . . you and Quinn, huh?" When Anna's eyes went wide, Hugh simply laughed. "Second-best news I've heard today!"

It was late in the afternoon when Quinn and Anna were back in Quinn's truck, heading home. The family had all stayed at the hospital long enough to visit with Aubrey and make sure she was okay before leaving.

"Do you think we should have stayed another night?" Anna asked as they pulled out of the hospital parking lot.

Quinn shook his head. "I think my brother is going to go home and get a good night's sleep — after he makes seventeen to-do lists about what he'll need to do to the house to prepare for the baby, and then he'll make spreadsheets to plan out the baby's life."

Anna laughed, mainly because she knew he wasn't exaggerating. "Eventually he'll learn to calm down a little with the planning. He's already gotten better."

"I know he has. Aubrey's been good for him, and I think the curveballs he's been thrown since meeting her have made a big difference too."

Anna relaxed against the seat. "Pregnant. I can't even imagine how shocked and relieved they must have felt when the doctor gave them the news. I'm sure my shock was nothing compared to theirs."

"I know. I was sitting there in the waiting room and when Hugh came out . . . Damn. I was certain it was bad news, and I felt sick for him. I hated even thinking of the two of them facing something so harsh."

"You know he's going to make her crazy, right?"

Quinn chuckled. "No doubt. He's going to want to put her in bubble wrap and not let her do a thing." Then he laughed harder. "She'll want to strangle him by the time the baby comes!"

They drove in companionable silence.

Anna watched the scenery go by, her mind wandering to all of the events of the last several days, when she sighed.

"What?" he asked softly. "What's the matter?"

She turned to him and smiled. "A baby. A Shaughnessy baby," she said with wonder. "This is going to be the first baby since . . . Darcy. The first grandchild for your father. It's all just so . . . so . . ." She was at a loss for words.

"I know," he said and reached over and took one of her hands in his. And they drove like that until they hit the outskirts of town. "You hungry?"

She nodded. The lunch at the hospital cafeteria had left a lot to be desired, and even though it was earlier than when she normally ate dinner, she was definitely ready to eat. "You know what? I kind of am. What do you have in mind?"

"We can stop at the pub and grab a burger," he suggested. "I know it's not the same since you're not there making them, but I think it will be okay." He winked at her.

"That sounds pretty good. Plus, you may not agree, but it's always better when someone else does the cooking."

"I don't know about that. I think it's bet-

206

ter when *you* do the cooking rather than me," he teased.

She couldn't help but laugh. Why had she thought he wouldn't agree? "Well, they're not as good as mine, but Johnny still does a pretty good job with them."

"Why didn't you just give him your recipe?"

Anna looked at Quinn with mock horror. "Give him my recipe? Are you crazy? It's a secret family recipe!"

Quinn rolled his eyes. "Anna, I've been going to barbecues at your parents' house since I was six. Their burgers have never tasted like yours. Clearly you created the recipe. Why does it have to be a secret?"

"Maybe I enjoy all the attention," she said saucily and winked at him, and they both laughed.

"Sweetheart, I will gladly give you all the attention you want as long as you feed me."

Instantly, sexy images of doing just that played in Anna's mind. Sleeping with Quinn last night had been wonderful. Waking up in his arms had been like a dream come true. It was sweet. It was innocent. And it was completely comfortable. It was almost as if they were an old married couple.

No! she corrected herself. *Don't think like that. It implies boredom.* She most certainly did not want Quinn to be bored with her already. Maybe . . .

"Maybe we should just stop at the super-market and get some groceries and I can make burgers back at my place. I wouldn't mind some clean clothes, and you could run home too if you want, while I cook."

"You just don't want me to see what you do to the burgers," he said suspiciously.

"Good grief! I was just saying —"

He chuckled. "I know, I know. You are just way too easy to tease." He picked up her hand again and kissed it. "I like your plan. I could definitely go for changing out of yesterday's clothes. I know we got to shower this morning and all, but a fresh set of clothes would have felt even better."

"Okay, so it's a plan. We'll stop at the store and then you can drop me off at home and —" She stopped and cursed.

"What's wrong?"

"My car! I totally forgot that my car is still crapped out at your shop!"

"Don't worry about it," he said. "I've got a loaner car you can use until we get yours taken care of."

She sagged with relief but frowned.

"Now what?" he asked.

"I just hate having to do that."

"It's not a big deal, Anna. You need a car

and I have one you can use. Don't worry about it, okay?"

She nodded but still wasn't happy about it. They pulled up to the supermarket, went in, and grabbed all the ingredients they needed for dinner.

"Do you have beer at your place?" he asked.

"I do."

"How about ice cream?"

"Beer and ice cream? It just sounds wrong. And a little disgusting." She shuddered at the thought.

He laughed again. "Well, not at the same time."

By the time they were back in the truck, Anna was feeling the first tingles of excitement. Cooking a meal for Quinn and eating together were no big deal. They did that at least once a week. But she couldn't help wondering how it was all going to be different this time. After all, they had kissed, they had spent the night together, and, if she was really lucky, they were going to again.

"You're quiet," he said as they drove through town.

"Just thinking." She kept her gaze focused on the passing scenery because she was certain her blush would give her away.

"Anna," he said, and when she didn't look

at him, he said it again. His smile was comforting. "Let's just focus on dinner for right now, okay?"

Right then, Anna wasn't sure if it was a blessing or a curse how he knew her so well. As friends, it was definitely a good thing, but in this new relationship — as lovers — it could get her into a lot of trouble.

In the past, they would talk about the relationships they were in. Quinn tended to overshare, but she wasn't going to think about it. Who was she going to talk to now? What if they had a fight or a problem or if things just didn't go the way she thought they would? He was her best friend and the one she turned to no matter what the problem was. Was she foolish for being willing to throw it all away on a relationship that may not work?

"You're doing it again," he said, pulling into her driveway.

"Get out of my head," she snipped, but there was no real heat behind the words. Anna was surprised when Quinn climbed out of the car with her and carried the groceries into the house. The house was dimly lit, as the sun was starting to go down, and Anna didn't turn on any lights and neither did he.

She turned to grab one of the bags and

found Quinn right behind her. "Oh!" she softly cried. "I didn't expect you to be right there."

His blue eyes darkened as he looked at her upturned face and slowly walked her backward until her back gently bumped the countertop. He placed the bags on the counter. Strong arms came around either side of her, boxing her in.

"I should go home," he said, his voice a low rumble.

Anna could only nod, but her eyes never left his.

"I need to get changed and make some calls." He was listing all the reasons for him to leave, but all Anna could think about were ways to make him stay.

"You could make your calls from here," she said, her voice a breathy whisper. "And Bobby keeps some clothes here. I'm sure you could find something to —"

It was all she could get out before Quinn swooped down and kissed her. Where last night's kisses had been slow and sweet, this time it was back to the fast and frantic kind they'd shared in his shop. Was it only twenty-four hours ago? she wondered.

Who cares? a little inner voice cried out. And that's when Anna's mind just shut off as she let the sensations take over. Quinn's

211

body pressed against hers. The feel of his lips on hers. The way his tongue slowly reached out and teased hers. It was sensory overload, and if they never got around to eating dinner, she'd be perfectly okay with that. Starvation was completely worth it.

Her hands roamed the muscled expanse of his chest, up over his stubbled jaw, and into the thick, blondish hair she loved. She could feel his body vibrating as he growled into her mouth, and that's when she knew they weren't waiting. They weren't going to talk or take it slow. Hell, they weren't even going to barbecue.

She'd be lucky if they made it to the bedroom.

Just then, Quinn lifted his head and took a minute to catch his breath. "I'm not leaving."

Anna couldn't help but smile. "Good."

One of his hands caressed her cheek, and his eyes followed its path downward — her jaw, her shoulder, before finally stopping and gently cupping her breast. He inhaled deeply while Anna almost melted on the spot. She sighed his name as her eyes fluttered closed.

"Look at me, Anna," he said gently, and she had to force herself to comply. "Are you sure about this? If you're not, I'll go. I don't want to, but I'll go."

She said his name again, and his hand moved back up to cup her jaw.

"This is different. You're not a casual hookup. You're not a one-night stand. I'm not just here for tonight, Anna."

Relief flooded her because on some level, she had worried about that. She knew the kind of relationships Quinn usually had. She'd been warned by more than one person that it was a good enough reason not to get involved with him. And yet, hearing him put her fears to rest was as much of a turn-on as his kisses were.

"I want you to stay," she said, her voice barely audible.

And before she could say another word, Quinn scooped her up in his arms and carried her to her bedroom. Excitement warred with disappointment. Part of her had been hoping they'd stay in the kitchen. She wanted to be the type of woman who caused a man to lose control — to the point where he had to have her right there, right now.

A goddess.

But this was good too, she thought as he placed her down on the bed. He straightened and pulled his T-shirt up and over his head, tossing it on the floor. His body was absolute perfection. For all the times she'd

213

seen him shirtless, it was quite another experience to know he was doing it specifically for her.

And in a matter of minutes, she'd be able to touch it, feel it.

Quinn kicked off his shoes and socks, but when his hands went to the button on his jeans, he stopped and looked down at her, a bashful grin on his face. "Is it weird how I'm nervous all of a sudden?"

Anna couldn't help the nervous bubble of laughter that came out. "Thank God you said it! I thought it was just me!"

He hung his head and chuckled. "Damn, Anna. I know this is what I want, and I . . . I just don't know what to do."

She pushed up on her elbows and looked at him, a smile of understanding on her face. And then she decided to have a little fun with him. "You mean you're a virgin?" she teased.

And that broke the tension. A bark of laughter was his first response, but he was able to reel it in quickly. "Why don't I prove to you how unvirginal I am?"

"Bring it."

Quinn shucked his jeans but left his boxers on as he crawled on the bed and covered her body — kissing her along the way. "I think one of us is still overdressed," he murmured.

She couldn't help but tease him. "I was wondering why you left your boxers on."

And then he rested his forehead against hers, closed his eyes, and smiled. "You're not going to make this easy, are you?"

She shook her head. "I was hoping to make it . . . hard. Very, very hard."

Slowly, Quinn lifted his head, his expression dark, serious. No more teasing. No more smiles. "Bring it."

And she did.

CHAPTER 7

Quinn was standing on Anna's back deck after midnight, manning the grill. If anyone had told him he'd be doing this — or how he'd be doing it wearing nothing more than his boxers and a grin — he'd have told them they were crazy.

And yet, there he was.

He stretched and flexed his shoulders, happy to be a little sore. The last few hours had been the best kind of workout he'd ever had.

Anna Hannigan.

He still couldn't wrap his brain around it. His best friend, the girl he'd grown up with, had completely rocked his world. Quinn found he was suddenly jealous of every guy she had ever dated, any guy who'd ever touched her. She was beautiful and sexy and, he thought with an even bigger grin, a goddess in bed.

Yeah, he'd said it — he'd actually spoken

those words to her while they were in bed, and she had blushed and then given him a sexy grin that had him getting hard all over again. He was hard now just thinking of it.

Damn burgers. He flipped them and made sure they were done before plating them and shutting off the grill. Walking back into the house, he found Anna wearing the T-shirt he had discarded earlier and nothing else. She was putting the rest of their meal together and hadn't noticed him yet.

How the hell had he been so blind for so long? When had he simply stopped paying attention to the woman she was becoming in favor of only seeing her as the girl she had once been? And how was it he was lucky enough that she wanted him?

Quietly, he stepped farther into the room and watched her. She spun around and moved with such grace that it left him mesmerized. And then she bent over to get something and . . .

Holy hell!

Stalking across the room, he put the plate down on the counter and came up behind her. Anna let out a little squeal of surprise. "I didn't even —"

Spinning her around, his mouth crashed down on hers as his hands went to her waist and lifted her until she was seated on the counter. Then she squealed again as the cold surface hit her bare skin.

"Quinn? What . . . ?"

"No talking," he said between kisses. "Just let me . . . I need . . ."

And then he was done talking for several long, breathless minutes.

Cold burgers certainly weren't a favorite, but knowing she was the kind of woman who made a man completely lose control certainly was!

Anna quickly heated up the patties before putting them on the buns and making up their plates. Quinn was sitting on the couch, flipping through the TV channels like she had asked him to. Not that she really wanted him to, but she needed a few minutes to pull herself together after their impromptu romp.

The look in Quinn's eyes as he'd made love to her had been better than anything she'd ever fantasized. *He* was better than anything she'd ever fantasized.

Picking up the plates, she thought of how this scene was so familiar and yet now so different. Quinn smiled at her when she stepped around and put their plates on the coffee table.

"There isn't a whole lot on right now, unless you want me to find something on Net-flix," he said and then reached for one of her hands and pulled her down on the couch beside him.

"It doesn't really matter to me. Any one of the late night shows is fine."

Quinn nodded, flipped to one of them, tossed the TV remote aside, and immediately picked up his burger. Before he took his first bite, he turned toward Anna. "I'm just warning you, this isn't going to be pretty. I'm starving."

"Ditto," she said, and then they each dug into their meals. They ate in silence for the most part, stopping to laugh or comment on what they were watching on television. When Anna was done, she slouched back on the couch. "Too. Much. Food."

He chuckled. "No such thing." Wiping his mouth, Quinn looked toward the kitchen. "You bought ice cream, right?"

She waved her hand toward the kitchen. "Help yourself. I'm too tired to move."

Standing, he stepped over her outstretched legs and then bent over and kissed the top of her head. "Rest up while you can. This is simply refueling!" Then he winked at her and walked to the kitchen.

Anna wasn't sure if he was serious or not, and as much as she really wanted sleep, her body was already humming and more than willing to stay up and play. "Traitor," she mumbled.

"Did you say something?" Quinn called out from the kitchen.

"Nope," she replied. "Just talking to the TV."

The next morning, Quinn took Anna to his shop and gave her the keys to his truck.

Anna looked at the keys and then at Quinn like he was crazy. "I don't understand. Why am I taking your truck? I thought you said you had a loaner for me to use."

He shrugged, but his gaze didn't meet her eyes. "It's no big deal. I want to make sure you're safe driving around."

She couldn't help but grin. "And the loaner isn't safe?" she asked playfully, nudging him with her shoulder. "Are your customers aware of this?"

"It's fine, but . . . this is better."

Leaning in, she kissed him on the cheek. "You're very sweet. Thank you." Then she looked around the parking lot. "What are you going to drive?"

"I'll probably use the Corvette," he said blandly.

Anna's jaw dropped. *"The Corvette?*

You're seriously going to drive the Corvette? You never take it out!" She took the keys to the truck and put them back in his hands. "I can't. I can't take the truck. I'll take the loaner or I'll call Bobby."

Quinn took her hands in his. He was momentarily distracted at how soft they were and remembered how incredible they'd felt roaming all over his body. Shaking his head free of the erotic images, he focused on Anna. "It's not a big deal. We'll look at your car today and hopefully have it back to you tomorrow. I can handle driving the Vette for a day or two."

"But you baby that thing," she reminded him anxiously. "You treat that car better than some people treat a real baby. I don't want you doing this on my account. Really. It's not a big deal. Please."

He pulled her into his arms and kissed her soundly. "No arguing. Take the truck and get going. I want to get your car up on the lift, and I'm sure you have calls to get caught up on since you were out of the office yesterday."

"Oh!" she cried. "That reminds me. I can't believe I forgot to tell you! Hugh decided to buy the property I showed him! Can you believe it?"

"Are you serious? That's great!" And then

he pulled her back into his arms and spun her around excitedly before kissing her again. "I knew you could do it!"

"This is huge," she said when he put her back on her feet. "Because it's a commercial property deal, the paperwork is a little bit more of a nightmare, but once everything is signed, sealed, and delivered, I can finally think about a new car. Just think — this will be the last time you have to patch the Honda up!"

"I just want you to be safe, Anna," he said, his expression going serious. "I'm sorry if I made you feel bad the other night. I was . . ." He shook his head. "It wasn't right. You know I'll do whatever I can to fix the car and make sure it's safe for you, and if I can't, I'll help you get another car."

She pulled back. "Quinn, I appreciate your helping me with the loaner for a couple of days, but if the Honda can't be fixed, I'll take care of it."

He threw his head back and let out a growl of frustration. "Why do you argue everything with me?"

"I do not argue everything," she said defensively and then frowned when Quinn gave her a pointed look. "Okay, fine. I argue some stuff, but this time it's legit. I don't expect anyone to help me get another car.

I'll make do until my commission on the property comes through. It's not a big deal."

As much as Quinn wanted to argue with her, he decided to bide his time. The car was a complete disaster, and he'd patched it up far too many times. Every time he gave her the keys back, he begged her to just sell it for scrap and get another car, but Anna held firm. He understood her reasoning — sort of. She didn't want to take on the financial burden of a car payment, but she wasn't thinking about her own safety.

He was.

And whether she liked it or not, Anna Hannigan wasn't going to get the last word this time.

A week later, Anna was still driving Quinn's truck. He wouldn't tell her exactly what was wrong with her car, just that he was waiting on parts. It all seemed logical, but she couldn't help but feel bad about it.

Quinn, on the other hand, was having a good time driving his beloved Corvette. He thanked her every time he saw her for forcing him to drive it. They would laugh about it, but deep down, Anna still felt guilty. Worse, she felt like a charity case and she hated it.

They had spent every night together and

each one had been hotter, sweeter, and sexier than the night before. Anna couldn't believe how easily they had transitioned from friends to lovers. She kept waiting for something to happen — for something to go wrong where they'd both look at one another and be like, "Well, we tried," and call it a day.

Not that she wanted to. Hell no. Quinn Shaughnessy had always had a knack for making her heart race, but now? She had to fan herself. The man was an incredible lover — not that she'd tell him so just yet; he had a huge ego as it was. No need to add to it. They were able to sit and talk about their days and joke and laugh one minute and then be tearing at each other's clothes the next. It was never boring and she was loving every minute of it.

Standing in her living room, she looked at her overnight bag that was waiting by the door. Quinn was due to pick her up any minute. They were heading to Hugh and Aubrey's for the weekend, so she and Hugh could go over the contracts for the sale of the property. They'd been emailing and talking on the phone, but when he asked if they could get together and talk, Anna was more than willing to do so. He extended the invitation to Quinn as well, so they were making a weekend of it.

Their first official outing as a couple.

It scared the hell out of her.

Not that she had any real reason to be scared or nervous. All the Shaughnessys had known about her feelings for Quinn for a long time. Hugh had even laughed about it when they had last seen him. But now that it was real? She just hoped Quinn was going to be able to handle the good-natured ribbing she was certain Hugh was going to throw his way.

Only time would tell.

The knock at the door made her jump, but she didn't have to walk over to open it — Quinn let himself in. "Hey, gorgeous," he said, sauntering over to her. "You all ready?" Without waiting for her answer, he leaned down and kissed her.

She loved that about him. It usually took less than ten seconds for him to take her in his arms and kiss her. Like he couldn't wait any longer to do it. She sighed against him. How had she survived all this time without being loved like this by him? When he lifted his head and smiled, her heart raced.

"Are you all packed?" he asked.

Anna nodded. "Sure am. I really didn't need much — Hugh said we were staying in. I don't think he wants to take Aubrey out just yet."

"Tell her to give us a safe word," he said with a chuckle as he stepped away and went to grab her bag, "and we'll break her out of there."

"A safe word?"

"Yeah, you know, like a code word to let us know she needs to escape."

Anna laughed. "You may need to take your brother out someplace so I can get Aubrey out of the house for a little while. Even if it's just to go and grab some groceries, I'm sure she'll appreciate it."

"No doubt."

"Although your brother just may surprise us. Maybe he's not being overprotective or hovering. Maybe —"

"You've met Hugh, right?"

Anna rolled her eyes. "Stop. He's been getting better!"

"Not that much better," Quinn replied. "Trust me. For all the progress he's made since meeting Aubrey, this whole situation has more than likely set him ten steps back." He looked around the house. "Is everything locked up?"

She grabbed her purse and her keys. "Yup." Turning off the kitchen light, Anna turned and followed Quinn out the door. "We're taking the truck, right?"

Quinn shook his head. "Nah. I figured we'd take the Corvette."

She stopped dead in her tracks. When Quinn got to the car and put her luggage in the trunk, he turned and noticed her standing there. "What?"

"You are freaking me out!" she said with a nervous laugh. "Who are you, and what have you done with Quinn Shaughnessy?"

He walked back over to her. "What's the big deal?"

"You've had this car for a year, and you drove it home from the dealership and that was it. Then you decided you could drive it to and from work until my car was ready — which, by the way, do you have any idea when that will be?"

He shook his head. "Still waiting on some parts."

She looked at him oddly. "It's taking an awful long time for them to come in. What's the hold up?"

Quinn took her hand and led her over to the car. "It happens sometimes, especially with older cars. Don't worry. We'll get it taken care of."

He was being evasive, of that she was certain. But why? He opened the car door for her and then she remembered her original question. "Oh yeah . . . so after a year of not driving this car, now you want to take it on a road trip?"

"It's not really a road trip. They only live an hour away."

"But still —"

"Anna?"

"Hmm?"

"Get in the car," he said lightly before placing a light kiss on her nose and walking around to his side of the car.

"Blink twice if you want me to slip a Valium in Hugh's tea," Quinn whispered loudly to Aubrey, and they all broke out in laughter.

Except Hugh.

"Not funny, bro. Seriously."

Quinn just laughed harder. "Dude, the doctors all said Aubrey is fine and you're treating her like an invalid!"

"It's not quite that bad," Aubrey said lightly, in defense of her husband.

"Don't let him keep going with this," Quinn said, leaning back in his chair and reaching for his drink. "You're going to start to go crazy before too long."

"I don't see anything wrong with pampering my wife," Hugh said as he smiled at Aubrey. "She deserves it."

"Oh my God, give me a break," Quinn whined. "You're making me lose my appetite." Then he looked down at his plate of grilled steak tacos. "And these are too good to skip out on."

Hugh grinned. "My baby wanted steak tacos, so I made steak tacos."

Quinn dramatically rolled his eyes and groaned.

"Oh, stop," Anna finally interjected. "I think it's sweet he's taking such good care of Aubrey, and look at her — she looks fabulous. Pampering obviously agrees with her."

Aubrey smiled and blushed. "I have to admit, it's not hard to get used to."

Quinn leaned over in his brother's direction. "You're creating a monster, that's what you're doing. You'll do this for nine months and then when the baby comes, you'll have two of them to take care of."

Hugh's smile broadened. "Can't wait."

"Fine," Quinn mumbled. "But don't come crying to me when you're feeling all left out and neglected, because I'm not going to be sympathetic."

"Like you ever are!" Hugh said with a loud bark of laughter. "You are the least sympathetic person I know!" Then he turned to Anna. "Seriously, what do you see in him? He's cranky, completely unsympathetic, and I'd bet you a month's salary he hasn't the first clue how to pamper you properly!"

It was all said in jest, but Quinn's spine stiffened a bit.

"Hey!" Quinn snapped.

"Don't even," Hugh countered. "Tell me I'm wrong! Tell me you've done anything that was solely for Anna and I'll apologize."

"Hugh," Anna warned playfully, "come on. Let's change the subject. Let's talk about your plans for the property and the new resort. Have you gotten any drawings on the design yet?"

"Wait, wait, wait," Quinn said, holding up a hand. He looked at Anna first and then his brother. "It's not a competition, bro," he said defensively. "All I'm saying is Aubrey isn't made of china, and it's okay for her to have a little time to herself doing the things she wants to do without you hovering over her. If the doctor said it's okay, then it's okay."

Hugh's grin faded. "I agree. But it doesn't mean I *can't* take care of her, either. If I want to cook her a meal or let her relax and rest, then I'll do it. Just because it's never once occurred to you to take care of someone other than yourself, it doesn't mean the rest of us have to be so selfish."

Seriously? This is what his family thought

230

of him? Quinn silently fumed.

"Hugh," Anna said quickly, "what did you use on the steak for these tacos? They're fabulous."

Quinn glared at her. "You agree with him, don't you?" he asked Anna harshly.

"What? What do you mean?"

He threw his napkin down on the table and stood up. "I can't believe this. You agree with him. You think I'm some sort of selfish jerk!"

"Quinn, that's not what I think," Anna pleaded with him.

"No, no, it's okay. It's fine," he said and took a step away from the table. "Clearly I'm the jackass of the family."

Now it was Hugh's turn to roll his eyes. "Quinn, knock it off and sit back down. Come on. I'm sorry. I was just kidding around. Let it go."

"No, I don't think you were kidding. You really think those things. You wouldn't have said them otherwise. You're the most honest one in the family," he mocked.

"Oh, for crying out loud," Hugh huffed. "Stop being such a drama queen and sit down."

"Come on," Anna said in a tone she always used when she was trying to tell him he was wrong. "Let's finish this delicious lunch and tonight I'll cook for us and we can eat out on the deck looking at the ocean. Won't that be nice?"

He wanted to argue; he really did. But then he'd be accused of being the guy who ruined lunch. *Fabulous.* Grabbing the back of his chair, he yanked it away from the table and then sat back down.

They all ate in silence for about a minute until he couldn't take it anymore. He would show them all he wasn't the jerk they all thought him to be.

"For your information," he said, looking at his brother, "I bought Anna a car! Hers crapped out and I bought her a new one because she didn't want a car payment. So now she'll have one free and clear. Tell me again how selfish I am!" Then he sat back smugly, crossing his arms over his chest.

"You did what?" Anna cried.

Uh-oh . . .

He turned to her, his arms dropping. He smiled at her reassuringly. "It was supposed to be a surprise. When we got home tomorrow night, it was going to be waiting for you in your driveway. One of my guys was going to deliver it and take the truck back." He noticed she wasn't smiling. If anything, her face was flushed with anger and embarrassment.

"And you didn't think to ask me before you did something like this? I told you how I felt about the whole car situation, Quinn!" she said and then jumped to her feet. "I'm not a charity case!"

She fled from the room and Quinn immediately jumped up to go after her, but Aubrey stopped him. "Let *me* go," she said, coming to her feet. "I have a feeling she's going to need a few minutes to herself. You two stay here and try not to start any more arguments." She walked away, leaving the brothers alone.

Quinn looked over at Hugh. "What did I do? Tell me what I did that was so horrible?"

Hugh chuckled. "Dude . . . sometimes I can't even believe we're related."

"What?" Quinn snapped. "Seriously, what did I do that was so wrong? Anna's car was on its last legs and she couldn't afford a new one yet. I'm just helping her out."

Leaning forward on the table, Hugh turned serious. "Did she ask you or even imply she needed help buying a car?"

He thought about it for a minute. "Not exactly."

"How long have you known Anna?"

Quinn looked at him dryly. "You know the answer to that."

"I do. And I was going for irony. You've

known Anna almost your whole life. She's very independent and doesn't like anyone helping her — no matter how much she may need it. It's a pride thing. Hell, even I know that about her! How did you think she was going to react?"

"I don't know . . . grateful?"

"Your lack of common sense is astounding," Hugh said, taking another drink of his tea. "If you had presented it to her as some sort of business deal or that you found a great deal on a car and managed to secure reasonable payments for her, she might not have gotten so angry." He paused. "She was going to be pissed off initially, but she would have eventually cooled off and gone for it. But what you did? Taking the matter out of her hands completely? It's going to take her a little while to get over that."

Damn it, his brother was right. Why hadn't he thought of it that way? And then it hit him. "I wanted to take care of her," he mumbled. "I really . . . I just . . ." He shrugged. "For once, I wanted to do something for her."

And then Hugh relaxed back in his chair and smiled. "Finally."

Quinn's head snapped up. "What?"

"I knew you had it in you somewhere."

"Had what?"

"The ability to put someone else first." He held up his hand when Quinn started to argue. "Before you get all pissy again, hear me out." He paused again. "You've always been strong-willed and a bit self-centered. It's not always a bad thing, but some-times . . . it's a little hard to take. Anna's been putting you first practically since the first time you met. And you know what? You always took."

"That's not —"

"Yeah, yeah, yeah . . . you helped her with her car or you beat up anyone who bothered her, but it wasn't a completely selfless act. I know your heart was in the right place with this car thing, and I'm sure she'll calm down about it, but you have to be able to explain to her why you did it."

"I would think it's obvious," Quinn said. "She needed a car and couldn't afford one. I could. End of story."

Hugh sighed and ran a weary hand over his face. "How it is that she fell in love with you and stayed there is absolutely astound-ing."

"Now what?" Quinn cried.

"How about explaining it to her as her boyfriend and not as her buddy? How about making her feel like she's special rather than some sort of burden? Maybe make it like a romantic gesture rather than a tax write-off?"

"Is that all? Maybe I should fill the damn car with roses while a full orchestra plays for her under a starry sky? Or maybe —"

"Just shut up," Hugh said. "You're killing me."

They sat in silence and picked at what was left of their lunches. "Okay, so what do I do?" Quinn finally asked. "How do I get her to . . . you know . . . not hate me?"

"Are you sure you want to ask me? After all, it was only a few minutes ago you were attacking the way I treat my wife."

"Well, I still think it's a bit much, but at least Aubrey's still talking to you."

Hugh laughed. "You may want to take notes on this because I have a feeling Anna's not going to be quite as easygoing."

"I know you're really angry right now, and rightfully so, but can I just say thank you for giving me an excuse to come down here and put my toes in the sand?"

Anna looked over at Aubrey and smiled. She had pretty much stormed out the back door of the house and down the deck steps that led to a path through the dunes to the beach. It left her breathless, but Aubrey looked completely at peace.

"It's beautiful down here," Anna said. "You and Hugh picked a great house."

"I'll admit, when we first found it, I was a little disappointed it was set so far back from the actual sand, but then after hearing about Zoe's first beach house, I'm kind of glad."

Anna nodded. "That was a nightmare. She had already been through so much with losing her mom and relocating, then to lose her house like that? In all the years I lived close to the beach, I never saw a house just fall into the ocean like that during a storm. It was horrible. I still can't imagine how she felt watching it happen on the news! Thank God Aidan had convinced her to leave." She looked around. "No, what you have here is perfect. You're set far enough back that you should be good in a storm."

Aubrey sat in the sand and tilted her head back so the sun could shine on her face. "I know it's the same sun I get up on the deck, but when you combine it with the feel of the sand between your toes, it's just better."

"I agree." She sat down beside her. "Am I being stupid? Did I overreact?"

Keeping her head back and eyes closed, Aubrey let out a sigh of contentment. "How bad was your car?"

"Really bad."

"How many times have you had to get it fixed?"

"Too many to count."

"Did you have plans to buy a new car?"

Now Anna sighed. "Yes. No. Kind of."

"Yeah, okay. That was clear."

"Fine. I knew I had to buy a car, but . . . I just kept putting it off. I don't want a car payment right now, and I figured once we closed the deal on the property, I'd be able to do something."

"That could still take some time, Anna. Are you sure the car would have held out that long?"

"Probably not. It's just . . . I wish he would have talked to me about it! He gets so high-handed and acts like some superior know-it-all." She fell back on the sand. "I swear he must think I'm some kind of idiot who can't take care of herself."

"Or maybe he really cares about you and your safety and wanted to make sure you would be okay," Aubrey said quietly. "Knowing what I do about Quinn, he acts first, thinks later. In this case, he saw you had a need and took care of it. It wasn't about proving you can't take care of yourself. It was about . . . maybe . . . him doing something nice for you."

"Well, crap," Anna muttered. "That does

238

sound like him."

"I'm not saying you can't be annoyed at him for not talking to you first, but maybe try and see his side of it." She lay back and turned her face toward Anna. "So now that that's out of the way . . . you and Quinn, huh? Is it awesome? Is it everything you dreamed it would be?"

Anna laughed out loud. "Oh God." She put her hands over her face in embarrassment.

"Come on, you've been wanting this since forever. Don't get shy on me now! Come on! Spill it! I want details!"

"You are so *not* getting details!" Anna said, forcing herself to sit back up and focus on the waves crashing on the beach.

"Okay, you can leave some things out. I don't need to think that way about my brother-in-law," she laughed. "Or you."

"Let's just say it's all good. Really good." Anna blushed. "Better than I ever really thought it could be."

"Yeah!" Aubrey squealed, waving her hands in the air. "I'm so happy for you guys! So what has everyone else had to say about it?"

Anna shrugged. "You guys are really the first to know. Or at least, you're the first ones we've been around since things started."

"Really? Wow. So when did things . . . start?"

Anna told her about the way things were before Aidan and Zoe's wedding and then about the incident with Jake.

"Oh my gosh, Anna! That's horrible! I can't believe nobody told me about this. Are you okay?"

"I'm fine. Luckily I only had a little bit to drink and was able to call Zoe to come and get me. She showed up with Aidan and Quinn. And, well . . . let's just say things got messy."

"I'm sure."

"When Quinn took me home afterward, we hung out until I fell asleep. He claims I kissed him."

"And did you?"

"I kind of thought I was dreaming."

"But you weren't," Aubrey said with a big grin.

"No, I wasn't. But he still left."

"Damn."

"Tell me about it." She sighed. "So a few days later, I was driving home after showing a house when my car started acting funky, and luckily I was near the shop, so I stopped in. Quinn was acting all weird, and next thing I knew, we were kissing."

"No!"

"Yes," Anna said, unable to stop her own grin. "And it was so hot and so amazing, and I couldn't believe it was happening."

"And then what? Did you guys do it right there in his office?" Aubrey asked giddily.

"Um . . . no."

She frowned. "Well, why not?"

Anna looked at her with a lopsided smile. "That's when we got the call about you. So we hopped in the truck and drove down here."

"Yikes . . . so I'm the reason you guys didn't get a hot and heavy first time. Damn. Sorry."

Anna chuckled. "Don't be. The actual first time was very hot and heavy and . . . perfect. And that's all I'm going to say about it."

"Good for you." Aubrey relaxed back in the sand again. "This really does feel good. Can you stay mad at Quinn for a little bit longer? Hugh thinks the walk to the sand is too much for me and makes me stay on the deck. I just need about fifteen more minutes of this bliss and then I'll be ready to go back inside."

"No problem. I'm just disappointed I didn't get to finish my lunch. Those tacos were awesome. I may have to ask Hugh for the recipe."

"We can reheat them when we get back inside," Aubrey said. "Or I can tell Hugh I want fresh ones." She looked at Anna with a wicked grin. "Don't believe for one minute I don't find ways to take advantage of all his hovering."

"You're an evil genius. I love it!"

No one mentioned the car — or the subsequent argument — again for the rest of the day. When Anna and Aubrey had gone back up to the house, Hugh offered to make them some fresh plates. The women looked at each other and giggled but refused to say why.

After lunch, they all sat out on the deck and talked about Hugh's plans for the property and the resort. There wasn't much Quinn could contribute to the discussion, but he loved watching how happy his brother was and how pleased Anna seemed to be.

Deep down, he knew real estate wasn't her dream. He understood — sort of — why she felt like she had to find a different career, but he knew that if she had her way, this wouldn't be what she was doing. So maybe she'd make enough money to get her to the point where she felt a little financially secure and then she could do what she loved.

Which was cooking.

She'd deny it till her last breath, but like he said, he knew her. She enjoyed the praise she received whenever she cooked, and she had loved running the kitchen at the pub. Hell, she should own the damn place! She had a head for business and the customers loved her. But for some reason, she didn't think it was something she should do. Something about breaking out of a rut, and not working in jeans . . . he wasn't sure, but he remembered all those things as parts of multiple conversations.

She made dinner for all of them, and they ate it out on the deck. Aubrey looked very relaxed and, for the first time since they'd arrived, so did Hugh. And Anna was positively glowing. That's how he knew he was right. If something as simple as making a meal for her friends put that look on her face, why was she wasting her time in real estate?

After the way he'd screwed up with the whole car thing earlier, Quinn knew tonight wasn't the time to bring it up, but he made a mental note to talk to her about it a little more. Soon. There was no reason for her to be miserable. Ever. He wanted to make sure she was happy — and that she stayed happy.

That made him stop and think. When had he ever been that considerate? No doubt he'd dated more than his share of women, but he had never been overly concerned about their happiness. Well, their future happiness. He was all about making them happy while they dated, but once they were done, he didn't give them another thought.

He was far from done with Anna. Wasn't sure he'd ever be. And not just because of their friendship, but because of the way he was beginning to feel. He'd always loved Anna — as a friend. He'd always been protective of her and loved spending time with her, just hanging out. But now it was different, in a good way. There was genuine affection. His need to protect her went deeper, and the need to spend time with her? Well, he almost wished he didn't have to go to work most days because he just wanted to stay in bed with her, holding her, touching her . . . just being with her.

By the time they said good night to Hugh and Aubrey, Quinn realized he and Anna hadn't really talked to one another since lunch. They'd talked as a group all day, but they hadn't had any one-on-one conversation all day. And it bothered him. A lot.

Closing their bedroom door, he leaned

against it and watched her move around the room. She was taking all the decorative pillows off the bed and pulling down the comforter. Then she went to her overnight bag and pulled out a T-shirt and the little bag that probably held her makeup and whatnot. Without a glance in his direction, she walked toward the attached bathroom. He reached out and placed a hand on her arm to stop her.

"Hey," he said softly and waited until her brown eyes looked up at him. They weren't twinkling like they normally did when she looked at him. Carefully, he maneuvered the two of them until she was in his arms. She held herself stiff, and he knew this wasn't going to be easy. "Dinner was excellent tonight. You didn't have to do that. It's good for Hugh to have to work a little," he teased, hoping to get a smile out of her.

He didn't.

Okay, new approach. "Aubrey looked great after you guys came back in. This pregnancy is really agreeing with her so far."

Nothing.

Not knowing what else to do, he released her and took a step back. "I'm sorry."

Anna eyed him warily. "For what?"

She knew him too well, knew he had a tendency to throw a blanket apology out there just to make a situation go away.

"For not talking to you about the car. I should have. I didn't mean for it to be a bad thing, Anna, I swear. I just . . ." He sighed. "For years, you've been the one taking care of me, and I let you. Hell, I even took advantage of it. And I finally found a way I could take care of you. I wanted . . . I wanted to do something that would make your life a little bit easier — to take at least one burden away from you. I know I didn't handle it right and —"

She immediately dropped her things on the floor and went up on her tiptoes and kissed him soundly on the lips. Quinn wasn't going to question it; he was just happy she was forgiving him. And she was kissing him. Anna was a spectacular kisser. One hand cupped her bottom while the other reached up to curl around the nape of her neck. God, she felt so good. All soft and warm and . . . everything.

Not wanting to break the kiss, he scooped her up in his arms and walked them over to the bed. Thankful the blankets were turned down, he immediately stretched out on top of her, kissing her, touching her, loving her.

Anna sighed his name when his mouth moved from hers. Quinn lifted his head and looked down at her. Her skin was flushed, her lips red from his kisses. "I want to take care of you, Anna," he said, his voice soft and low. "Let me."

A slow smile spread across her face as she relaxed beneath him. "I'm all yours," she said.

They were the three sweetest words Quinn had ever heard.

CHAPTER 8

"Oh, Quinn," Anna said the next day as they drove up to her house. "What did you do?"

"What? We already covered this."

She leaned forward in her seat as they pulled into the driveway. "I wasn't . . . I didn't think . . . Oh my God." She sighed as he parked.

Yes, she knew there was a car waiting for her, and yes, she knew it wasn't going to be something old like her Honda, but . . .

Quinn climbed from the car and walked around to the passenger side to help her out. He opened the door and held out a hand to her. "You promised not to be mad. Remember that."

Anna took his hand and stood. His name came out on another sigh. "I can't believe . . ."

"You seemed to have some sort of weird connection with your old Honda, so I figured I couldn't go wrong with a newer one." He let go of her hand as she began to walk around the new car. "It's not brand-new, but it's only two years old and has under five thousand miles on it. My guys checked it out, and it's in perfect condition. I tried —"

But he never got to finish because Anna launched herself into his arms and kissed him. This was a much better reaction than what he had been expecting, so he readily jumped on board, banded his arms around her, and held her close. When she lifted her head, her smile was dazzling. "So . . . you like it?" he asked, gently lowering her to her feet.

"It's perfect. It looks like it just rolled off the showroom floor! And I love the color! That blue is just so beautiful!" She gave a little squeal of delight. "Where are the keys? Can I look inside? Can I drive it?"

Quinn nearly sagged with relief and laughed as he reached into his pocket. "Here you go. The second set should be in the car, under the driver's seat. It's where I told Tommy to leave it."

But Anna wasn't listening. She had the car door open and was sitting in the driver's seat and starting the car. "Ooo . . . power windows! I almost forgot what those were! Mine stopped working last year."

"I remember," Quinn mumbled, shaking his head.

"And power seats and mirrors!" She pushed buttons until the seat was in the perfect position for her and then worked on getting the mirrors just right. "This stereo is better than the one I have in my house!"

Quinn walked over to the passenger side and climbed in. "You've got every option available — cruise control, back-up camera, the radio has satellite, there's a USB port here for your phone, and there's Bluetooth —"

"This is amazing! I never thought I'd have a car this new." Turning toward Quinn, she smiled, leaned in, and kissed him on the cheek. "I'm sorry I was a bit of a brat the other day about this. This is incredibly generous of you, and I . . . well . . . I want to say it's too much but I love it already!"

"I figured we've got about twenty-plus years of you feeding me and helping me out," he teased. "Now we're kind of even."

She shook her head and reached out and cupped his face in her hands. "It was never a competition. I wasn't keeping track. I enjoy taking care of you and helping you."

"Oh yeah?" he asked quietly. "I have to be honest, Anna. I really enjoy taking care of you too. I just wish I had been smart enough to start doing it sooner." Then his expression turned serious, somber. "I should have paid more attention and not been so selfish. I don't deserve you."

A slow, sweet smile crossed her face as her thumbs skimmed over his cheeks. "Don't talk like that. I don't see it that way at all."

"Then you're the only one," he said.

"Why would you even say that?"

"Trust me. I've heard it a lot over the years."

"From whom?" she asked, pulling back slightly.

Quinn took one of her hands from his face and pulled it around so he could kiss her palm. "It doesn't matter."

"Damn right it doesn't," she said firmly.

"You sound pretty fierce there, Anna Hannigan," he said with a grin.

She nodded. "It's true. You're stuck with me and there's nothing you or anyone can do about it."

Quinn wasn't sure what to say to that. He kissed her and was about to go for something light and funny but she cut him off.

"Now close the door so we can take this baby out for a ride!"

For another week, they managed to stay somewhat cocooned in their own little world. While Hugh and Aubrey knew about the change in their relationship — and Anna was certain the rest of the Shaughnessys had an idea — Anna had managed to avoid her own family.

It was early on Saturday morning, and they were lying side by side in her bed catching their breath. "This is the best way to wake up," Quinn said, turning his head and kissing her bare shoulder. "Let's throw out our alarm clocks and stick with this."

Anna playfully swatted him away. "We'd never get up if that were the case."

Quinn sat up. "Nonsense. I'm energized and ready to go." He looked over at the clock. "Holy shit . . . it's after nine already?"

She chuckled. "See? I told you."

He stood up and reached for his jeans. "How about some breakfast? I happen to make some great French toast."

"You're on," she said and snuggled back under the blankets.

"Oh no," he said, reaching for her hand and forcing her to sit up. "No going back to sleep. You've got about fifteen minutes and then breakfast will be on the table."

"What? Not in bed?" She pouted. "Seems to me the least you could do is bring me breakfast in bed."

"And I promise I will — another time,"

he added. "I've got to go in to the shop today. Those two classic cars are supposed to get picked up at noon and I need to be there to sign some papers."

Anna stared at him for a minute. "You mean Jake Tanner's cars?"

Quinn nodded.

Guilt washed over her. She hated that she had managed to cost Quinn some very lucrative business. She reached for the hand that had just let hers go. "Quinn, I . . ." She sighed. "I'm really sorry. I didn't expect you to lose such an important job because of me."

His gaze hardened as he looked at her. "You're kidding, right? Did you honestly think I'd still want to do business with that guy after — ?"

"Look, what happened with Jake was awful and horrible and I hate it, but the bottom line is I'm okay. I was lucky. Nothing happened to me other than getting sick and feeling embarrassed."

"Anna, what the hell are you saying?"

She shrugged. "I just think you should, you know, still do the work. I'd double the price if I were you," she said in an attempt at humor, "but I'd still do the restorations. It would be great for your business. You know it, and I know it."

"I don't know," he said hesitantly. "The thought of ever dealing with Jake Tanner again —"

"I know," Anna interrupted. "Believe me, I know. But . . . just think about it, okay? I know how much you were looking forward to working on those cars. It meant a lot to you and the business."

"You mean more to me than that, Anna," he said fiercely, leaning on the bed toward her. "I can always find other restoration jobs, but if anything happened to you?" He stopped when Anna placed a finger over his lips.

"Don't, okay?" she whispered. "Don't think like that." She kissed him and then smiled. "Now go and make me some breakfast. I'm starving."

Quinn stood and still looked a bit unsure of himself, but he watched as Anna rose from the bed — naked and beautiful — and walked to the bathroom.

He was shirtless, his hair was a mess, and his pants weren't buttoned. He raked a hand through his hair and walked out to the kitchen. He was pulling eggs and butter from the refrigerator when a sound by the front door caught his attention.

"Hey, Anna! What's with the —" Bobby Hannigan stopped dead in his tracks at the sight of Quinn in his sister's kitchen. "What the hell are you doing here?" he snarled, slamming the door closed.

For his part, Quinn did his best to remain calm. He had known they were going to have to deal with Bobby eventually — and Bobby's intense dislike of him — but he had been really hoping it wasn't going to happen quite like this.

"Hey, Bobby," he said casually. "I'm making French toast. You want some?"

"You son of a bitch," Bobby hissed as he stalked across the room, tossing his keys on the ground as he went. When he got close enough, he lunged at Quinn.

Quinn managed to dodge him, but a plate crashed to the floor in the move. "Look, let's just talk for a minute, okay?" he said, trying to reason with Bobby.

"Are you sleeping with my sister? Is that why you're here?" he growled, doing his best to back Quinn into a corner.

"Seriously, just calm down. I don't want to fight with you."

"Too bad," Bobby snapped. "You couldn't just leave her alone, could you? It's not enough you've been taking advantage of her for years, or that your friend drugged her. No. You had to just swoop in and do this now!"

"It wasn't like that!" Quinn yelled. "And it's really none of your damn business what's going on between me and Anna."

"She's my sister. That makes it my business." He shook his head in disgust. "I really hoped she'd outgrow the stupid crush she had on you, but you just kept dragging her along."

"No one was getting dragged! We were friends! Shit, Anna's the best friend I've ever had! I would never hurt her, and as for what's going on right now —"

"Shut up!" Bobby interrupted. "You just shut the hell up. I've been waiting a long time for this. I've been waiting for the opportunity to punch you in your damn smug face."

Quinn stopped. His hands dropped to his sides. "You want to hit me? Would that make you feel better? Then go ahead. I'll stand here and I'll take it. If that's what it takes for you to realize I'm not just fooling around with your sister, that she means something to me, then go ahead. Take your best shot."

Bobby's eyes narrowed.

"So help me, Bobby, if you do it, you'll have me to deal with," Anna yelled from the bedroom doorway. Slowly, she walked into the room. "What in the world is going on here?"

Bobby turned and looked at her. "I've been driving by your house for the last couple of days and haven't seen your car. Finally I decided to stop in and see what was going on. Where's your car? Did it break down again?"

"Actually," she said hesitantly, "that's my new car out in the driveway."

"New? How?" Bobby stammered. "I thought you said you couldn't afford a new car right now?"

She shrugged. "I couldn't. But my old one crapped out, and Quinn helped me out and —"

"You bought her a car?" He cursed under his breath and took a few steps away. "You seriously bought her a freaking car?"

"Um . . . help me out here," Quinn said quietly to Anna. "I can't tell if he's angry or impressed right now."

"Yes, he bought me a car," Anna answered instead. "I didn't ask him to, and at first, I was really annoyed he did it, but . . ." She looked at Quinn and smiled. "But he knew I needed the help."

"I knew you needed the help too!" Bobby said defensively. "I would have helped you get a car, Anna! You don't need him doing it for you! You don't have to sleep with him because he bought you a car!"

"Okay, that's enough," she said and walked over and gave her brother a shove until he fell back on the couch. "You need to understand and accept that Quinn and I are together. I don't know what your deal is with him, but it's got to stop."

"You're too good for him, Anna," Bobby said through clenched teeth. "All these years you've waited on him hand and foot and he never gave you a second thought."

"That's not true," Quinn protested. "I've always been there for Anna! We've been friends our whole lives!"

"That's not what I'm talking about, jackass," Bobby snapped at him. "She's been pining after you since you were teenagers and you never noticed. Do you have any idea how many times she cried after you started dating someone new?" He didn't wait for an answer. Slowly, he stood up and began stalking Quinn again. "Or how many times she would come home brokenhearted and disappointed because you didn't thank her or appreciate the things she did for you?"

"Bobby," Anna warned.

"No! It's time he knew just how awful he was!" Slowly, he walked around Quinn. "How many times did you call her and ask her to make you food or bake you cookies, and she did it only to find you with another girl when she arrived?"

Quinn watched him warily at first and then with defeat. "If I could go back and change any of it, I would," he said quietly. "I know I can't and it kills me. I had no idea Anna felt that way about me."

"Yeah, well . . . maybe if you paid attention to someone other than yourself —"

"Look, I get it!" Quinn finally snapped. "Do you think I like knowing how much I hurt her? Do you think it's easy for me to stand here and listen to this?"

"You're not good enough for her," Bobby snarled. "You're having fun right now and everyone's happy, but I know you, Quinn. You don't stick around. You don't have staying power. Eventually, you're going to get bored, and you'll start treating her exactly like you used to. And I'll be the one whose shoulder she'll cry on."

"It's not like that," Quinn said.

"We'll see."

Anna stepped in between the two of them, facing her brother. "Thanks for the vote of confidence, Bobby," she said sadly. "Thanks for believing I'm the type of girl who isn't enough for someone to stay with."

And then she stormed from the room, slamming the bedroom door behind her.

"Way to go, genius," Quinn said, raking a hand through his hair.

"*Me?* This is all your fault!"

Quinn shook his head. "Uh-uh. No way. You came in here and started this. And by the way, why not try knocking next time instead of just barging in?"

"Barging . . . ?" Bobby let out a growl of frustration. "You do realize I used to live here too, right?"

"Whatever. That was like . . . two years ago. This is Anna's house now, and you have no right just letting yourself in. She's entitled to her privacy."

"Don't you dare lecture me about my sister."

Quinn threw up his hands in defeat and frustration. "You know what? We're done. You need to leave so I can go and make sure Anna's okay."

"I'll go and see —"

"No, you won't," Quinn said firmly. "You need to leave." Then he sighed. "Honestly, Bobby, let me go and take care of her."

"I don't trust you, Shaughnessy."

"That's fine. I don't really care what you think of me, but you'll respect your sister. Just go. I'll make sure she calls you later."

Bobby hesitated for a full minute before he simply nodded and bent to pick up his keys on his way out the door.

Once it was shut and Quinn heard Bobby's car pull way, he walked over to the bedroom door and lightly knocked. "Anna? Can I come in?"

"Sure."

He opened the door and found her lying on the bed, one arm flung over her face, covering her eyes. "You okay?"

"Oh, yeah. Just great," she mumbled.

Quinn sat down beside her. "You know he's just looking out for you."

"It didn't feel that way."

"Yeah, well, trust me. I think if I walked in on Darcy and found some guy in her place, I'd probably kick his ass first and ask questions later."

She moved her arm away from her face. "It's not like that at all. Bobby knows you. He's known you as long as I have. What he said out there — and what he implied — was pretty insulting." She sat up. "And Darcy's still a child. Any guy you found with her would be a complete stranger to you, so you'd better punch first and talk later."

He loved how she was just as protective of his little sister as he was. "I'll remember to tell her it was your idea, should it ever happen." He pulled her into his arms and kissed the top of her head.

"And I'll completely deny it. No one would believe you over me. Your family thinks I'm very sweet."

Quinn tucked a finger under her chin. "I think you're very sweet too." He kissed her nose, her cheek, and then her lips. "Everything about you," he murmured before kissing her again.

Soon they were lying down on the bed and he was rolling her beneath him. It would have been easy to distract her — and him. With very little effort, Quinn knew he could have them both naked and lost to the world outside. But he knew it wasn't the way to really make her feel better.

Instead, he lifted his head and looked down at her solemnly. "I really am sorry, Anna. All this time I thought I was a good friend to you, but I wasn't. I hurt you and I didn't even realize I was doing it."

One of her hands came up and caressed the side of his face. "It wasn't your fault, Quinn. I could have handled things differently too. I should have said something a long time ago."

"No. I hate that you got hurt because of me, but I think where we are now, here like this, it wouldn't have happened unless we went through all we went through. Does that make sense?"

She nodded.

Rising from the bed, he pulled her up with him. "Now come on. It's your turn to sit and watch me do all the cooking." He took her by the hand and led her from the bedroom.

Of course, once the cat was out of the bag — compliments of Bobby — the phone started ringing. First it was her parents, and then some of their friends, and eventually the Shaughnessys chimed in. But in their defense, it was a family dinner invitation, and Anna never turned one of those down. This would be the first one — kind of — that she and Quinn would be going to as a couple.

Ian Shaughnessy was hosting a barbecue because all of the restoration and remodeling on his home was officially done. At one point or another, each of his six children had come home and helped with the work, but this was the first time everyone was going to be there to see the finished product.

Quinn had to work that morning, so Anna told him she'd meet him at his father's. It wasn't unusual for her to go there on her own, and if anything, it was no different from going home to her parents'. Well, it could also be because her parents lived right next door to Ian, and if they were in town, she had no doubt they'd be joining the family for the festivities.

Ian greeted her at the door with a big smile and a kiss on the cheek. "There's my girl," he said and took the large bowl from her hands. "What have you made for us?"

"This is some potato salad," she said with a proud grin — it was one of her specialties and she knew the Shaughnessys all enjoyed it. "And I happen to have several trays of brownies out in the car. I just need to —"

"Did someone say brownies?" Riley asked as he came over and kissed her on the cheek too. "I'll just go and grab them from your car."

"It's the blue Honda," she yelled over her shoulder as Riley walked out the door.

She made her way into the house, saying hello to everyone as she went until she was in the kitchen. Zoe and Darcy were in there slicing vegetables and talking. "Hey, girls! How are you both doing?"

Zoe looked up and smiled while Darcy continued to look down at the tomato she was slicing. Anna walked over and hugged Zoe and looked at her questioningly. Then she turned to Darcy. "Hey, kiddo. What's going on?"

Darcy shrugged and Anna looked back at

Zoe. "Am I missing something?"

There was a moment's hesitation before Zoe sighed. "Darcy asked if she could go on a trip to Florida for spring break and Ian said no."

Darcy looked up at Anna. "Honestly? *Everyone* said no." She glared at Zoe.

"O-kay," Anna said and put her purse down on the kitchen table. "So who's going on this trip?"

Slamming down the knife she was using, Darcy huffed. "Everyone! All of my friends are going — Michelle, Diana, Amy, Jennifer, Mike, Rob —"

"So it's a coed trip?" Anna asked, grabbing a celery stalk and munching on it as she leaned a hip against the counter.

"Well, yeah . . . it's college. Of course it's a coed trip."

Anna chuckled. Oh, to be young and think everyone around you was a moron. "Were you planning on flying or driving?"

"Driving. Why?"

"And where were you going to stay?"

"We were going to rent a house in Daytona," Darcy replied.

"Hmm . . . and how much was it going to cost?"

A shrug was her only response.

"Come on, Darce," Anna said. "Out with it."

"Okay, so I was going to need about fifteen hundred dollars for everything. But it would cover everything! Gas, food, the house — all of it!"

"And do you have that much money saved?" Anna asked.

Darcy looked at her like she was crazy. "No, why?"

"So basically you not only asked your dad for permission to go, but you wanted him to finance it too?" She didn't wait for Darcy to answer. "And you were foolish enough to ask for way more than you could possibly need for the trip. That's a huge red flag to me."

"What are you talking about?" Darcy asked defensively. "We worked out the budget. That's how much it's going to cost."

Anna finished her piece of celery, rested her elbows on the counter, and looked at Darcy with a mixture of sympathy and condescension. "Sweetheart, I hate to break it to you, but whoever worked that budget up probably failed fifth-grade math."

"What do you mean?"

"The cost of driving from here to Florida — in one car — would maybe be a hundred bucks tops. Split that between however many are in the car and you're maybe at twenty dollars a person." She paused. "Then if seven of you are going in on a house and are splitting the cost of the house — a three-bedroom one would be completely sufficient — you're looking at about three hundred per person."

Darcy sputtered a little bit but couldn't seem to get a word out.

"Then food and whatnot for one person, you're looking at maybe — at most — about two hundred. And that's only if you are eating out every day. Renting a house means you can stock the fridge to cut costs." She straightened. "Sorry, baby girl, but honestly, had you said six hundred dollars, you might have had a chance."

"No," Darcy said. "They all said no because of the guys. If it were all girls, I'm sure Dad would have said yes."

"Dad would have said yes to what?" Ian asked as he strolled into his newly designed kitchen.

Anna didn't have a problem dealing with family matters head-on, and this family was like her own, so she knew it wouldn't be a big deal to throw herself into the middle of this mess. "What was your biggest issue with the spring break thing, Ian? The cost or the boys?"

Ian looked at Anna for a minute and then glanced at his daughter. "Honestly? The cost. I'm not an idiot, Anna. She goes to school and lives on campus and is even in a coed dorm. The cost of that trip was just excessive." He looked at Darcy again. "Sorry, sweet pea." Then he kissed her on the head, grabbed a beer from the refrigerator, and walked back out to the living room.

"Holy cow." Darcy sighed and then stared at Anna. "How did you do that? How did you know?"

Anna walked over and put her arm around Darcy. "Believe it or not, kiddo, you're not the first college girl to try and con her way into a sweet spring break. Mine was Hawaii. I thought my dad was going to have a heart attack. Had I aimed small — like Florida — he might have gone for it. But I got greedy." She ruffled Darcy's hair. "Lesson learned."

"Well, shit," Darcy said and pushed the plate of tomatoes away.

"Language," Aidan said as he strolled into the room.

"Oh, for crying out loud," Darcy muttered. "Unclench."

He went to Zoe and kissed her soundly on the lips. "And here I thought a big family get-together wasn't going to be any fun. Who knew my baby sister would be so entertaining?" He turned and grinned at Darcy and almost choked when she flipped him the bird and stormed from the room.

"Aidan," Zoe admonished. "That wasn't very nice. You know she's already upset."

"And it's all her own doing. She still hasn't outgrown the need to make a scene when there's an audience. She chose today to ask about that ridiculous trip because she figured Dad would be too distracted to question it. We're all here for a nice day and to see the house as a finished product, and she had to ruin it."

"I wouldn't say she ruined it," Anna chimed in.

Aidan gave her a bland look. "Anna, come on. As much as Darcy has grown up, she's still very immature." He shrugged. "Hell, we all were at her age, and it just sucks for her that there are so many of us who've been there before her." He reached over and grabbed a beer. "We should be thankful Quinn wasn't here to witness the whole thing. There would have been a lot more screaming and crying."

"Yikes," Anna said and walked over to grab herself a bottle of water.

"Speaking of which — when is he supposed to get here? I figured he'd be here by now."

Anna looked at her watch. "Yeah, I thought so too, but he probably lost track of time. He had to go into the shop this morning to do some work on a car he's restoring."

"Not Jake Tanner's, I hope," Aidan said and then shook his head. "If it were me, I would have put those cars out in the middle of the road with the keys in them after what happened." Zoe elbowed him in the ribs. "Sorry. Didn't mean to bring that up."

"It's okay, Aidan. Really. I told Quinn he should do the work on the cars."

"What?" Aidan and Zoe cried at the same time.

Anna nodded.

"Sweetie, are you crazy?" Zoe asked. "Why would you want him to work for that jackass? After what he did, I'd think you wouldn't want Quinn to have anything to do with him!"

"I thought about it, but it's a really big opportunity for his business. It isn't like Jake's going to be working beside him." She shrugged again. "It's really not a big deal. Quinn's business is more important."

"Um . . . no," Aidan said. "*You're* more important." He stopped and cursed under his breath. "So is that why he's not here? Because he's working on one of Jake's cars?"

At this point, Anna was afraid to confirm or deny it.

Riley walked into the kitchen with the trays from her car. "I'm not going to lie to you," he said with a grin, "I ate two of them before I closed the car door."

Anna chuckled. "You didn't need to confess. The chocolate crumbs on your shirt gave you away. You're forgiven."

"Excellent." He put the trays down and walked over to hug her and then kept his arm around her shoulders. "My brother's a lucky man." Then he looked around a bit. "Come to think of it, it looks like most of my brothers are lucky men."

"And don't you forget it," Zoe said.

Riley looked from person to person and noticed the conversation had stopped. "Okay, what's going on? Why'd everyone clam up when I came into the room?" He paused. "It's the new song I sent, isn't it? You guys hate the new music." He stepped away from Anna and cursed. "Just come out and say it. I can take it."

Anna immediately reached out and touched his arm. "No one hates your music, Riley. Relax."

"Then why is everyone so damn quiet?"

"It's . . . it's nothing," Anna said.

"I'll tell you what it is," Aidan began.

271

"Quinn kept those classic cars that belong to Jake Tanner. He's still going to do the work on them!"

Riley's eyes went wide. "Wait . . . Jake Tanner? The guy who . . ." He looked at Anna and then back to his brother. "Are you kidding me?"

"It's really not a big deal," Anna murmured, but no one seemed to be listening.

"I have no idea what's wrong with him," Aidan said, shaking his head with disgust.

"Why would he do that?" Riley asked, brows furrowed.

Before anyone could reply, Anna stepped in between the two brothers and held up her hands to stop them. "Look, I told Quinn he should keep the cars and work on them. The publicity he's going to get once the cars are done will be a real boost to his business. So if I'm okay with it, then you all should be too. I don't want anyone giving him any grief when he gets here." Her voice was firm, as was her expression.

Wordlessly, Riley held up his hands in defeat. Reaching over, he grabbed one more brownie, and with the grin he was famous for, he left the kitchen.

Anna turned to Aidan and Zoe. "Promise me," she said. "Promise me you're not going to say anything to him." She paused.

"Today is about your dad and the house. I don't know if any of you noticed, but he didn't invite Martha, so that should tell you how important it is that the family is here. I'm sure it would be helpful if everyone got along. Darcy already got everyone riled up. Let's not add to it, okay?"

Zoe nodded, and when Aidan didn't say or do anything, she elbowed him in the ribs. "Fine," he finally said. "But I'm still annoyed —"

"I get it," Anna interrupted. "Just let it go for today. Please. For me."

He nodded and kissed his wife on the cheek, and then kissed Anna on the cheek as well before walking from the kitchen to join the rest of his family in the living room.

"You won't be able to keep them quiet forever, you know," Zoe said when they were alone.

"I know. But for today I just want everyone to get along."

Zoe laughed. "You know that's not very realistic. Whenever you get more than two Shaughnessys in the room, they're bound to disagree about something. It's just the way it is."

"Oh, you don't have to tell me. I know it's the norm, but maybe they'll find something else to argue about."

Zoe sighed. "I wouldn't hold my breath if I were you."

"Hey, a girl can dream."

He could barely hear himself think, the room was so noisy. It was full of conversation and laughter and, yes, arguments. With ten people around the table, dinner was boisterous to say the least.

There was steak and chicken Ian had grilled on the barbecue, salads, corn on the cob, dinner rolls, and baked potatoes. There was enough food for a small army — which they kind of were. Plates and bowls were passed around almost continuously.

Aubrey updated everyone on her health and how she was feeling with her pregnancy. Hugh grinned as he watched his wife, making sure she had everything she could possibly want to eat. Darcy talked about school, Riley talked about the possibility of a tour to promote his new album — if he ever finished it — and Owen shared how he had been offered the opportunity to teach at UC Berkeley at the Lawrence Hall of Science.

The only problem with all of this was everyone was talking at once.

Quinn looked around the table and caught a couple of words of each conversation. He thought about talking about how business was going, but he kind of felt like flying under the radar right then. Not about work, but he had a feeling he and Anna were under the microscope. It was their first time with everyone, and he suddenly felt uncomfortable in his own skin.

"So, Anna," Ian said loudly to be heard over all his kids, "I hear you and Hugh are working on the contracts for the coastal property here. It's very exciting!"

She nodded. "Things are moving along and my bosses are very pleased."

"I'm sure. I know we're all looking forward to having him work close to home for a while. So thank you for helping to make it possible."

"Hey," Hugh protested with a laugh, "I would have come around eventually."

Ian laughed and shook his head. "Not soon enough."

"Yeah, we'll see how you feel when I'm around all the time," Hugh challenged.

"I still think I'll be okay with it," Ian replied.

"Well, I can't take all the credit," Anna said. "I wasn't really the one to approach him with the potential property. Quinn presented it to him first."

"Dude," Riley said with a grin, shaking his head. "Not cool. You totally stole Anna's thunder."

Quinn looked around and found the conversation had calmed down and everyone was looking his way. "What?"

"That was totally Anna's place to present the property deal to Hugh. Why'd you interfere?" Riley asked. His tone was light, but it still rubbed Quinn the wrong way. Then he added, "Seriously, Anna, what do you see in this guy?"

Everyone laughed. "I always pictured you with a guy in a suit," Hugh said with a playful grin. "You know, a businessman."

"I agree," Aidan chimed in. "You can do way better than our resident grease monkey here." He looked over at Quinn and saw the tension there and then winked at Anna. "I bet a businessman wouldn't horn in on your job."

"I did not horn in!" Quinn snapped, slamming a hand down on the table. "I was simply trying to move things along to help her!"

"Call it what you want, Quinn," Riley said. "But you still stole her thunder." He shook his head and made a tsk-ing sound before focusing on Anna again. "I wouldn't tolerate it if I were you."

"It really wasn't a big deal," Anna said quietly, looking down at her plate.

And it hit Quinn for the first time — had he really done that? Had he stolen her thunder? Had he interfered when he shouldn't have? He thought about it for a minute and shook his head. *Hell no!* This was the dynamic of his and Anna's relationship — they helped one another out. They always had. That's what friends did. And technically, when he had called Hugh, he and Anna had still been just friends.

Did she resent him for interfering?

Would she even tell him if she did?

No. Anna had a way of keeping certain things to herself — especially when it applied to things he did that upset her.

Which, apparently, was a lot over the years.

Knowing he wasn't capable of participating in any more conversation, he ducked his head and focused on his meal, thankful the conversation turned to Hugh and his plans for the new resort.

Out of the corner of his eye, he could see Anna was eating and she was even participating in the discussion, but Quinn couldn't bring himself to. Right then, his head was messed up.

What if everyone was right? What if he wasn't right for Anna? What if she did deserve to be with someone else? Instantly, an image of some corporate guy in a suit sprang to mind and it made him angry. The guy was faceless and yet Quinn could feel the rage building.

What was so wrong with him that made everyone so damn certain he was wrong for her? Granted, he hadn't been the most observant guy over the years, but he was working on it! Why wasn't he getting any credit for trying to be a better person?

He was so lost in thought that he didn't notice everyone standing up and starting to clear the table. In the Shaughnessy house, it was a group effort. No one person had dish duty; everyone did. For once, Quinn was glad to get lost in the shuffle. Conversation flowed around him, and when things were almost done, he ducked out and went to the backyard. The sun had gone down, and for a minute, all he could do was stand there and breathe, his head thrown back.

"I wish I had my telescope with me."

Quinn didn't need to turn his head to know Owen was coming up beside him.

"The sky on a clear night offers an ever-changing display of fascinating objects you can see, from stars and constellations to bright planets, the moon." He sighed wistfully. "If you want, I can point out some of the things you're seeing."

Shaking his head, Quinn straightened and looked at his brother. "Thanks, but . . . not tonight."

"They're all wrong, you know."

"About what?"

"You," Owen said simply. He wasn't looking at Quinn; his attention was still on the sky.

"Oh yeah? What makes you so sure about that?" Quinn asked, curious to get his brainiac brother's spin on the whole thing.

"For starters, there's more to you than just being — what did they call you? A grease monkey?" He looked at Quinn with confusion. "I'm guessing it's a play on words because you work on cars."

Quinn couldn't help but chuckle and nod.

"Anyway, I don't understand why they say it like it's a bad thing. Aidan builds houses, Hugh builds resorts, and Riley builds songs." He shrugged. "You build cars — and not just one kind of car, every kind. You need to have a working knowledge of how every kind of car works. Most people don't understand how an internal combustion engine operates. You do." Then he turned and looked at Quinn. "Seems to me that makes you smarter than they are."

Well, hell. "You think I'm smart?" Quinn asked quietly.

Owen nodded. "You're one of the smartest guys I know. You've mastered so many different things already — and you didn't go to school for any of them. I mean, I know you had to get certified to be a mechanic, but for you, that was just a technicality. You already knew how to do everything. You put your mind to something, and you make it happen. It's impressive."

Wow. His genius brother was seriously standing there telling him he was impressed. Damn. "Yeah, well . . . no one else sees that."

"Does Anna think that?"

"What?"

"That you're just a grease monkey?"

Quinn chuckled. "No," he said, smiling. "She's never thought that. It doesn't matter what I'm doing or what I'm trying, she makes me feel . . . hell . . . she makes me feel like I'm the best at it."

"It's because you usually are," Owen said simply.

"Dude, knock it off. I'm blushing."

Owen looked at him oddly. "I wouldn't really know. It's dark out here."

Leave it to Owen to take him literally. "Can I ask you something?"

"Sure."

"Do you think I'm wrong for Anna?"

"No."

"Care to elaborate?"

With a sigh, Owen faced him. "People like to argue how opposites attract. And in some ways, it's true. But it seems to me what you and Anna have is something most people only hope to attain."

"And what's that?"

"You genuinely like each other."

Quinn's eyes went a little wide. "That's it? No scientific facts or figures?"

Owen shrugged. "From the first time the two of you met, you clicked. You were instant friends and you've stayed that way. Why? Because you have a love and respect for one another. Granted, it didn't turn into a romantic love until recently, but I think it's always been there. It just needed time to be nurtured."

"I wish I could believe that. My track record is really working against me here — at least where everyone else is concerned."

"It shouldn't matter what everyone else thinks. What do you think? Do you think you're the right man for Anna? Do you believe you have staying power even if you don't wear a suit to work?"

Quinn didn't know what to say.

His confidence was slightly rattled after

dinner, and he wasn't so sure of anything right then.

CHAPTER 9

Something was becoming blazingly obvious to Anna — she and Quinn spent most of their time alone at her place.

After the dinner at Ian's, Quinn had been a little sullen and withdrawn, and she normally had to work at getting him to relax. They spent almost every night together, but she was beginning to realize they had gone out more when they were just friends than they had since they'd started dating.

Not that she was complaining — not really. The time they spent alone after work was her favorite part of the day. They'd share dinner, watch movies, and make love. The man was insatiable, and she was finding her inner goddess was too! But there was going to come a time when they both needed something more. Neither of them was antisocial, and next week they had their monthly softball game. They'd been on the local league together for years, and it was something they'd always enjoyed. She could only wonder how Quinn was going to handle it. Maybe she needed to nudge him out of their routine and see how it went.

It was after six on a Thursday night when he showed up. He looked exhausted and sexy as hell. Anna's original plan had been to grill a couple of steaks and watch the Yankees game, but after her realization earlier, she changed it.

Quinn kissed her thoroughly before walking over to the refrigerator and grabbing a beer. It was a very domestic scene — including the "Hi, honey! How was your day?" and it normally made Anna smile. Unfortunately, she didn't feel much like smiling. She felt like shaking things up.

"I don't feel like cooking tonight," she said casually, grabbing a bottle of water for herself out of the refrigerator. "I was thinking we'd go into town and grab something to eat, maybe some pizza or something."

Placing his beer down on the counter, Quinn looked at her. "You should have called me. I would have picked one up on the way home."

She shrugged. "Nah. I really want to get out and eat someplace. Come on. We'll keep it casual. Just go and get changed, and we'll go."

He looked completely uncomfortable. "Seriously, Anna? It's been a crappy day. The Camaro is giving me fits, and we have cars parked all over the property waiting to be worked on and not enough space or manpower to get to them all. I was really just looking forward to staying in tonight."

"We stay in every night," she reminded him. "We went out more before we started dating." Then she chuckled. "Although I don't really think we can call this dating since we haven't gone out on any dates, so I guess I should rephrase and say we used to go out more before we started sleeping together."

His anger was apparent. "What the hell's gotten into you?" he demanded. "So we haven't gone out much. I didn't think you minded."

She shrugged. "Normally, I don't. But tonight I'd like to go out. I didn't think it was a big deal. Obviously I was wrong."

He huffed and raked a hand through his hair, sending his hat flying. "Look, if you had mentioned it earlier, I would have been a little more mentally prepared for it, that's all."

"Since when do you need to be mentally

prepared to go for pizza? For crying out loud, Quinn, I'm not asking you to take me to the Four Seasons; it's just a quick dinner so I don't have to cook!"

He studied her hard for a minute and then seemed to relax. "You're right, you're right. I'm sorry. Like I said, it was a crappy day. Give me a few minutes to wash up and change." He walked back to her bedroom and she heard the bathroom door close.

For a minute, she almost felt bad. Almost felt the need to go and tell him to forget about it and she'd cook for them instead, but she had a feeling that's what he was hoping for. The old Anna would have done it, and she was done being that girl. Why, all of a sudden, she didn't know. But right then, the only thing she was certain of was that she was tired of being kept locked up and not seeing anyone.

Well, anyone other than the Shaughnessys.

Fifteen minutes later, they were in his truck heading into town. "So . . . pizza?" he asked.

"Sure. Unless there's someplace else you'd like to go."

When they drove past Main Street, Anna questioned it.

"There's a really good seafood place I've

286

been wanting to try," Quinn answered. "We can get pizza anytime. What do you say?"

She wouldn't have minded if he'd asked before they'd passed the pizza place, but whatever. "Sure. That sounds good."

Thirty minutes later, Anna was a little suspicious. "This is kind of far, don't you think?"

Quinn shrugged and parked the truck. "Yeah, but sometimes the good places are worth it. Come on. All the guys at the shop have been talking about this place and telling me how good it is."

She supposed it made sense. It was a small place — barely more than a shack — and she could only hope the inside was more appealing than the outside.

Quinn took her by the hand and pulled her in close, kissing her deeply. "Maybe after dinner we can go for a walk on the beach. There's supposed to be outside seating in the back that overlooks the sand."

And then she relaxed. She was being suspicious for nothing. Maybe he really did just want to take her someplace different and have a date that wouldn't include a dozen interruptions from everyone in town.

"I think it sounds absolutely perfect."

And it was. She was completely dazzled by this side of Quinn. They talked all through dinner, and she was pleasantly surprised at how amazing the food was. The place certainly didn't look like much, but it more than made up for it with its meals.

After dinner, they walked along the beach hand in hand. The sky was clear and the breeze coming off the water was refreshing. They'd kicked off their shoes, and to Anna, it could quite possibly have been the most perfect date.

"I'm glad we did this," he said after a few minutes.

"Me too."

"I know you may not believe this, but . . . I really just don't think of things like this. I'm not usually that kind of guy." He shrugged.

"I don't know about that. In the past you've told me —"

He cut her off. "I don't want to talk about my past. I was a completely selfish jackass, Anna. I never should have talked to you about my dates, and I certainly don't want to be reminded of them."

She looked at him and smiled softly. "I don't think you were a selfish jackass, Quinn. I just miss going out places with you. We used to go to the movies or bowling or . . . anyplace. I'm beginning to feel like you're embarrassed to be seen with me."

That stopped him in his tracks. "*What?!* Why would you even say such a thing? I would never . . . could never —"

"You have to admit it seems pretty suspicious," she interrupted with a nervous chuckle. "You never want to go anywhere anymore."

He reached up and cupped her face in his hands. "Did it ever occur to you that I don't want to share you with anyone else? That maybe now that I've realized how much you mean to me, I want to show you as much as I can? Or maybe because you're so damn sexy and my every freaking fantasy that I can't wait to get you alone, so I can touch you, kiss you, and love you from head to toe?"

His words made her weak. "Oh my . . ."

"Even standing here right now, all I can think about is getting you home, undressing you, and making love to you until neither of us can move." He leaned in and kissed her cheek. "All day long, I think about you." He kissed her forehead. "The drive home seems to take forever because all I can think about is being with you." Another kiss on the tip of her nose. "And it's not just the sex. I just want to be with you. You're my home. My heart. I love you."

And then she couldn't breathe. It was

everything she had ever dreamed of — only it was better because it was real. She sighed his name as she reached up and touched his face. Tears swam in her eyes. "I . . . I never thought . . . I just . . ."

"Shh . . . I know. I don't deserve you. I know that. But you're everything, Anna. Everything."

She shook her head. "I feel the same way about you. I always have. I love you too."

And then, finally, his lips claimed hers, consumed her. They stood locked together with the waves crashing on the shore and stars shining in the sky, and Anna lost all track of time. When Quinn raised his head, the look of pure need there almost brought her to her knees.

"Let's go home," he said huskily, taking her hand in his again as he began to lead her back to the truck.

She could only nod.

The entire drive home, Quinn kept her tucked close to his side, his hand playing with her hair and skimming up and down her neck. Anna had to fight the need to climb into his lap and beg him to pull over and have his way with her right then.

As if reading her mind, he turned and gave her a sexy grin. "Patience. I promise you we'll be home soon."

"Not soon enough," she said, snuggling closer.

By the time they pulled into the driveway, she was ready to explode. She needed to touch him, to have his hands on her, and it didn't matter if they made it to a bed or not. A slow smile crept across her face.

Reaching over, she ran a hand up his denim-clad thigh. She loved the way his eyes closed as he sighed. "So . . . I've always had this . . . fantasy," she said softly, her hand roaming up and down his leg and up his stomach and chest.

"Really?" he said in a low voice.

"Mm-hmm," she purred. "I always thought you looked very sexy driving this truck. I remember you had another one in high school, and I used to imagine what it would be like if it were me you were fooling around with in it."

Quinn opened his eyes and scanned her face. "You wanted to fool around in my truck?" He looked toward the house and then back at Anna. "There's a bed just a few feet away."

"Yeah, but . . ." she began, "we can finish up in there. I think it would be really hot if we got things started right here." Shifting, she got up on her knees and started kissing his neck. "You don't even have to do much.

This is more about me . . . and what I always wanted to do."

"Anna," he sighed. "Baby, you're killing me."

"I'm just getting started." She gently bit him and then ran her tongue over the same spot. Quinn hissed in a breath, and in the blink of an eye, she was sprawled out across the seat with him stretched out on top of her.

"Now you're just teasing," he growled before kissing her roughly, his tongue dueling with hers until she began to whimper beneath him. He raised his head. "Tell me what you want, Anna — anything, and it's yours."

"I want you to make love to me right here, right now." Her eyes never left his as she issued her sexy challenge. She waited for him to argue. She waited for him to try and change her mind.

Then she squealed with delight as he quickly began to work on the button of her jeans.

"Your wish is my command," he said before his lips claimed hers again and made one of her long-time fantasies come true.

A week later, her suspicions were not only back, but they were pretty much like a giant neon sign she couldn't turn off. Since their dinner and walk on the beach — and subsequent hot sex in his truck — they'd gone out four more times, each place farther from home than the last. She was seriously beginning to get a complex.

Anna tried to remember all the things Quinn had said to her about why he enjoyed being alone with her, and sometimes it was enough. But she couldn't help but be a little annoyed by some of it. She was all for being alone with him and not wanting to share him with anyone — particularly the little fan club of women who seemed to flock to him whenever they used to go anyplace local — but she was still willing to try. It would mean so much to her to see him willingly ignore the women and claim her as his in front of people they knew.

After each date, they'd come back to her house, and just when she was ready to comment on where they'd been and how far away it was, he'd seduce her to the point where she barely knew her own name.

It was a gift he had.

But one she was starting to really resent.

"I thought you had a house to show tonight?" Quinn said, coming out of the bedroom dressed to play softball.

Anna had done the same while he was in

the shower. She shook her head. "Nope."

"Are you sure?" he asked, grabbing a couple of bottles of water from the pantry. "I thought you said something about showing the two-bedroom place over on Billings."

"Quinn, I think I would know if I had an appointment. If you don't believe me, look at my calendar." She took her phone out and slid it over to him and then walked over and found her day planner and did the same. "No showings."

"Oh."

"Besides, I wouldn't miss a game. I've never missed a game." She chuckled. "And I think the team would miss me if I wasn't there. I'm the queen of first base. You guys would lose without me." She said it with a smile but noticed he didn't seem amused. Sighing, she leaned against the countertop. "Okay, spill it. What's wrong?"

"What? Nothing. Nothing's wrong. Why would you even say that?"

"Um . . . maybe because you're acting like a complete tool. You're making it seem like you don't want me at the game tonight and I want to know why."

"You're imagining things, Anna. That's not it at all. I'm just . . . I guess my head's just not in the game, that's all. These restorations are harder than I thought. Maybe I shouldn't play."

Yeah, her suspicions were almost blinding her now. "Don't be ridiculous. You've never missed a game no matter what was going on in your life." She reached for her duffel bag and slung it over her shoulder. "Come on. Let's get going or we'll be late."

"I left my mitt at home. Why don't you go ahead and I'll meet you there?" he suggested.

Anna wanted to argue but found she couldn't. All she could do was sigh. "Just make sure you're there in time for the first pitch," she said wearily and walked out the door. Quinn followed silently behind her.

He gave her a distracted kiss on the cheek.

And he didn't respond to her statement.

Anna sat in her car and watched him drive away, wondering what in the world she was going to do. There was a time when they'd told each other everything — even if it wasn't comfortable. But for some reason, Quinn was keeping this to himself. It was obvious he was uncomfortable with the game tonight, and she couldn't understand why. Did he think she was going to demand sex in front of everyone?

These were their friends! There wasn't anything for them to worry about. No one was going to make any snarky remarks like his brothers had, and no one was going to say anything stupid.

At least . . . she hoped they wouldn't.

The mitt was in his truck and Quinn had no place to go. He just needed to get his head on straight. Normally the thought of going out on the field and playing the game was exciting, something he looked forward to.

And right now, he didn't.

This was going to be one of those moments that was a game changer — no pun intended. Taking Anna to his father's house for dinner and getting ribbed by his brothers was one thing. It was what they all did and it was normally done in good fun. But to face a bunch of their friends tonight and have everyone witness the change in his relationship with Anna scared the hell out of him. Why? Because he had a feeling he'd get a lot of the same comments and it wouldn't all be said in fun.

It would be the truth.

He wasn't good enough for Anna and she deserved better.

Slamming his hand on the steering wheel, he cursed. He was the most confident member of his entire family. Hell, he was probably one of the most confident people he even knew. Why was it then that this situation had him feeling so insecure?

Because Anna does deserve better.

Better than what? He was truly committed to her — and not just as her boyfriend, but as her best friend. Her happiness meant everything to him, and now that he knew all the ways he'd hurt her in the past, he was doing his damnedest to make up for it. Wasn't everyone entitled to a second chance?

Yeah, but you're pushing, like, your thirtieth chance where she's concerned.

Okay, fine. This was still all kind of new to him. He didn't do long-term relationships. He'd never seen the appeal of it, but now . . . now he did. Being with Anna had him thinking of his life differently. He used to enjoy his freedom, his independence. Now the thought of being alone wasn't all that appealing. He liked going to sleep beside her and waking up with her in his arms.

He loved her.

And even saying the words to her hadn't scared him. He'd never said them to anyone before — shouldn't that count for something? And she'd said it back! So they were solid on that front, but . . . why couldn't they just be . . . them? Just the two of them?

Why did everyone else get to have an opinion and butt in?

He thought of how sad she looked when he'd suggested they take separate cars to the game. Yeah, he was pretty much scum. *You can't be in love one minute and push her away the next,* he chided himself. A little too late for that now.

The field came into view, and he pulled into the parking lot. There weren't any open spots near Anna's car, and Quinn had no choice but to park on the other side of the lot. He climbed out and slowly made his way toward the dugout. Everyone was there already and talking strategy.

"Nice of you to join us," Billy Harper called out. He was the team captain and could be a real pain in the ass, but the man had a pitching arm that was a thing of beauty.

Looking around, he saw Anna standing in the back of the group with a couple of people — mostly guys — and frowned. There were three other women on the team. Why did she have to be surrounded by men? Then he thought about it and realized she normally did hang out more with the guys and knew he was going to have to deal with it, no matter how much it peeved him.

When Billy finished his lengthy spiel about

teamwork and kicking ass, the group broke apart and everyone finished getting their gear ready. Quinn walked over to Anna and felt a pang of regret when she merely gave him a cursory glance and went about her business.

"Hey," he said softly.

"Did you get your mitt?" she asked, not even bothering to look at him.

"Uh . . . yeah. Look, I'm sorry. I was a jerk and —"

"Anna!" someone yelled. "Come and toss a few with me!" Quinn looked over and saw Mark Brady standing on the first base line grinning. Quinn normally liked the guy, but right then, Mark's grin was pissing him off.

"In a minute!" Quinn yelled back and then saw the look of irritation on Anna's face. "What? What did I do?"

"I can answer for myself," she said tartly as she straightened and faced him. "Say what you have to say because I have things to do."

He sighed with frustration. There was no way he wanted to create a scene here. "I'm sorry, all right?" he snapped. "Sometimes this shit freaks me out. I'm not perfect, Anna, and you of all people should know that. So . . . are we good?"

She eyed him warily. And it seemed like

there was a war going on inside of her. When her shoulders relaxed, his did too.

"Neither of us is perfect, Quinn," she said quietly, "but at least we used to talk to each other when there was a problem. You know damn well I didn't have a showing tonight, and I can guarantee you your mitt was in your truck." She let out a growl of frustration. "Not so long ago, you accused me of shoveling bullshit, and that's what I'm saying right now to you. You're shoveling it. So when you can be honest with me and tell me the truth about what's freaking you out, I'll listen. Until then, just . . . leave me alone."

And then she walked out of the dugout, and Quinn had a feeling that if he didn't get his shit together, she'd walk out of his life just as easily.

It was the bottom of the ninth, and their team needed one more run to win. Anna was on third base and knew she could do it — she'd be the one to get the win. Suzi Hall was up at bat, and the woman was one of their best hitters.

With her heart threatening to pound out of her chest, Anna began to slowly inch off the base as the first pitch was thrown.

Strike one!

Inching back, her toe on the base, she waited for the second pitch.

Strike two!

Dammit. She was so close to making this happen. Anna was never the one in this position, and it felt pretty freaking fantastic. If Suzi could just hit the ball out of the park, Anna could fly across home plate, and their team could officially claim the victory.

Another pitch and . . .

A hit!

At the crack of the bat, Anna took off and didn't even bother to look and see where the ball went. All she knew was she had to run and run fast. People were cheering her on and as her foot touched home plate, she was immediately whisked up in Billy's arms.

"You did it! You did it!" Everyone crowded around her as the rest of the team rounded the plates. When Suzi ran over home plate, she was hailed for her spectacular hit. Everyone was cheering and high-fiving one another.

Anna made her way through the crowd, and when she spotted Quinn, her smile grew. They lived for games like this. The victory, the celebrating. She was about to launch herself into his arms when he stopped her, his hands on her shoulders.

Then he high-fived her.

"Good job!" he said and then blended into the crowd, leaving her standing there dumbfounded.

Good job? Good freaking job? That was it? It wasn't as if Anna was expecting a make-out session, but seriously, a high five? With a snort of disgust, she allowed herself to get caught back up in the excitement of the win before she ended up punching Quinn in the face. *Jerk.*

The usual routine after a win consisted of everyone going to the pub to celebrate, and while normally that was extremely appealing, Anna couldn't help but feel a sudden lack of enthusiasm. Everyone started walking toward their cars, and she spotted Quinn standing near the dugout alone. She was tempted to just ignore him and keep walking, but that wasn't their thing — sex or no sex. Anna wasn't one to shy away from a fight with him.

"You going to the pub?" Quinn asked when she approached.

She noted that almost everyone was out of earshot and that made her frown. "I don't think so. I'm probably just going to head home."

"Why? You had the winning run. I would have thought you'd want to go and celebrate."

She shrugged. "Yeah, it wasn't as exciting as I thought it would be." They stood there in awkward silence for a few moments before she couldn't take it anymore. "What about you? Are you going?"

"I was thinking about it . . ."

She knew what he was doing and couldn't decide if it was sweet or annoying. "You don't need my permission to go to the damn pub, Quinn. If you want to go, then go. We don't have to go everywhere together."

"That wasn't what I was saying —"

"No," she interrupted. "You were probably making sure we both weren't going to be there at the same time. We don't want our friends to actually know we're involved, right?"

"Anna, it's not —"

"Hey!" Mark Brady came walking over with a big grin on his face. "Great game, Anna." He looked between the two of them. "Am I interrupting a lovers' spat or something?" Then he broke out laughing. "Sorry, couldn't help that one."

"What the hell is that supposed to mean?" Quinn snapped.

"The two of you looked like you were fighting, and I was being sarcastic about the lovers thing." He laughed again. "As if the two of you would ever hook up."

Anna felt her skin heat with embarrassment.

"And why the hell not?" Quinn demanded.

"Look, no offense, Anna," he began, and then focused on Quinn, "but you're more of the blond-bimbo type, and Anna's . . . well . . . not." He shrugged. "You guys coming?"

"Not me," Anna mumbled, and reached for her duffel bag and slung it over her shoulder.

"Anna," Mark said, "I didn't mean it as an insult to you. Quite the opposite, really. You're better than those girls. I know you wouldn't be crazy enough to get involved with our resident playboy here. You're smarter than that." He pulled her into a bear hug and kissed her on the head. "I hope you change your mind and come to the pub. Drinks are on me!" Then he jogged away.

Well, if the silence was awkward before, it was downright painful now.

Anna couldn't help but think of the way Quinn's brothers had teased him at the family dinner, and now with the things Mark said . . . she suddenly understood some of his reluctance to go out places with her.

"Quinn —"

He held up his hands. "You know what? You should go to the pub with everyone. I think I'll be the one to skip it." He collected his gear and walked away.

Her first impulse was to go after him, but she didn't have the first clue as to what to say. She knew the real Quinn — and that was really all that mattered. Unfortunately, she also knew what it was like to live with people's preconceived impressions and opinions. Wasn't that one of the reasons she had started to make changes in her own life, so other people would stop seeing her as nothing more than the tomboy they all grew up with?

They were going to have to talk about this. And soon.

But for tonight, Anna knew it was probably for the best for them each to retreat to their own corners and be alone.

Quinn sat in the darkness. He'd been home for over an hour and didn't see any point in turning on any of the lights. Hell, it had been a while since he'd spent more than a few minutes there. Almost every night for weeks, he'd been staying at Anna's. He had loved coming home to this space — it was all his — but tonight, all he felt was loneliness.

For years, he'd been so busy just living life on his terms that he hadn't given much thought to how it would look to others. Worse, he hadn't really considered how his actions affected others.

Particularly Anna.

Well, it was becoming pretty damn clear now.

People thought he was a complete asshole.

Great.

It was one thing for his family to think it — they still had to love him — but he was slowly beginning to find out it was a more widespread opinion. He could have handled it if it just came from someone like Bobby — he'd always hated Quinn and he was Anna's brother; of course he was going to have issues. But Mark? That one stung a little. Mark liked everyone. Hell, Quinn had never even heard the guy say a bad thing about anyone.

Until tonight.

There was a reason he'd been avoiding going out on dates with Anna to any local place, but it had been based on his own insecurities and what he thought *might* happen. It was completely different when it became a reality.

He loved Anna. Loved her more than he'd thought possible. But was he being selfish?

Was he banking on their years of friendship and the way she'd always felt about him to keep her in a relationship that wasn't good for her?

Not that she'd even complain — he knew that about her. She might have been pissed at him at that moment, but Quinn knew it wouldn't take much for her to get over it. Hell, he could have probably gone over to her house right then and sweet-talked her into forgiving him for acting so stupidly.

And that's when he knew he had a real problem.

There comes a time when you're forced to take a look at your life and you have to decide if you like what you see.

And Quinn didn't.

He now realized how, even though he and Anna were friends, he had manipulated her all those years. He knew exactly how to act and exactly what to say to get her to do whatever he wanted. It was usually stupid stuff, like cook for him or, back in school, do his homework for him, and it just made him feel sick inside.

Scrubbing a hand wearily over his face, an image of his mother came to mind. How many times had he sweet-talked her to try and get himself out of trouble? It had never worked, and she'd always called him out on it, but that had never stopped him from trying.

"But Aidan and Hugh are getting to stay up late! Why can't I?"

Lillian smiled down at him. "Because they're older than you and this is their reward for doing well in school today."

Eight-year-old Quinn looked up at her, and even though he was mad, he gave her his sweetest smile. "I did good in school today too! I helped Mrs. McGrath wipe down all the chalkboards, and then I got to bring the TV and VCR back to the media center all by myself."

"You did? Well, good for you, Quinn!" She ruffled his hair and then cupped his cheek. "And I am very proud of you for it."

"So I can stay up and watch movies too?"

She shook her head. "No can do, blue eyes. Not tonight."

He frowned and then inspiration hit. "If I do good in school next week, can I get a special night?"

Lillian considered it. "That depends."

"I'll do all my homework and make my bed and help with the twins and . . . and . . . I'll help Mrs. McGrath again, and then can I stay up late while Hugh and Aidan go to bed?"

Chuckling, she pulled him in close for a hug. "We'll see. Why don't you finish getting ready for bed and I'll let you have an extra fifteen minutes so you can read your new comic book. How about that?"

It wasn't a movie, but it was something. "Thanks, Mom," he said. "And when it's my special night, I'll even let you pick the movie."

"You will?" she said with exaggerated enthusiasm. "So if I want to watch . . . say . . . *Mary Poppins,* we can?"

Quinn wanted to make a gagging sound but decided against it. "If that's what you want, then sure." He knew he'd get her to change her mind by next week. And he could probably convince her to bake some cookies too. "You're the best and prettiest mom in the whole wide world. I love you."

Bending down, Lillian kissed the top of his head. "I love you too, blue eyes. Now go and see how the Amazing Spider-Man gets out of trouble this week and tell me all about it tomorrow, okay?"

And he had. And she had listened.

And she had known he was trying to con her into getting his own way.

And she had loved him anyway.

His chest felt tight, and for a minute he felt as if he couldn't breathe. So basically he'd been manipulating people his entire life. Great. Yeah, that felt real good. A loud sigh escaped as he rubbed the place over his heart. Two of the most important women in his life, and he'd spent most of his time with them essentially conning them into doing what he wanted.

"I'm surprised there hasn't been an angry mob after me sooner," he muttered.

There was no way he could change the past, no matter how much he wanted to. He could apologize to Anna from now until the end of time. But unless he started making some changes now and started showing her — and everyone — how he wasn't selfish and he was a different person, all of his apologies would mean nothing.

"No pressure," he said into the darkness.

Now he just had to figure out how he was going to accomplish it.

"He high-fived you?"

Anna nodded. "He high-fived me."

"Wow . . . just . . . wow."

"Yeah, that was pretty much my reaction too."

Zoe sat back in her seat and frowned. "I don't even know what to say to that. Even when Aidan was being a complete jerk when we started dating, he never would have —"

"High-fived you when you were looking to hug him?"

Raising her glass of iced tea, she saluted

Anna. "I give you props for not picking up a bat and slugging him."

"It was tempting, but there were too many witnesses."

Zoe chuckled. "So . . . now what? What happened when you guys got home?"

"Nothing. I came back here alone, and Quinn?" She shrugged. "I have no idea where he went. Probably to the pub with everyone."

"You didn't go?"

"Between the high five and Mark's comment . . . I just needed to get away."

"Okay, but you've talked to Quinn since then, right? I mean, it was four days ago."

Anna shook her head. "He texted me the next day and said he needed to put in some serious time on the restoration job."

"I still can't believe he's doing it," Zoe said with disgust. "After everything Jake did —"

"I don't want to talk about it," Anna interrupted. "I told everyone I didn't mind and I don't. Sort of." She cursed. "Not really."

"Anna, come on! How can you sit here and tell me you honestly don't care? That guy is a creep! And what he tried to do to you was criminal! How can you sit here and tell me you want to encourage Quinn to do this job? There will be other restorations!

Does he really want the recognition so badly he's willing to do a job that is nothing but a constant reminder of what Jake Tanner did?"

Anna hadn't really thought of it that way. With a sigh, she rested her head on the back of the sofa. "He's only doing it because I told him to. I know how important getting this restoration part of the business is to Quinn. This job was not only a big deal because of the kind of cars they are, but also because Jake had already lined up magazine interviews and deals for the big reveal. How could I take that away from him?"

"How could he not offer to?" Zoe snapped. "Honestly, out of all the Shaughnessys, Quinn really is the most clueless. And that's saying something!"

"He *did,* but I talked him out of it. So I'm partially to blame. I'll be all right," Anna said, but she didn't honestly believe it, and the look Zoe gave her said she wasn't buying it either.

"So what are you going to do?"

"I don't really know. We had a couple of weeks when we were inseparable, and that's never happened before. I know he has a lot of work that needs his attention at the new shop, and I guess when he has the time, he'll let me know."

Zoe stood, clearly agitated. "You're too good to him, too forgiving."

"What am I supposed to do?" She paused. "And besides, I told him to leave me alone."

"Oh, please. You were upset. Now, you're supposed to drive over to the shop and demand he talk to you, for starters! Then, you get in his face and tell him to man up and stop hiding when things get tough! And lastly, tell him if he ever high-fives you again instead of accepting the hug you're offering, I'll come over there and hit him over the head with one of those giant wrenches!"

Anna chuckled. "Man . . . does Aidan ever win an argument with you?"

A slow smile crept across her face. "Not if he knows what's good for him."

CHAPTER 10

By the time Zoe left, Anna felt pretty riled up. Not that she hadn't been for several days, but there was something about a good pep talk that really seemed to help. She'd been sitting at home, wavering between self-pity and being pissed off, and at that moment, all traces of pity were gone and her anger was fresh and ready to be unleashed.

"High-five me, will you?" she muttered as she grabbed her sneakers and slipped them on. "I didn't think I was an idiot before, but if you're going to go out of your way to make me look like one now, then be ready for my wrath!" In her mind, Quinn was right there and practically quivering from her words. Anna knew the reality was going to be very different, but right then, she pretty much had a whole "I am woman, hear me roar" thing going on.

Storming across the living room, she snatched up her purse on the way to the front door. She yanked it open and froze.

Quinn.

"Hey," he said, almost sounding shy and uncertain of whether or not he was welcome there.

"Hey, yourself," she replied, and a little of the fight went out of her. He was dressed in clean clothes and he'd shaved and there wasn't a cap on his head. That told her he'd put in a bit of an effort before coming over. "I was just coming to see you. I figured you'd still be at the shop."

"I practically slept there all weekend."

"Oh." They stood there in the doorway for several long moments until Anna finally took a step back. "So . . . um . . . do you want to come in?"

He nodded. "Thanks." As Anna shut the door, Quinn walked into the living room and sat down on the couch, waiting for her.

Honestly, Anna was a little disappointed he was so mellow. Looking at him sitting so meekly on her couch took the last of the fight out of her. With a disappointed sigh, she sat down. "How've you been?"

He shrugged. "Busy. I put an ad out for more mechanics. I can't believe how crazy things have been at the shop. It feels like everyone in town needs their cars looked at."

"That's a good thing, right?" She hated small talk. And worse, she hated forced small talk. With a steadying breath, she looked at him. "You really pissed me off Thursday night. I can't believe you freaking pushed me away when I was trying to hug you!"

She waited for his flash of temper and for him to argue with her — which he always did in an attempt to make it seem like he hadn't done anything wrong. She waited for it. She welcomed it.

But it never came.

"I know," he said quietly. "And I'm sorry."

Well, damn. Her shoulders sagged. "If you're this uncomfortable with this relationship, Quinn, then maybe we need to . . ." — she swallowed hard — "just let it go. I hate feeling like you're ashamed to be seen with me. I deserve better than that."

His blue eyes sparked with anger when he looked at her. "You think I'm ashamed to be seen with you? What the hell, Anna?" He stood up. "Has it ever occurred to you that maybe I'm ashamed of myself? That maybe it's less than flattering to have everyone look at me like I'm some sort of loser who isn't good enough for you?"

"That's bullshit and you know it," she snapped. "For as long as I've known you,

you've never given a damn about what other people say — and you've preached it to me plenty too! And now you're going to stand here and tell me the reason you've been such a jerk is because of other people?" She snorted with disgust. "When did we start lying to each other?"

"I'm not lying!" he yelled. "Jeez, first I had your brother on my back, telling me I'm not good enough, then my whole family pretty much tells you how you can do better than me, and then at the game —"

She held up a hand to stop him. "Yeah, yeah, yeah. None of that stuff has ever bothered you before! And do you think it's easy for me? You don't think I'm afraid that when we go out people are going to look at us — and look at me! — and think 'What the hell's Quinn Shaughnessy doing with her?' I mean, look at me! I'm not your usual *Playboy* playmate wannabe like you usually date!"

"There is not a damn thing wrong with you, and I dare anyone to try and say there is!" He walked over to her and grabbed her by the shoulders and gave her a small shake. "Don't ever think that! You're ten times more beautiful than any of those women!"

Just the feel of his hands on her, the fierceness in his eyes, was enough to bring that sizzle of attraction to the surface. All she wanted to do was wrap her arms around him and jump up and wrap her legs around his waist while he kissed her.

Focus!

"Oh, please," she said with disbelief and pulled out of his grasp. "It wasn't until I was practically naked that you even noticed I was a woman! It's no different with every guy in this town. They look at me and they see Anna Hannigan, the tomboy, the chick who serves burgers and beers at the pub! That's why I had to get out of there! I'm tired of people looking at me like I don't measure up as a woman! Do you know how much it used to kill me to see you with those other girls and know that you — and everyone else — would never look at me that way?"

"Jesus, Anna . . ."

Tears stung her eyes and she cursed them. "I was finally starting to have a little confidence in myself and you shot it all to hell, Quinn!"

And then he pulled her into his arms and held her tight while she quietly sobbed. "I'm sorry, baby. I'm so, so sorry," he murmured as he kissed her temple and simply held her.

Anna's hands clutched the front of his shirt as she pulled herself together. When she finally lifted her head and looked at him, the look of utter devastation on his face made her knees almost buckle. With one hand, she reached up and cupped his cheek, simply needing to touch him.

"They're all right, you know," he said solemnly. "You deserve better."

She shook her head.

"It's true," he said. "We can go around in circles about this, but the bottom line is it's my fault you seem to have low self-esteem, and it's my fault you're standing here crying right now. I can't bear it, Anna. I never want to be the reason you cry."

"Walking away from me isn't the way to accomplish that," she said quietly. "That's something I couldn't bear."

He gave her a sad smile. "So what do we do? Where do we go from here?"

It may not have solved any of their problems, but Anna didn't care. She knew what she wanted — what she needed — right then. And that was Quinn.

Straightening, she looked him in the eye. "We go to my bedroom," she said, her hand caressing his face. "And you make love to me."

"Anna," he said, and it sounded like a mixture of agony and ecstasy.

"I've missed you so much, Quinn. And I

need you. I really need you."

He cupped her face. "Baby, I need you too. More than you'll ever know. But . . . we haven't resolved anything here."

"There is no quick fix," she said. "And I don't want to fight with you. I want us to go inside and close the door and turn out the lights and just . . . forget about the rest of the world for a little while. Can we do that? Please?"

He looked ready to argue but didn't. Instead, he leaned forward and gently kissed her lips. "We can do whatever you want, Anna. Always."

Her heart felt ready to burst with love for him. There may have been times when she didn't like him, but in her heart, she was always going to love him.

She just wasn't sure if that proved she was weak or if it proved she was strong.

If Quinn had to guess, he'd have said they were fine for a couple of weeks. They went back to their usual routine of him spending the night at Anna's almost every night, but they did start going out more.

At first, it was with people he felt a little more secure with — like Aidan and Zoe — but eventually they did go back to hanging out with their friends. And, as Quinn had figured, he took a lot of ribbing about the turn in the relationship. He had laughed along with everyone, but it was slowly eating him up inside.

It was a boring Tuesday at the shop, and he couldn't focus on anything. Deciding to just call it a day, he hopped in his truck and began to drive around aimlessly. After about an hour, he ended up at the jobsite Aidan was currently working at. He drove through the streets of the new subdivision until he spotted his brother's truck.

He parked and climbed out, and was relieved when Aidan spotted him. "Quinn! What brings you out here? Is everything okay?"

Raking a hand through his hair, Quinn looked around a bit. "Yeah . . . I guess. Listen, do you have time to go and get some lunch or something?"

Aidan looked at his watch and shrugged. "Sure. Just give me a minute to wrap things up. You want to ride together or meet someplace?"

"I'll wait and we can ride together." One look at Aidan and Quinn knew his brother could sense something was up. He jogged off and talked to some of his crew and then came right back over. "You don't need to rush, man. Really. If you need to talk to your guys —"

Aidan waved him off. "Everyone's good. Come on. The pub?"

"No," Quinn said a little too quickly. "Maybe someplace . . ." He shook his head. "Just someplace else."

Without questioning it, Aidan walked over to his truck and climbed in. Quinn joined him and they drove out of the heart of town to a small diner while doing nothing but talking about the latest sports scores and the weather.

Once they were seated inside and had placed their orders, Aidan cut to the chase. "Okay, I may be way off base here, but if I had to guess, I'd say you didn't ask me to lunch because you missed me." He shook his head. "I know that look, Quinn. I've had that look. What's going on with Anna?"

There was no point in playing dumb — this was exactly why he'd asked his brother to lunch. He sighed wearily as he played with the salt and pepper shakers on the table. "No one thinks I'm good enough for her."

Aidan sat back in his seat and studied his younger brother for a solid minute. "And what about you? Do you think you're good enough for her?"

Quinn shrugged. "I want to be."

"But?"

Pushing the shakers aside, he looked at Aidan. "You've all said it. Everyone thinks Anna should be with someone . . . someone better. I'm a screwup. I didn't pay attention all those years. I was a serial dater who avoided relationships like the plague. I mean, take your pick. It doesn't matter who I am now, everyone, including you, can't see beyond my past. I can't outrun my reputation."

"Okay, okay, just hang on a minute. What do you mean 'including you'? How did I get involved in this?" Aidan asked with genuine concern.

"Not just you — you, Hugh, Riley, Bobby . . . hell, everyone we know. You're all reminding me of the stupid things I've done and how badly I treated Anna and how she deserves better." And then, much to Quinn's annoyance, Aidan laughed. "What's so damn funny?"

"You are! Jeez, Quinn, when did you get so damn sensitive?"

"What the hell are you talking about?"

Aidan rested his arms on the table and leaned forward. "You know, out of the entire family, you have the biggest damn mouth."

"Hey —"

"Shut up," Aidan interrupted. "Every time

we all get together, you're the first one to pick a fight or tease someone about something, but when we do it back, you get all bent out of shape! You've done more than your fair share of teasing me about being whipped where Zoe's concerned, and not so long ago, you told her she should leave me and marry you. Don't you think I found *that* a little insulting?"

"Dude, I was teasing!"

"Yeah, and so were we! Do you not see the irony here? It's what family does, dumbass. We tease one another. And Anna's been family practically since we all first met! Why wouldn't we all get a kick out of picking on the both of you? You need to lighten up, man."

"Yeah, well . . . what about everyone else?" He told Aidan about the incident at the softball game.

The waitress brought their plates out and smiled as she walked away. "Look, the fact is you do have a rather colorful past. You can't change it. And you can't expect people to simply forget it either. All you can do is your best, Quinn. You need to make people see who you are now and how much you've changed."

"What if I can't?"

"What? Change?"

He shook his head. "No. What if I can't make anyone forget or see I'm not that guy anymore?"

Aidan looked at him and gave him a sympathetic smile. "Then they're not trying hard enough to see who you really are."

"And who am I?"

"Only you can answer that."

They ate in silence for a few minutes before Quinn could speak again. "I don't want Anna feeling like she made a mistake. We've been friends for too damn long, and I don't think I'd know how to live my life without her."

Putting his burger down, Aidan's expression was serious. "What if it doesn't work out, Quinn? What if the romantic part of the relationship doesn't work? Do you really think the two of you could go back to being friends?" Before Quinn could answer, Aidan continued. "I'm not going to lie to you. I think it was a big risk to change the dynamic. The two of you were closer than any two people I know. Personally, I don't know if I could have been that brave."

"You think I'm brave?"

Aidan nodded. "You're one of the bravest people I know, Quinn. You go after what you want. You always have. I've seen you take on every kind of sport, and you were a damn legend when you were racing, and now you've got your own chain of shops. Dude, nothing scares you. But this? This thing with Anna? I can see that it does. That's not a bad thing, but you're going to have to get to a point where you're okay with it."

"You mean to tell me nothing about your relationship with Zoe scares you?"

"At one time, sure. Hell, everything about my relationship with her scared me in the beginning, and because of that, she almost moved back to Arizona. I had to come to grips with my fears and insecurities, my crazy beliefs about how life was supposed to be. And, if memory serves, you made fun of me because of them."

"Yeah, well —"

"Bottom line: Do you see yourself marrying Anna? Having kids? Settling down, buying a home, and doing the forever thing? Or do you see yourself with Anna in your life the way things were?"

"Why can't the two be combined?" Quinn asked, his throat tight.

"Because they can't," Aidan said simply. "It's always a great thing when you marry your best friend, but there needs to be more, Quinn. You can't expect Anna to be content with having you just as a sex buddy for the rest of her life. You need to figure out how you really see your future. And then you have to figure out if it only benefits you — or you *and* Anna."

Unfortunately, Quinn felt like he already knew the answer.

It had been a crappy day.

Anna had shown six houses to an extremely demanding couple, and she was mentally exhausted. There had been a problem with some of the permits for Hugh's property, and he had called her having a bit of a panic attack because he thought everything was already lined up for him to move forward with his plans. On top of that, as low man on the totem pole at the agency, it had been her turn to pick up everyone's afternoon coffee, and she had dropped the tray getting out of her car. The amount of ribbing and teasing she had gotten — on top of dealing with her coffee-drenched clothes — had been all she could stand.

The only bright spot in her day was that she and Quinn were going out to dinner that night. And not to the pub or for pizza, but he was taking her out to one of her favorite steakhouses — in town. They would have dinner and do a little dancing, and just the thought of it was enough to get her through the drive home and put the thoughts of her day behind her.

She took her time getting ready — showering and shaving and using enough scented moisturizer to make sure she was smooth and silky all over. Her hair was beginning to get on her nerves because it was longer than she'd ever worn it, and rather than being able to simply blow it dry, she had to take out her curling iron and do something with it.

"Well, this sucks," she murmured after she burned her fingers for the third time and gave serious thought to grabbing a pair of scissors and just hacking it all off.

Looking over at the clock, she knew Quinn would be home soon. They'd already talked about him coming over directly from the shop and getting ready at her place. Even though Quinn still had his place, he spent most of his time at Anna's and even had a small collection of clothes he kept there — including the suit he was going to wear tonight.

Just the sight of it hanging in her closet made Anna smile.

How many years had she dreamed of this? Of finally having Quinn love her and being in the kind of romantic relationship that made her heart skip a beat and her toes curl? They'd made the transformation from friends to lovers with such ease, she knew they were destined to be.

With her hair and makeup complete, she walked over to her closet and pulled out the dress she had purchased especially for tonight. Red silk with spaghetti straps, the bodice hugged her almost like a second skin. It hit right at her knees, and she'd found the perfect pair of matching sandals to go with it. It was so different from anything she'd ever worn, and yet when she saw it in the little dress shop she drove past every day, Anna had known she had to have it.

And she couldn't wait to see the look on Quinn's face when he saw her in it.

Her phone rang and she smiled when she saw Zoe's face on the screen. "Hey! What's up?"

"So tonight's the big date night," Zoe said giddily. "Did you get the dress?"

"I did! I still can't believe I really bought it, but once I went in and tried it on, I was sold. It's so bold and sexy and —"

"Sweetie, you should have started show-casing your curves a long time ago," Zoe interrupted. "Quinn is going to swallow his tongue when he sees you."

"That would be something," Anna said. "I think the last time I really gave him that kind of reaction was before your wedding when he saw me in the bikini."

Zoe chuckled. "That was a great day! I think it was almost cartoonish the way his eyes popped out!"

"Yeah, well . . . he wasn't so happy about it then. I can only hope he'll have a better response tonight."

"You and me both."

"Anything else going on?"

"Actually, yes. I just got off the phone with Aubrey, and Hugh has to be out of town for a few days. She's going to be home alone and asked if maybe you and I would come and hang out with her. My schedule's fairly flexible, but I wasn't sure about yours."

"I can definitely move things around," Anna said, going over her next set of appointments. "Is she all right? Is there a reason why she can't travel with Hugh?"

"Yeah, he's making her crazy!"

That had Anna laughing. "No!"

"Yeah, apparently she needs a little time without him hovering, and she's hoping with him away for a few days, he'll see she's not an invalid."

"I can see how his behavior could start to get annoying."

"It's sweet, don't get me wrong, but she's not allowed to just enjoy being pregnant because Hugh is so worried and cautious. She wants to prove she can still do all the things she loves to do and be pregnant at the same time."

"I'll definitely move my schedule around. When did you want to leave?"

"Hugh's leaving tomorrow — which is Wednesday — and I figured she'd want at least a day to herself to do whatever it is around the house that he won't let her do, so maybe Thursday afternoon? What do you think?"

"That should work. That will give me tomorrow to get my stuff in order. Is Aidan okay with you going?"

"Absolutely. I admit I'll miss sleeping beside him, but it's for a good cause. Besides, he's putting in a lot of extra time on this new subdivision because he wants to get a little ahead of schedule."

"How come? Everything okay?"

"We kind of started talking about going on vacation — a real one this time, when we seriously get out and leave the hotel room."

"Oh, really? Where to? Please tell me you're not going back to Mexico because that would just be sad. You blew your chance with that one. You need to move on."

"No, no, no, we're thinking either Hawaii or checking out Hugh's place in Sydney."

"Wow! Either of those would be amazing."

"I know! So if we do it, Aidan wants to make sure he's leaving at a point when things are somewhat under control. I mean, he knows anything can happen, but he's trying to get everything in order now in hopes it will stay that way."

"That's great, Zoe. I'm so happy for you guys." Anna looked over at the clock. "But I need to get moving. Quinn's going to be home soon, and I want to be dressed when he gets here."

"I'm going to want all the details on his reaction!"

"You got it! I'll see you Thursday! Your car or mine?"

"Yours," Zoe said with a chuckle. "It's new and pretty."

"Yes, it is. Okay, I'll talk to you later!" She hung up and immediately jumped up and finished getting dressed. Looking at herself from every angle in her full-length mirror, Anna was feeling pretty damn confident in herself.

She looked longingly at the jeans and sneakers in her closet. She missed them, missed being comfortable all the time. This being a girly-girl thing was exhausting — the hair, the makeup, the shoes! Why did society act as if it were all a good thing? Then she looked back at her reflection and smiled. "Oh yeah," she said. "Because I look really good!"

With nothing left to do, she went out to the kitchen and got herself something to drink and then waited.

And waited.

And waited.

She knew Quinn could easily lose track of time when he was working on a car, but she couldn't help but be annoyed that he'd do it tonight. They hadn't ever gone out on a real romantic date, and the fact that he would choose this night to be late really ticked her off.

Calling the shop, she cursed when no one answered. She got the same result when she called his cell phone.

That's when she began to worry.

Certainly he wouldn't ignore his cell phone — he kept it on him at all times. What if something had happened to him? What if he was hurt and alone in the shop? All of her anger instantly fled as she scooped up her purse and ran out the door. His shop was only a few minutes away, and she knew she could get to him quickly.

Dressed in her killer dress and heels, she pulled up in front of the garage and saw his car was still there, along with several others. Climbing from the car, she immediately walked around to the back of the property where Quinn did the restorations.

Pulling open the door, she was struck by the sound of male laughter. The loud slam of the door behind her had the space going quiet for a second. Quinn looked over at her, and she knew the instant he realized he'd screwed up. He jogged over to her.

"Shit, Anna. I'm sorry. I lost track of time and —"

"Who is he?" she asked, motioning to the man Quinn had been talking to.

"That's Ken Bishop. He's with *Classic Cars* magazine. He came to check out the cars and see what I'm working on and get some preliminary stuff out of the way for the article he's going to write. It's going to be a series, and he believes this kind of exposure will lead to me getting more clients. These two cars will —"

"Jake's cars?"

He nodded.

"You do realize we had plans tonight?" she said with a little snap to her tone.

"Yeah, yeah, I know. But he showed up here unannounced and we got to talking and the time just got away from me." He wanted to touch her, but his hands were dirty and he reconsidered. Then he finally noticed what she was wearing. "Damn, Anna. Your dress is amazing. Red looks really good on you. You look beautiful."

"You're joking, right?"

"What? I'm serious. You look amazing. I've never seen you in anything —"

"No, you haven't," she snapped. "I bought this dress especially for tonight. I thought tonight was a big deal. Apparently I'm the only one."

"Okay, look, give me five minutes and I'll get this guy out of here and —"

"It won't matter! We've missed our reservation!"

"So we'll go someplace else. Really, just let me —"

She held up her hands and took a step back. "You know what? No. I have tried to be understanding, and I have tried to be supportive. Always. Everyone told me I was being too generous in not making a big deal out of you working on Jake Tanner's cars and I sided with you. I *defended* you. And when it came time for you to choose between those damn cars and me, you chose the cars."

"Anna, if you'd just listen —"

She shook her head. "No. I'm done listening to you. You'll always have an excuse. You'll always have a reason why you're right and I'm wrong. God, I'm such an idiot!" she cried. "I knew this about you and I still let it happen!" Her brown eyes welled with tears as she poked him in the chest. "I knew you would never put me first, and I let myself believe you would change!"

"I have changed! I made a mistake. I screwed up!"

"Yes, you did," she said sadly.

"Baby, I'm sorry. Let me get rid of Ken and we'll talk. Let me make it up to you. Let me —"

She shook her head again. "I can't. I can't do this anymore, Quinn. That's your go-to line: 'Let me.' Let me explain. Let me make it up to you. I need someone who doesn't have to keep explaining why I'm not a priority and why I'm not enough."

"But you are enough! Anna, you're everything! Please, you have to know that!"

"It's what I try to keep telling myself, but even I don't believe it anymore." Her heart ached and she knew if she didn't leave soon, she would simply crumple to the ground. "It hurt when you did things like this when we were just friends, but it's killing me now." She took a few more steps away from him. "We could have been so good together, Quinn. I gave you everything — I always have — but it's never going to be enough."

At least he was smart enough to know to stop arguing and trying to correct her.

"I don't want you to come by my house. I don't want you to call. I'll make arrangements to get your things back to you."

Quinn's expression was of pure devastation. "Don't do this," he said quietly, his voice shaking.

Anna took a steadying breath. "I have to. It's the only way I'll survive." She didn't allow herself any more time. Carefully, she turned around and walked to the door and out of the garage.

And out of Quinn's life.

"Are you sure Aidan doesn't mind? I hate dragging him into this."

Zoe smiled sadly. "He doesn't see it like that. You're like a sister to him, and if doing this one little favor helps you, then he's happy to do it."

Anna had packed for her stay at Aubrey's and had also packed up all of Quinn's things and brought them over to Aidan and Zoe's place. "I feel like a coward."

"Don't you even think that! I think you're handling this incredibly well. I know you're hurting, and I'm sure getting all this to-gether wasn't easy."

"It wasn't, but it was worse having to look at it all over my house."

In truth, it wasn't that much stuff — a couple of changes of clothes, some hats, toiletries — nothing major. She just knew she didn't want it there when she came back from Aubrey's. Maybe by that time, she'd be a little more in control of her emotions, but the fewer reminders she had, the better.

The pictures that were scattered all over her house had all been taken down and packed up in a box and put away. She'd replace them all eventually, but she couldn't bear to keep looking around and seeing Quinn's face everywhere.

Zoe took the box and placed it in the house before locking up. "I texted Aidan so he knows it's here. He'll take care of it."

"Thanks." They climbed into Anna's car and she sat there silently, not starting the car, not moving.

"Anna? Sweetie? Are you okay? What's go-ing on?"

"The car."

"What about it?"

"I can't keep it."

Zoe sighed. "Let's not think about it right now. Do you want to take my car? We can move everything into it pretty easily and then hit the road."

Shaking her head, Anna turned the key. "I'm being stupid. I don't have to have all the answers right now, right?"

"No, you don't. Just don't do anything hasty."

"I just . . . I need to sever all ties. I can't . . . I don't want . . ."

"I know." Reaching over, Zoe squeezed Anna's hand. "I'd say this little getaway was perfectly timed."

"You got that right."

"Come on. The sooner we get there, the sooner we can help you figure out the best plan for your future."

Right now, the only plan Anna had for her future was remembering to breathe.

"I'm not sure what we're supposed to do in this kind of situation — drink, eat, cry, throw things. Seriously, I'm clueless," Aubrey said when she and Zoe were alone for a minute. Anna had gone to the guest room to put her things away, so they were taking the time to discuss strategy.

"If it were up to me, we'd leave her here and go and beat Quinn upside the head with a heavy object," Zoe hissed, checking over her shoulder to make sure Anna hadn't come back into the room.

"I don't think it would solve any of this."

"Yeah, but I'd feel a lot better." With a sigh, Zoe sat down on the sofa. "The thing is, I'm proud of her."

"What? Why?" Aubrey looked completely confused as she sat down next to her sister-in-law.

"I've known Anna for a while now, and I've watched her fawn over Quinn for most of that time. Don't get me wrong. I love Quinn. I really do. But he is beyond clueless."

Aubrey nodded. "Aren't they all?"

"Oh, absolutely! But out of all the Shaughnessys — hell, out of all men — right now, he takes the cake."

"I thought he had potential." She looked over at Zoe with a sad smile. "I really did. The weekend they came and stayed here with us? I watched the two of them and thought, 'Okay, he's finally getting it.' Even Hugh kept commenting on how nice it was to see his brother finally get his head out of his butt."

Zoe laughed. "Yeah, Aidan thought the same thing. I'm sure most people would look at the situation and think it wasn't that big of a deal. So he forgot about dinner. It happens. Hell, there are times it still happens to both me and Aidan — you get caught up in work and next thing you know, you're late."

"I don't know. I don't think it's so much the dinner as much as what he was doing. I knew those stupid cars were going to come back and bite them eventually. He should have walked away from them right after the whole incident with Jake."

"I agree. Hell, we all think that, but Anna — being Anna — didn't want to jeopardize the chance of Quinn getting some publicity for his restoration business. Personally, I would have just told him to suck it up and find another classic car enthusiast to do business with, but that's just me." She shook her head. "Quinn's just used to doing things his own way and not really having to think about anyone else."

"We all can have that tendency, Zoe," Aubrey said. "But once you get into a relationship, you tend to make an effort to change. He's too smart not to know that by now. It's almost as if he sabotaged the relationship on purpose."

Zoe shifted in her seat and faced Aubrey, her gaze narrowing. "Go on."

A small smile crossed Aubrey's face. "Okay, Quinn's been upset about how everyone keeps bringing up his past, that he's selfish, blah, blah, blah . . . It bothers him."

Zoe told her about the lunch Aidan and Quinn had had. "I know he told me in confidence, but I don't think the rules apply here. So, okay, Quinn was upset and feeling insecure. But why would he just jump ship like that? It seems cowardly."

"Or maybe he was being proactive. You know, forcing her to leave him now before things got serious."

"Please, they've been serious for a long time — long before they started dating, the two of them were serious. It was weird, and Quinn was the only one who didn't see it."

"Wow, he really is clueless," Aubrey said and sighed. "Well, then I'm stumped. I'd like to think he was being a gentleman and hurting her now rather than devastating her later."

Zoe shook her head. "Anna's been in love with him for so long, she was going to be devastated no matter what. I hate that for her."

"But you said you're proud of her. Why?"

"She always made excuses for him — or accepted the excuses he gave her. In the end, she knew she was going to be devastated and knew walking away was going to hurt. But she did it anyway. For once, she really stood up for herself and put herself first. It's not an easy thing to do."

"Tell me about it."

Zoe smiled. "Exactly! You did it with Hugh, so you know exactly how it feels. You walked away because you wanted Hugh to have the life you didn't think you could give him. It hurt and you were miserable, but at the time, you were being selfless. Our girl had to do something she'd never done before; she had to be selfish. And she's the least selfish person I've ever known. And I know it's killing her."

"So my original question stands: What do we do? Eat, drink, cry? Are we supposed to find pictures of him and throw darts at it or something?"

With a sigh of her own, Zoe rested her head on the back of the sofa. "Unfortunately, I think we're going to have our hands full with all of the above."

Aubrey stood and stretched. "I'll get started baking the brownies."

Zoe followed her into the kitchen. "What other kinds of junk food have you got?"

"Not much. Hugh's been a bit militant about what kind of things I eat and drink. He wants to make sure the baby and I are healthy."

Zoe glanced over at her. "Come on, you

know you've got a secret stash hidden somewhere. And if you don't, I'm going to the store and making sure you have one after we leave."

With a laugh, Aubrey reached into one of the kitchen drawers and pulled out a pad and pen. "You have no idea what a lifesaver you are! I was planning on going to the store while he was gone, but I was enjoying the peace and quiet too much to get out yesterday." She began to quickly make a list and soon tore the paper off the pad and handed it to Zoe.

"Chips, dip, caramels, muffins, doughnuts," Zoe read off the list. Then she looked at Aubrey and smiled. "Baby steps, little mama. We can't have you gaining ten pounds while your husband's gone. He'll never let me visit you again!"

They were both laughing hysterically when Anna walked into the room and eyed them curiously. "What's so funny?"

They walked over and flanked her on both sides. "We're going food shopping," Zoe said, "to make sure Aubrey has a secret stockpile of junk food to tide her over for a while when Hugh gets back."

Anna chuckled and took the list from Zoe's hand. "You might want to add fried chicken, mashed potatoes, ice cream, peanut butter, and gummy bears."

"Um . . . that's kind of specific," Aubrey said. "And I don't think I'd be able to hide all those things from Hugh. And I'm not particularly fond of gummy bears."

"Oh, that wasn't for you," Anna said and walked over to grab her purse. "That's for me. And that's just to get me through lunch. We'll decide the rest while we're roaming the aisles at the grocery store."

Zoe looked over at Aubrey and shrugged. "You wanted to know how it works? We'll go in stages. Eating is obviously going to be phase one. Remind me to add tissues to the list because the crying phase will be here before you know it."

CHAPTER 11

For more than thirty years, Ian Shaughnessy had been there to pick up his kids when they fell. It almost became a full-time job after his wife died. And at that moment, he'd have given anything to have been dealing with something more straightforward, like a scraped knee or losing the big game. When he stepped into the restoration garage his heart broke.

His son — his strong and confident son — was sitting on the floor in the middle of an empty garage. He looked beyond sad — he looked broken. Ian wasn't a fool. He had found out what had happened a week ago, but he knew that his son was going to need a little time before anyone would be able to talk to him. From the looks of it, maybe he'd waited too long.

Without a word, Ian walked over and sat on the floor beside him — not an easy task for a man his age, but sometimes you had to take the pain. They sat in silence for a few minutes. Quinn didn't even blink when Ian sat down. If there was one thing Ian knew about his son, it was how stubborn he was, and he had a feeling that if he didn't say something soon, Quinn would be content to just let them stay like this.

"Business is booming up front," Ian said mildly. "There're a lot of cars lined up to be looked at. This town's needed a quality mechanic for a long time. I'm glad we have that now with you."

No response.

"You missed dinner with everyone Sunday. Owen surprised us all and showed up just as we were sitting down." He chuckled. "I haven't seen this much of that boy in I don't even know how long. It's nice that he takes the time to get away and come home more often. Of course, I wouldn't mind a phone call or two in between visits so I'd know when he's coming home."

Nothing.

It was time for a different approach. "Your mother used to call you her all-or-nothing child."

Quinn turned and silently faced him.

"Did you know that?"

Quinn shook his head.

"We used to laugh because there was

never any middle ground with you — from the time you were a baby, you were the one who took things to extremes." He chuckled. "You'd spite yourself and I don't even think you were aware of it."

"What —" Quinn cleared his throat. "What do you mean?"

"Well, there was the bicycle thing. You were told you could ride it as long as you didn't race it." He looked at his son. "But you wouldn't compromise, and you raced until the bike got taken away." Ian shifted to try and get a little more comfortable. "Then there was baseball. My God, were you gifted. You were one of the best players I ever saw. But when your coaches reminded you how they had to let everyone play, you quit."

"Yeah, well . . . some of those guys had no right being on the field."

"Oh, I agree. But part of good sportsmanship is letting everyone have a turn — even if it means losing the game. You can't tell me you didn't miss playing."

Quinn nodded. "What's the point in playing if you aren't allowed to win?"

Ian chuckled again. "I can see your point, but you're missing the bigger picture here. Rather than follow the rules, you chose to walk away. The team went on without you.

The only one missing out was you."

"It wasn't that big of a deal."

"And what about racing?"

Quinn frowned. "What about it?"

"You walked away at the height of your career. Why?"

"My best friend got killed in a crash, Dad. It was horrible. I didn't want to put you and everyone through what his family was going through."

"How many crashes had you witnessed during your time on the circuit?"

"I don't know . . . dozens."

"How many deaths?"

Quinn shrugged. "A few."

"Over the course of your life — just your everyday life — have you seen people get hurt and die?" Ian asked quietly.

"Dammit, Dad!" Quinn shouted and jumped to his feet. "What the hell kind of question is that?"

Slowly, Ian stood up. "Accidents happen all the time, Quinn. Whether you're on a racetrack or running errands or standing in your own home. Your mother was a perfect example of that. Did you love racing?"

"You know I did!"

"Then why leave?"

"I just told you," he replied with an angry huff. "What's your point?"

"The point is you have a tendency to walk away when things get tough or they don't go your way."

"I didn't walk away from anything," he said with a low growl.

"And yet I'm standing here in the middle of an empty garage." Ian gestured to the open space around them.

"Yeah, well, that wasn't walking away. It was the right thing to do. I should have done it months ago. I got so caught up in something that could possibly happen two years down the road that I wasn't paying attention to what was happening right now."

"You've turned down a couple of decent restoration offers since though," Ian pointed out.

"I wasn't feeling them."

"You love cars. You've always loved cars. I think you're full of crap."

Quinn's eyes went wide. "Excuse me?"

"You heard me. I think you're full of it."

"Dad," Quinn said with a slight stammer, "what's gotten into you?"

"I think sending those cars back to Jake Tanner was the right thing to do — and so was telling that reporter the reason why."

"I didn't . . . I never said . . ."

"Yeah, well, you're not the only one who was going to be part of that interview."

Quinn rolled his eyes. "Dad, please tell me you didn't tell Ken what Jake did."

"Why not? Why shouldn't I? What that man did was criminal, Son! And all he got was a slap on the wrist and probation! He pulled the celebrity card and got to go on his merry little way! I don't think it's right, and I certainly don't think it's fair to Anna."

At the sound of her name, Quinn winced.

"Now I don't think Ken's going to write about what I told him, but I'm pretty sure his magazine won't be doing a story on Tanner either."

"I guess that's something."

"Anyway, he sent you two potential clients and you blew them off. Why?"

Quinn walked over to his tool bench and began moving things around. Ian came over and stood beside him, waiting. "I just . . . I can't."

"Why?"

"It's because of my selfish behavior and because of this business I was so hell-bent on having that everything went wrong. Maybe it just wasn't meant to be."

"Hmm . . . maybe," Ian said with a shrug. "Or maybe you're just following form and running because it didn't go your way."

Quinn threw a wrench across the garage with a feral growl before facing his father again. "You know, why is it that you're compassionate and loving when everyone else has a problem, huh? You give everyone these heartfelt pep talks to lift them up, and all you've done since you got here is kick me while I'm down!"

"It figures you'd see it that way," Ian said. "Because I see it as giving you the lift you need to get up off your ass and finish something!"

All the fight left Quinn as confusion took over.

"When Aidan came to me about his fears about Zoe, we talked. He didn't sugarcoat it and he didn't lay blame on anyone. We talked until he figured it out. Then we cried." He paused. "When Hugh came to me about Aubrey, I had to point out to him how his obsession about always wanting to be safe played a big part in why they didn't work out. But in the end, I encouraged him to take a risk. Do you think it was easy for either of them to admit they were at fault in any way? Do you think it's easy for any of us to admit to that?"

"I don't like to think about having any weaknesses," Quinn said. "I don't want anyone to see that side of me." He looked up at his father sadly. "Anyone."

"You're human, Quinn. We all have weak-

nesses. It doesn't make you less of a man."
He looked around the garage. "You've
always required a bit of a different approach. Aidan and Hugh are a little more
sensitive. Don't get me wrong. They're
tough and dependable men, but in their
own ways, they were always ostensibly cautious."

"But you're basically telling me I am too,"
Quinn reminded him.

"You're cautious in a way that doesn't
make you seem like you're cautious. Only
someone who really looks would see it." He
smiled. "I'm really looking, Son." When
Quinn didn't respond, Ian continued. "I'm
not going to sit here and wax poetic with
you. I didn't do it with your brothers either.
I can only guide you to the best of my ability. And you don't need to hug it out. You
don't need to cry. But you do need a solid
kick in the ass."

"Hey!"

"It's true! I want you to finish something,"
he shouted — and Ian never shouted. "Just
once, I want you not to walk away because
something got tough. Here's a bit of news
for you, Son: not everyone gets their way all
the time, and they don't all take their toys
and go home." He huffed and raked a hand
through his hair. "That's not who I raised

you to be and that's not who your mom wanted you to be."

Quinn took a shaky breath. "Oh man . . ."

"She said you were her toughest — and she meant it in the best possible way. You do hate to show weakness and sometimes that's a good thing. Other times, well . . . not showing your weaknesses is what makes you weak. Make her proud, Quinn. Show her, and the whole world, how tough you are."

"What if the business fails? You know, on its own, because I'm not as good as I think I am?"

"What if it succeeds?"

Quinn frowned. "Things fail all the time, Dad. Even with all the attention in the world."

"That's true. But then you can look back and know you did everything possible and gave it your all. And when that's the case, no one can look at you like you're a failure."

They stood in companionable silence for a few minutes. Ian walked around the shop, touching tools and simply checking things out. He turned back toward Quinn. "Martha and I had dinner with the Hannigans last night." He almost smiled at how Quinn paled, although he wasn't sure if was the mention of Martha or the Hannigans that did it. "It was kind of nice. We barbecued and played cards and just visited."

A weak smile and a nod were Quinn's only response.

"By the time we got done talking about all of you kids and how everyone is, half the night was gone. Bobby's thinking of transferring to South Carolina," Ian said with a shrug. "He says it's just time for a change."

"Good for him," Quinn mumbled.

"And we talked about Aidan and Zoe planning their Australia trip, Aubrey's pregnancy, Riley's music, Owen's promotion, Darcy's school, your shop, and . . . Bobby's move . . ." He paused and sighed. "Hard to believe there are so many of you." Once again, his son's reaction was pretty funny. "Oh, I know who I forgot."

Quinn seemed to perk up.

"Stanley."

"Excuse me? Who's Stanley?"

"He's Martha's French bulldog. He's the funniest little thing!" Ian chuckled. "Honestly, that dog has the personality of a human. I never considered myself a dog person, but he has me reconsidering. Sometimes I think he's going to just get up and talk to me!"

The poor boy looked deflated. "That's nice, Dad."

"Anyway, I guess I should be going. Martha and I are going to the movies tonight." He pulled Quinn close and hugged him. "Think about what I said."

With a nod, Quinn said, "Okay. I'll make some calls and get those cars in here."

Ian shook his head and patted his son on the arm. "You don't really think this was all about some cars, do you?"

"Hell no. But I've got to start somewhere, don't I?"

Life was moving on — just barely.

Hugh had finally closed on the property and Anna had received her commission. It was really quite exciting to get that large of a check. After paying off some bills, she put another chunk into savings and then knew what she needed to do next.

Picking up the phone, she called the car dealership she knew Quinn had purchased her car from. After thirty frustrating minutes, she wasn't able to convince them to let her pay off the car. "Well, now what?" she murmured. A knock at her door had her looking up just as her brother walked in.

"Hey, squirt! What's going on?" he said with an easy smile. He kissed her on the head and noticed her frown. "Seriously, what's up?"

She explained the situation about the car. "I know I don't have to do anything, but I need to. Every time I get in the damn thing I think of Quinn." She looked up at him helplessly. "What do I do?"

Bobby quietly studied her. "This is just a suggestion, but . . ."

"But?"

"I'm going to be out of town for a while, so why don't you take my car?"

She looked at him oddly. "Why? Aren't you taking it with you? You're only going to South Carolina, not South America."

He chuckled. "Yeah, but . . . I'm sort of ready for a complete change. I already have a new car picked out, and the financing is good to go without using my car as a trade-in. So why don't you take my old car and give the Honda back to Quinn."

Unable to help herself, she lowered her gaze to her hands. "I don't think I could handle seeing him, Bobby. Not yet."

His arms came around her as he hugged her tight. "No worries there. I'll drop the car off."

Anna immediately lifted her head. "Oh . . . no. I don't want you to do that."

"Why not?"

"Because you'll just use it as an excuse to

start a fight with Quinn."

"So? He deserves it! Dammit, Anna, I hate seeing you like this!" He looked like he was about to say more and then stopped and seemed to relax. "You know, you should come with me to South Carolina."

"Are you crazy? Why?"

"I would think it was obvious — you need a fresh start too. Look, I don't want to upset you but it needs to be said. This is a small town. You're not going to be able to avoid Quinn forever. There's gonna come a time when he moves on and, true to form, he's not going to give a damn if it hurts you."

"He wouldn't —"

"Just stop, okay? Are you prepared to run into him and one of his bimbos?"

She sighed with irritation. "Do people even use that term anymore?"

"Trust me, I'm toning my choice of words down to be nice. Think about it, Anna. If you stay here, there's always going to be that possibility. The two of you have been in each other's pockets since you were kids. He's always going to be there — or here. With this new shop he's got, it seems like he's going to be here even more than he used to be. He's not traveling as much and he's not in a rush to go anywhere. How are you going to handle it?"

"I don't know, Bobby!" she shouted. "But that doesn't mean I want you to go to the shop and pick a fight with him!"

He huffed with frustration. "Fine. I won't fight with him. I promise. I'll drop the car off, give him the keys, and leave."

"You promise? Really?"

"Unlike some people, I'm not looking to make you upset on purpose, Anna. I may be a jerk a lot of the time but not to you."

She rolled her eyes. "You did not just say that."

He chuckled. "Okay, fine. I'm a jerk to you too, but this time I promise not to be. It's part of my whole makeover." He smiled. "You inspired me."

"And why are you suddenly giving yourself a makeover?"

He shrugged. "I've been here my whole life, kiddo. It's the same thing day in, day out. I'm just ready for something new. Nothing's happening for me here. You said the same thing about yourself when you left the pub."

"How do you know something's going to happen for you in South Carolina?" she asked quietly.

"I don't. But I'm willing to give it a shot." He pulled her in and kissed her. "Come on. Give me the keys and I'll take care of this car thing right now."

"How will you get home after you leave the shop?"

"I'll give my partner a call."

"Wait . . . you have a partner? Since when?"

"Since about a month ago." He made a face. "There have been some changes in the precinct and I feel like I've taken about ten steps backward."

"Ah . . . so there's more to this makeover story than meets the eye."

"Sort of. Anyway, I'll get a ride. I don't want you to worry about it."

Slowly, Anna went and got both sets of car keys and handed them to Bobby. "I'll walk out with you and clear all my stuff out." Together they walked outside, and within five minutes, she had her few meager belongings in a pile on the grass.

"You sure about this?" Bobby asked.

"It's the last tie to him," she said and cursed the fact that she was close to tears.

Bobby pulled her in for one last hug before getting in the car and driving away.

"What the hell do you mean?" Quinn angrily tossed a rag aside as he approached Bobby Hannigan.

"I thought I was pretty clear, dude. Anna

doesn't want the car, so I'm bringing it back for her."

Everything inside of Quinn went cold.

Then he looked at Bobby's smug face and that instantly changed. "You talked her into this, didn't you?"

"Sorry to disappoint you, Shaughnessy, but it was her choice. She even tried talking to the dealership first about paying the car off, but they wouldn't let her do it." He glared at Quinn. "I'm sure you had something to do with it."

"Hell yeah I did!" Quinn snapped. "The car was a gift to make her life easier! If she knew she could just swoop in and take over the payments she would have done it sooner." He cursed. "She needs a car, Bobby. You know it and I know it. Just . . . convince her to keep it. I'll transfer the payments over to her if she really feels so strongly about it."

Bobby shook his head. "She already has another car and she doesn't want any reminders of you. For once, do the right thing and just let her have her way."

Even though Quinn knew Bobby was right, it still irritated the hell out of him. "You're loving this, aren't you?" he finally asked.

Bobby laughed darkly. "Believe it or not,

I'm not. You think I enjoy seeing my sister this upset? I really thought this was going to be the one time you proved me wrong." He shook his head. "I thought for her . . ."

Quinn looked away.

Bobby shoved him on the shoulder to get Quinn to face him. "Hey, I'm not here to gloat and it doesn't do shit for me to be proven right. I would have put up with your sorry ass forever if it made Anna happy."

"Yeah . . . well . . . now you won't have to."

"You just don't get it, do you?" Bobby said in disgust. "All these years and you haven't figured it out." When Quinn just stared at him, he continued. "Ever since she started crushing on you in the seventh grade, I've wanted to kick your ass. At first, it was just on principle. My sister liked you, and you didn't like her in return. Then the older we got, and the more she refused to move on, I started to resent you. By now I should hate you, but all I can do is pity you. You're the one who's going to miss out on an amazing life, because there's no one better than my sister."

Quinn couldn't have uttered a word even if he'd wanted to — his throat was so tight he almost couldn't breathe.

Bobby tossed the keys at him, which he

readily caught.

"Most guys would kill for what you had," Bobby said, almost with a hint of sadness. "And they wouldn't have been stupid enough to let it slip away."

When Quinn was alone in the shop, he looked at the keys in his hands and closed his fist around them. He'd gotten all of his clothes back, Anna had quit the softball team, and now she'd given back the car. Short of hiding in the bushes with a pair of binoculars, he had no excuse to see her. And what was worse, no one would talk to him about her, either. It was almost as if they were all trying to make him crazy.

He'd seen Aidan and Zoe several times over the last few weeks, but no matter how many hints he'd dropped, neither of them had talked about her. Even after Bobby's little speech, Quinn was no closer to knowing how Anna really was other than her not wanting the damn car.

He'd respected her wishes and kept his distance — everyone thought he was doing it of his own free will, but he wasn't. No one could possibly understand how hard it was to stay away.

Just as no one could possibly understand how much he really did love her.

Could barely breathe without her.

Hadn't slept in weeks because of her.

Tossing the keys on his workbench, he stalked across the garage and out the door, locking up behind him. He needed to get out and clear his head. He needed to get out and find something to do that wouldn't have him thinking of Anna. Aching for Anna.

He cursed. There was no such thing and he knew it.

He could drive from one coast to the other and back again and nothing was going to be better. Nothing was going to be right. Unfortunately, he knew he had to keep moving forward. The pain he felt was self-inflicted and he had to learn to live with it.

He drove through town in his truck. It was a quiet Tuesday afternoon. No traffic. No distractions until . . .

He'd have known that blond hair anywhere.

Sitting at a table of one of the café's that had outdoor seating, he saw Anna. Carefully, he pulled over and just . . . watched. He knew it was wrong and creepy, but it had been so long since he'd seen her that he couldn't stop himself.

She was sitting alone, talking on her phone. Even from this distance, he could see she was sad. She was laughing at something, but Quinn knew her well enough to know her heart wasn't in it. He knew her body well enough to know that her fidgeting was because she wasn't comfortable. The constant toying with her hair was because its length was annoying her. When her shoulders sagged, he wanted nothing more than to jump out of the truck and go over and hold her.

Quinn watched as she put her phone down on the table and looked around. He hoped she didn't see him. Then she stood and smiled at someone . . . a guy. What the hell? She was sitting there waiting for a guy? Like a date? He's sitting there like some lovesick puppy and all the while she'd been waiting for her new boyfriend?

Unable to watch anymore, Quinn pulled back onto the main road and drove away.

"Congratulations," Anna said with a bright smile. "You've bought yourself a house!"

She had been saying that phrase a lot lately and found that it was fun to see the smiles on her clients' faces. Anna had been on a bit of a selling streak. In the last month, she'd sold four houses on top of closing on Hugh's property. She still didn't love real estate, but right now it was being very good to her. Sitting at the café table, enjoying the sunlight, she collected all the paperwork and put it in her folder.

Dan Michaels leaned back in the chair and smiled back at her. "It certainly looks that way." He paused. "I can't thank you enough, Anna. You really listened and found me my perfect house. How about we go out and celebrate?"

Celebrate? Hell, it had been weeks since Anna had wanted to celebrate anything. It was one thing to not see Quinn when he was traveling or when they were each away at college, but this? This variation they had going on, where they were deliberately not seeing each other, was slowly killing her.

Her smile fell slightly but she forced herself to keep her tone light. "I wish I could but I'm supposed to meet up with some friends after work for drinks."

"Anyone I know?"

She should have said no, but her mouth got away from her. "Aidan Shaughnessy and his wife, Zoe."

"Oh, wow. I haven't seen Aidan in years. I heard he's got a construction company now."

Anna nodded. "He's the best in the area."

"I considered calling him if I didn't find what I was looking for and seeing if he could custom build something for me. Looks like

I won't have to now."

"I'm really glad you like the house, Dan. It's beautiful."

"Listen," he began as he leaned forward, "I know this sounds forward but . . . would you mind if I tagged along? I really would like to see Aidan, and even though I don't need a house built, I do have some business projects in the works that might be of interest to him."

Her immediate thought was to tell him no, but how could she deny Aidan a potential opportunity for his business? So with her smile — stiff though it may be — still in place, she agreed.

"I do need to run by the office and get these processed. Why don't you follow me and we'll go from there?"

Dan readily agreed and Anna was thankful to have a few minutes to herself. Back at the office, Dan sat and made some calls while she finished with the paperwork. When she couldn't delay any longer, she went into the ladies room and freshened up and then walked out to tell him she was ready.

Twenty minutes later, they pulled into the pub's parking lot — separately — and Anna was relieved to spot Aidan's truck already there. For some reason, she was uncomfortable with the entire situation. She didn't really want to be out, and she certainly didn't want to be out with Dan, but Zoe had been after her pretty much since the breakup to leave the house and engage in life again.

So here she was. Engaging in life.

And hating it.

Dan walked over and met her as she was climbing from the car. "I don't think I've been here in years," he said with an easy grin, taking her hand to help her. "I actually came here for my twenty-first birthday and had my first official, legal drink." He chuckled. "A bunch of us came here and drank until they threw us out. It was a great little bar."

Anna chuckled. "Well, brace yourself. It hasn't changed much."

Together they walked in and she stiffened slightly when Dan's hand rested on the small of her back as they made their way through the crowd toward where Aidan and Zoe were sitting in a booth.

"Hey!" Zoe said. "Glad you made it." She looked past Anna and her eyes landed briefly on Dan before zeroing back on Anna as if to say, "WTF?"

"Oh, sorry," Anna said as she stepped away slightly from Dan. "This is Dan

Michaels. We went to school together and he just signed a contract on a new house on the beach."

"Dan, how are you?" Aidan asked, standing up and shaking his hand. "You used to play ball with my younger brother, right?"

Anna could tell Aidan was deliberately trying not to say Quinn's name, and as much as she appreciated it, she just wished everyone would act normal.

Or just let her go home where she could curl up in a ball and be by herself.

"I did, way back when," Dan replied. "It's good to see you." He reached over and shook Zoe's hand, and then they all took their seats in the booth.

"So . . . I take it Anna sold you the house," Zoe said, grinning.

Dan nodded. "It was the very first one she showed me over a month ago. I kind of dragged my feet a bit — I had several business trips to take that sidetracked me — but luckily the house was still available when I was ready for it."

"It's a beautiful house," Anna said and then launched into all the amenities. "You would go crazy for all the finishes, Zoe. It was all done over just before the house went on the market. And the view is breathtaking."

Dan turned to her and smiled. "It certainly is."

Zoe arched a brow at Anna who, in turn, blushed. "So," she said brightly, "have you ordered yet? Are we just doing drinks? Or food? Or . . ."

Zoe shook her head. "We just got here about five minutes before you did, so we figured we'd wait and see what you were in the mood for."

Aidan motioned to the waitress and once they all gave their drink orders, Dan immediately began talking business with Aidan. Anna was grateful for the reprieve, but she desperately wanted to talk to Zoe — alone. Unfortunately, they were on the inside of the booth and sort of trapped in their spots. So she went for small talk — the beach, the weather, shopping.

"I was talking to Aubrey last night and she really wants to come for a couple of days and visit."

"Is Hugh going out of town again?"

Zoe nodded. "Although I kind of think Aubrey orchestrated this one."

"Uh-oh."

"Nah. It's nothing bad. She really wants to do a little shopping for the nursery and wants to get a feel for things before she and Hugh go together."

"Okay. As long as they're fine and happy and still in love."

"Almost sickeningly so," Zoe laughed.

"So when is she coming?"

"I was thinking maybe we'd hit the outlets next weekend if . . ." Zoe began and then her eyes drifted to the door of the pub and she stopped.

"If . . . what?" Anna asked and then followed Zoe's gaze.

Quinn.

It was the first time in weeks that she'd seen him, and her heart seemed to kick her in the chest right before stopping altogether.

He looked good. Really good. He must have gotten out of the shop early because he'd obviously showered and shaved, and he had on clean clothes. She watched as he shook hands and greeted a couple of people, and then she felt as if she were going to be sick.

He wasn't alone.

She didn't want to stare — she really didn't — but for some reason she couldn't seem to look away.

The girl was her every nightmare — tall, thin, big boobs. The centerfold they used to joke about. And she seemed to need to have her hands all over Quinn. And he didn't seem to mind.

"We can go someplace else," Zoe whispered as she reached across the table and squeezed Anna's hand.

But Anna shook her head. No. She was going to have to get used to this. Hadn't Bobby warned her of this exact scenario? They lived in a small town and they were bound to run into one another.

She just had hoped it wouldn't happen quite so soon and that her heart would be a little more intact to handle it.

Slowly, she leaned back in her seat and nearly jumped when Dan's arm came to rest behind her.

Worst. Night. Ever.

The waitress delivered their drinks and they toasted the sale of the house. Neither Dan nor Aidan were aware of her emotional state, and she hoped it stayed that way. Anna couldn't help but smile — it was a great thing for Dan and it was a huge commission for her. Between this commission and the one from Hugh's property, she finally had some breathing room to get part of her life on track. The sensible part.

The emotional part was still a mess.

"Best of luck to you with the house, Dan," Aidan said.

"Hear, hear!" Zoe chimed in.

And as they all clinked glasses, it seemed

as if all the noise in the room faded away. Anna took a sip of her beer, and when she looked up, her eyes met Quinn's. His gaze narrowed at her, and when he spotted Dan, his gaze turned dark and thunderous. It was all she could do to not slide under the table and hide.

"Actually, this might be of interest to you too, Zoe. Aidan says you're a decorator. I've got a building downtown that I was thinking of . . ." Dan was saying.

Anna knew they were all talking. All around the room, people were talking and there was music playing in the background, but all she heard was her heart pounding in her ears. The beer tasted vile in her mouth and she knew if she took another sip, she certainly would get sick.

"Excuse me," Anna interrupted, hoping she sounded normal and that no one detected the tremor in her voice. "I just need to run to the ladies' room." Zoe gave her a sympathetic smile and normally Anna would have wanted Zoe to go with her, but right then, she needed a minute to herself to calm her nerves and break away from Quinn's stare.

Anger built with every step she took. He had no right to look at her that way. This was what he wanted whether he admitted it or not. What did he expect — that she'd just sit at home and mope for the rest of her life? Well, that was kind of exactly what she wanted to do, but no one needed to know that.

Maybe Bobby had been onto something — maybe she did need a fresh start someplace else. She'd hate moving away from her parents and Zoe and all her friends, but there was no way she wanted to keep feeling like this every time she happened to cross paths with Quinn. Maybe it would get easier over time, but somehow Anna doubted it.

Her mind flashed back to a conversation she and Zoe had had way back when, while Zoe and Aidan were broken up and Zoe was all set to move back to Arizona.

"It's just too hard. I don't want to have to look over my shoulder and wonder if I'm going to run into Aidan, or any of the Shaughnessys for that matter. This is for the best," Zoe said.

"For whom?" Anna asked.

Only now did she fully understand just how much Zoe had been going through, and she knew if she went to her friend and told her how she felt, Zoe would support her. Aidan would too. Hell, half the town probably would.

And it just made her feel even more pitiful than she already did.

Inside the ladies' room, she took several deep breaths to calm herself down and then washed her hands just for the sake of having something to do. Looking up at her reflection, she wanted to cry. She didn't even look like herself — her eyes were sad; she looked pale — it was as if Quinn had taken all the life out of her.

And he was here on a date.

With a centerfold.

Bastard.

Turning off the water, she reached for a paper towel to dry her hands and forced herself to relax. She breathed through the nausea rolling through her as she kept envisioning that woman with her hands all over Quinn. "You can do this," she murmured. "It's not like you haven't seen him on a date before." All she had to do was go back out to the booth, finish her drink, and leave. No one could accuse her of hiding out or being rude. She'd come, she'd socialized, and that was that. Zoe would explain to Aidan why she was leaving so soon and she'd deal with Dan another time.

One last look at her reflection and she fussed with her hair — not that it was helping. Just another delaying tactic. Maybe she could escape out the back door and just text Zoe that she'd left. She sighed. No, that was just rude, and it wasn't who she was. Dammit. One last attempt to finger comb her hair, and then she just gave up. It was getting too long and it occurred to her she no longer liked it. She wanted her old hair back. Hell, right now, she just wanted her old life back. *One thing at a time.* "Note to self, call the salon," she muttered as she took a steadying breath and opened the door.

And immediately walked into someone. "Sorry," she mumbled and moved to walk around them. Then she noticed it wasn't another woman trying to get into the ladies' room, but Quinn.

He didn't say a word; he simply moved forward until they were both in the bathroom and he locked the door behind him. The look in his eyes was murderous.

"You can't do that," she said lamely, pointing at the door. Quinn continued to advance on her until her back hit the wall. Her brown eyes went wide looking up at him and her throat went dry. Her fingers twitched with the need to touch him, but instead she just inhaled deeply. Then cursed herself because she loved the scent of his cologne. Up close, he looked weary, tired, and she wanted to stroke his jaw, his temple, like she used to, to ease his tension away.

"I guess everyone was right," he said, an edge to his voice. "You do belong with a guy in a suit."

"What? No, I'm not . . . I mean, we're not . . ." she said weakly as she shook her head. "That's Dan Michaels, remember? We just signed the papers on the beach house. He wanted to talk to Aidan about some business and so . . ." She couldn't finish the thought; her heart was racing and she could feel herself trembling.

"And you couldn't just give him Aidan's number?"

She rolled her eyes. "I mentioned how I was meeting Aidan and Zoe here and Dan asked if he could join us." Then she paused. "Why the hell am I even explaining myself to you?"

He shrugged and crowded her in even more. "Habit," he said, his voice sounding gruff. "You used to tell me everything. There was a time when you didn't turn and run away when things didn't go your way."

Anna raised her hands to shove at his chest, and he grabbed her wrists to stop her. "You have a hell of a nerve."

"I never claimed otherwise," he said. "If you're not dating him, he hasn't gotten the memo yet."

"What are you talking about?"

"You looked pretty cozy in the booth."

Anna rolled her eyes. "Oh, that's rich coming from you, the man who was getting felt up at the bar. How long have you been dating Miss September out there? An hour? Twenty minutes?"

He chuckled but there was no humor. "An hour. Why? Keeping track?"

Beyond angry, Anna pulled her wrists free of his grasp. "No. It's just humorous to see how quickly you reverted to type."

His gaze hardened as he leaned in closer, until they were almost nose to nose. "If memory serves, I was more than willing to go against type and I loved it." He cursed under his breath and looked away for a minute. When he lifted his head, his expression was unusually calm. "And really, the same could be said for you. Dan's exactly the type of guy you used to always go for — the type of guy everyone thought you'd end up with. I guess they were right. So why is it all right for you to revert and not me?"

She didn't have an answer — mainly because she knew he had a point. Her mind was screaming for her to just move around him and leave — she knew Quinn wouldn't hold her there against her will — but being this close to him after so much time apart was almost a sweet form of torture.

"Quinn . . ." She meant to put a little force behind her words, to make it seem like she was strong, but it came out more like a breathy plea.

"Yeah . . . I know," he said as he lowered his head and captured her lips with his. His hands immediately cupped her face, his thumbs stroking her cheeks. Over and over his lips slanted over hers, his tongue teasing hers.

A helpless moan came out before she could stop it as her arms came up and wrapped around him. In the back of her mind, she knew this was wrong, this wasn't going to make walking away again any easier, but right now she wanted him, needed him. Her hands came around and rested on his chest and just as they were about to curl into his shirt, he pulled away.

His breathing was just as ragged as hers, and she knew immediately that he was frustrated and angry but didn't understand why. Instead of speaking, Quinn turned and punched the wall. The sound echoed in the small confines of the room, causing her to jump. He reached for the door and looked at her over his shoulder.

Tears almost blinded her as she looked at him.

"Good-bye, Anna," he said, his voice low, broken.

Once the door closed behind him, Anna sank to the floor and cried.

CHAPTER 12

Two weeks later, Anna was back at the pub.

The only reason she was able to convince herself to do it was because it was a private party. Her brother was leaving, moving, and they were having his going away party. Steve, the owner of the pub, was standing with his arm around Anna as they watched everyone mingling.

Steve was a sixty-five-year-old Navy vet, and this place had been in his family since forever. He'd always treated Anna like the daughter he never had. Steve had no kids, no family left, and it always made Anna feel good to help him out and take care of him.

"You know, this place hasn't been the same since you quit," he said. She'd had more than her fair share of guilt since leaving, but Steve had understood her reasoning.

"You seem to be doing okay," she said, smiling up at him.

He shrugged. "I'm getting too old for this. I'm thinking of moving someplace tropical."

"And then what would you do?"

"Open a bar," Steve said with a big grin.

Anna elbowed him in the ribs. "Then why move? You already have a bar!"

"Anna, I'm getting old. Other than my time in the navy, I've lived here my whole life. I think I'd enjoy someplace tropical. Plus, a couple of buddies of mine are thinking of going in on it with me."

"Not you too! What is it with everyone suddenly needing to move away from here? This is a great place to live!"

He nodded. "No one's saying it isn't, but I'm ready for a change."

She sighed. "What about the pub?"

"Well, I heard there was this sassy new Realtor on the block who seems to be responsible for selling half the houses around here." He looked at her with pride. "You did good, kid. I know it's not your dream job, but as usual, you totally rocked it."

Tears welled in her eyes. "Yeah, well . . . sink or swim, you know?" She shrugged. "I chose to swim."

"You always do." Steve looked around the room and took a step away from Anna. "I need to go and check on the food and make sure Johnny's okay in the kitchen. I hate leaving that kid alone back there."

"He's not so bad, Steve."

"Yeah, but he ain't you, Anna," he said with a wink. "Do me a favor? Hang around after the party. I really want to talk to you."

"You got it." Watching Steve get swallowed up by the crowd, Anna couldn't believe just how many people were there. Besides her own family, Ian and Martha were there along with Aidan and Zoe and Hugh and Aubrey. Hugh and Aubrey had surprised her, but it seemed Hugh was finally starting to relax with his wife and come to grips with the fact that she was more than capable of leaving the house without being encased in bubble wrap.

It was incredibly sweet.

There was a large percentage of the local police force in the room, and while Anna knew most of them, there were a few unfamiliar faces. Zoe stepped up beside her. "How's it going?"

"Good," Anna said. "I still can't believe he's leaving. I thought he was just going to go for a week and check it out and decide it wasn't all he thought it would be. I never thought he'd really move."

Aidan walked over and kissed Anna on the cheek before putting his arm around his wife. "What are we talking about?"

"I was just saying I can't believe Bobby's really moving," Anna said with a bit of a pout.

"He's not going to be that far away. It's going to be good for him and he seems happy about it," Aidan said.

"I suppose." Anna looked around the room and spotted a woman she had never seen before. "I wonder who she is?"

"She's Bobby's partner. On the police force," Aidan said as if it were obvious.

"Wait . . . *what?* But she's a . . . a . . . She's, um . . ."

"A she?" Zoe said.

"Exactly!" Anna cried. "No wonder he was freaking out."

Aidan looked around uncomfortably. "Anyone need their drinks refreshed?"

"What?" Zoe asked. "What do you know?"

"Nothing. It's . . . it's nothing."

"Uh, yeah. Okay," Anna said with a chuckle. "You know something, so spill it."

"You mean you know something and you didn't share it with me?" Zoe asked with mock offense. "I thought we told each other everything!"

"Okay, fine." Aidan sighed dramatically. "Bobby was a little put out that they paired him up with a woman and at the same time they almost demoted him while they re-structured the department."

"That's just crazy. I can't believe my brother is so sexist."

"It's not that," Aidan said and began to look around for an escape.

"Then what is it?" Anna asked impatiently.

"He kind of . . . He's . . . Well . . ."

"Oh, just spit it out, Aidan!" Zoe demanded.

"He's kind of really attracted to her!" he hissed.

"No!" Anna and Zoe said in unison.

Aidan nodded. "But you did *not* hear it from me," he warned them both and then rolled his eyes. "Honestly, when did I become the town gossip?" he mumbled as he walked away.

"That was fun," Zoe said as she watched her husband's retreating back. "So you really had no idea about this female partner thing?"

Anna shook her head. "Not a clue. Bobby hasn't said a word. At least not to me." She sighed. "I guess I've been so busy having my own pity party he didn't think he could talk to me. I hate that. I'll have to make sure we get some time to hang out, just the two of us, before he leaves."

Zoe nodded and took a sip of her beer. "I

saw you talking to Steve earlier. Was he begging you to go and help out in the kitchen?"

"No." Anna chuckled. "But he did mention wanting to move to someplace tropical and open up a bar with his navy buddies."

"But what about the pub?"

Anna shrugged. "I think he's going to sell it. He asked me to stick around after the party to talk to him about it and he was praising my real estate skills, so I'm guessing that's what he wants."

"Wow . . . just . . . wow. Too many damn changes lately."

"You got that right." And as true as it was, Anna knew not all of them were bad. She was surrounded by so many amazing people, and even though she contemplated jumping on the moving truck with Bobby, she knew she would miss all of this far too much if she did. The people. The places.

Quinn.

Dammit. She had sworn to herself she wouldn't think about him tonight. That lasted all of thirty minutes. Good grief, when was that going to end? If she was going to stay in town — and she was — she was going to have to learn to coexist with Quinn. They'd known each other too long and knew too many of the same people to avoid each other forever.

"So what about you, my friend? What's next for you?" Zoe asked as she maneuvered the two of them to a quieter corner.

"I'm not really sure. Things are finally going well with real estate. It's not my dream job, you know, but I'm finally out from under the mountain of debt I had."

"I know that's got to feel good." Zoe smiled.

"It does. But other than that, I don't have any plans. Work, work, and more work. I think I may want to do some renovations and updates on the house."

"Why don't you sell it? You can afford something a little bit newer and bigger now."

"What do I need a bigger house for? It's just me," Anna said sadly. "Maybe I'll get a cat. Or two."

"Oh no you don't. You're not going to become that person. I won't allow it. There's no need to do anything drastic!"

"For crying out loud, Zoe," Anna laughed, "it's just a cat!"

"That's how it starts! Then it's two cats, then four, and the next thing you know, you're sleeping on the couch because the cats have taken over your bed!" She grabbed Anna by the shoulders and shook her. "Don't do it!" They broke out in fits of laughter and Zoe pulled her in for a hug.

"It's gonna get better, sweetie. I promise."

It was two in the morning and Anna was exhausted. She was helping Steve clean up — all of the guests were gone and only a couple of pub employees were still there. She yawned widely and Steve chuckled. "Subtle, Anna. Come on, come sit down and talk with me."

She followed him over to a booth and sat. "So I'm guessing you want me to get the ball in motion for you to put the place on the market."

He shook his head. "No. I've been thinking about this for a while, and this place has been in my family since I was a kid. My grandparents started it — hell, my grandfather built it. It's not a great place, but it's been good to me and my family." He shrugged. "I worked hard to keep up with everything and I'm proud of all I accomplished."

Anna reached over and squeezed his hand. "And you should be! This place is a local legend. An institution! Everyone who grew up here has a memory of coming to the pub. You and your family created something great, Steve."

"That's why I can't sell it, Anna," he said, smiling sadly at her. "I'd rather see it close down than have strangers in here changing everything. Or worse yet, having some big corporation buy it and turn it into one of those chain restaurants or something."

She didn't think he had to worry about that but decided to keep it to herself. "I hate the thought of this place closing, but I understand."

Again he shook his head. "But I'm not going to close it. I'm going to give it to a family member."

She looked at him oddly. "But you don't have any family left. You've always said that." Then she gasped. "Did you find some long-lost cousins or a secret child you didn't know you had?"

The bark of laughter nearly shook the walls. "Oh, Anna! You have quite the imagination!"

"I don't think it's so out of the realm of possibility," she said primly. "You hear about things like that happening all the time. You watch daytime TV. You know I'm right."

"Sweetheart, believe me, there are no Steve Jr.'s running around in this world. I can guarantee it."

"And the long-lost cousin?" she prompted.

"Afraid not."

Anna leaned back against her seat. "Well,

then I'm stumped."

Steve seemed to blush a little as he fidgeted in his seat. "Anna," he began, "I took a risk hiring you when you were fresh out of college. But you were a fast learner and you always knew how to make everyone around you smile. Hell, I was a grumpy old man even back then, and you came in here like a breath of fresh air and a ray of sunshine rolled into one."

"Steve," she said with a soft sigh.

He reached out and took one of her hands in his. "I watched you grow up here. You came here at a time when I was ready to call it quits. I was tired and unmotivated and pretty much resented everything and everybody."

"You weren't so bad."

He tugged on her hand and laughed. "You don't need to sugarcoat it. I was a pain in the ass, and you used to call me on it daily." He paused. "You turned this place around and breathed new life into it. Now, I know you've been working in real estate for a while, and I know why you went into it, and if you're happy, then we'll just forget we ever had this conversation. But if you . . . you know . . . if you want to take on something else, something of your own, I want to sign the business over to you."

"What?" she gasped.

He nodded. "You're the only family I have, Anna. You are like the daughter I never had, and I would be honored if you'd let me do this for you."

"But . . . but . . . Steve, I don't have the kind of money it would take to buy this place! I couldn't possibly —"

"You're not listening to me, Anna. I'm not asking you to buy me out. I want to sign it all over to you. We can just put your name on the corporation and all the accounts, and it would be a done deal. I'm debt free," he went on. "The business has been doing really well, and I have an account set up for business expenses that would be yours. There's enough to cover all the monthly stuff for at least a year, plus money to do any improvements you'd like."

She stared at him wide-eyed, certain she must be dreaming. "I . . . I don't know. I mean, it's not a big secret that I'm not in love with selling houses, but . . . wow. This is huge, Steve. This is really, really huge."

"I know," he said solemnly. "And I don't want you to answer me right now. I want you to take some time to think about it. I'm not in a rush, and we can take our time transitioning, and then when you're ready, you can throw me out."

"I would never do that," she said, unable to help the smile on her face. "I don't even know what to say."

He squeezed her hand one more time. "Promise me you'll think about it."

As if she'd be able to think about anything else.

For three in the morning, Anna was pretty wide-awake. She'd left the pub after hugging Steve until her arms went numb and then sat in her car for several minutes still trying to wrap her brain around what had just happened. At one time, she had considered the possibility of buying the pub from Steve, but she knew, financially, she couldn't do it.

I want to sign it all over to you.

Right then, she really wished someone would pinch her so she'd know she hadn't had too much to drink and was only dreaming. "I need to get home," she murmured, starting the car. Sitting still, Anna let the car warm up a bit. She was grateful to her brother, but this car wasn't in as great condition as Anna would have hoped. There was a bit of a chill in the air, and it took a few minutes for the heat to kick in.

Dammit, she missed her Honda.

And not her old Honda, but the new,

shiny one she had stupidly given back to Quinn. "Should have kept it," she said in disgust. "I'd be on my way by now, and warm."

Pulling out of the parking lot, Anna drove the deserted streets with a smile. This was her town. Her home. What Steve was offering her was an amazing opportunity and, if she was honest, a dream come true. She wasn't happy selling houses, but it had helped her achieve financial stability. Anna knew if she did take over the pub, she'd not only have the financial backing from Steve and his business accounts, but she'd also have breathing room because of her own smart decisions from her commissions.

Maybe she'd hold on to her real estate license and do it as an on-the-side thing if need be but put her primary focus on the pub. "Okay, pros and cons," she said out loud. "Pros, no more dresses and high heels. Cons, go back to everyone looking at me as Anna the tomboy."

Hmm . . . not off to a solid start.

Racking her brain, she tried to think of more pros. "I can cook as much as I like — pro! I'll never have to be the low man on the totem pole — pro!" She giggled, feeling a little bit giddy. "I'll be spending every day surrounded by friends! Pro!" She laughed

again. "This is kind of fun! I could redeco-
rate a little bit with Zoe's help and then —"

POP!

Anna let out a small scream as the car immediately began to swerve. She tried to
regain control but wasn't sure what exactly
had happened. She hit the brakes and carefully pulled over to the side of the road.
Cursing under her breath, she shut off the
car and took a few seconds to let her heart
rate slow back down.

"Holy crap." Climbing from the car, she
walked around it and found she had blown
a tire. "Well, this just sucks." Stamping her
foot, she popped open the trunk and was
grateful she had taken the course that
taught her how to change a tire.

The only problem? It was pitch-black
outside and she was on a side road with
nothing around, and she was majorly
freaked out. Jumping back into the car, she
slammed the door, locked it, reached for
her cell phone, and immediately called
Bobby. She hated to do it at such a late
hour, but it was an emergency.

"Hey, you've reached Bobby. I can't take
your call right now —"

"Dammit!" she yelled and disconnected
the call. She thought about calling her dad,
but she knew he'd never even hear the

phone at this hour. With no other choice, she dialed Zoe's number and prayed their friendship could withstand a middle-of-the-night tire change.

"H'lo."

"Hey, Zoe, it's me," Anna said softly.

"Anna? You okay?"

"Yeah . . . kind of. I blew a tire and I'm over on Elm and it's pitch-black, and I was wondering if you could send Aidan to help me."

No response.

"Zoe? Zoe, you there?" she asked a little louder.

"What? Oh, shoot . . . Sorry, Anna. I sort of dozed for a minute."

"Crap, I'm sorry. I know it's late but I don't know what else to do. I think I can change the tire myself, but it's so dark out and it's freaking me out."

"Okay, okay . . . o . . . kay . . ."

Anna heard a very distinct snore and then the connection was lost. "Well . . . shit!" Unwilling to give up just yet, she tried her parents and got no answer and even went so far as to call the pub, but Steve was already gone and she knew he'd had enough to drink that she wouldn't feel good about having him driving around any more than he had to tonight.

She wanted to cry. How was it possible that she knew so many people and there wasn't anyone to help her? The clock on her phone now read three forty-five and all she wanted was to be home in bed.

Her last resort was to call AAA. She waited through all the recorded messages, and when she finally got a live person on the line, she told them her issue, her location, and her member ID number and was finally feeling optimistic.

"We'll have a tow truck to you in three hours," the operator said.

"What! How is that even possible?"

"There was a multicar accident on Route 74 and all the local trucks responded to it. There's a chance one can get to you sooner, but I can't guarantee it."

Anna groaned. Her first thought was how she hoped no one was injured. And while she desperately needed help right now, her only problem was a flat tire. A multicar accident usually meant much more extensive damage. There was no way she could begrudge them for getting the help they needed. The reality was that she could change the tire. She just didn't want to.

"Ma'am? Are you still there?"

"I am."

"Someone will call you when they are

thirty minutes out. Will that be all right?"

"You know what? It's okay, just cancel the request."

"Ma'am, are you sure?"

"Yeah. I'm sure. I'll . . . I'll just find another option. But thank you."

"Okay. Have a good night!"

Anna wanted to reach through the phone and slap the operator upside the head. "Have a good night"? For real? This was a nightmare and she had clearly exhausted all of her options.

With a huff, she climbed from the car again with her phone in her hand for light and began to search in the trunk for everything she'd need to change the tire. On a good day — as in full daylight — it took her almost thirty minutes to change a tire. There wasn't a doubt in her mind she was going to double that.

Ninety minutes later, she was done.

She was exhausted, sweaty, and filthy, and was practically seeing double from lack of sleep. Slamming the trunk closed, Anna stumbled to the driver's side door and pulled — and almost fell back on her ass. On her second attempt, she managed to get it open and then just stood there as if trying to remember what she was doing.

Off in the distance, the sun wasn't even

close to being up but she did see a light. "This is it," she sighed wearily. "This is how it ends. I'm seeing the light. Changing a tire killed me." She yawned and rested her head on the roof of the car. "I hope they don't put that on my headstone."

Somewhere nearby, she heard a car door slam and her head shot up as she looked around. Was she in the car? Did she close the door?

"Anna? What the . . . ?"

Quinn? Now she knew she was dreaming. Or dead.

Quinn didn't talk to her anymore and that was just fine with her. She looked over her shoulder and saw him sprinting toward her just as her knees gave out and everything went black.

Quinn drove with one eye on the road, the other on Anna. She had taken twenty years off his life when he watched her eyes roll back in her head and she started to fall to the ground. All night, he had cursed how he couldn't sleep but now he was thankful for it. It was why he was driving around at this hour — he was going to the shop because he couldn't stay in bed staring at the ceiling any longer.

He wished he knew what had happened

to her but she was out cold. Pulling up in his driveway — his house was closer than hers — he quickly jumped out and ran around to the passenger side and picked her up. Once he had her inside, he strode through to his bedroom and placed her down on the bed.

"Anna? Anna, baby? Come on, wake up for me, sweetheart." He stroked her cheek and looked for any signs of injury. Other than being dirty — like she'd been working on a car — she appeared unhurt.

Running from the room, Quinn went to the kitchen and poured her some water and then was immediately back at her side. "Anna, please, honey. Open those eyes. Let me see those beautiful brown eyes. Please."

She didn't stir. Not sure of what else to do, he was about to call 9-1-1 when she moved. He whispered her name and watched as she tried to open her eyes and focus on him. He said her name again.

"Dream Quinn . . . you need to stop talking," she mumbled and rolled over.

Dream Quinn? "Wait . . . Anna . . . what happened? Why were you on the side of the road?"

She sighed loudly and rolled over. "Jeez, even in my dreams you can't just be quiet and let me have my way, can you?"

She was so adorable and obviously not really awake and yet Quinn couldn't stop looking at her, talking to her in hopes of figuring out what had happened. "Baby, I need to make sure you're all right. Are you hurt?"

A loud yawn was her only response.

Quinn repeated the question.

"Just my heart," she said as her eyes started to close. "You broke my heart."

"I know," he said quietly, and leaned in and placed a kiss on her temple and then watched in mild amusement as she kicked her shoes off. She was dressed in a pair of jeans and a plain blue T-shirt and looked every inch the girl he'd always known.

"Sleep," she slurred. "Flat tire. Too hard to change . . . even with the classes, but I did it." Another yawn. "I don't need you anymore, dream Quinn."

And with that one statement, he felt his own heart break again. Unable to help himself, he ran his fingers through her hair and caressed her cheek. She hummed for a minute — just like she always had in her sleep when he'd touched her. With a sigh, he rested his forehead against hers and whispered her name.

"But I miss you," she whispered and then her head lolled to the side and she let out a soft snore.

It wasn't much.

Hell, it was barely audible.

But those few words gave Quinn more hope than he'd had in a very long time. Standing up, he covered her with a blanket, turned out the light, and left the room so she could sleep. Out in the living room, he got things in motion to get her car towed to the shop and to have all the tires checked.

Once that was done, he made a few other calls — and woke a bunch of people up — to let them know he wasn't coming in to the shop today, he'd be in touch, and he wasn't to be disturbed unless it was an absolute emergency.

He put the phone down and looked toward his bedroom door. Anna was here and he wasn't going to let her leave until they finally talked things out. He'd given her the space she asked for, and ever since that kiss two weeks ago, he'd barely been able to think straight.

He loved her.

That wasn't going away, and it wasn't going to change.

And after hearing her small admission that she missed him, Quinn was hopeful that maybe Anna still loved him too. Somehow, they had to make things work out. Yeah, he had a little explaining to do — like why he'd been out on a date — but she'd been out on one too! After seeing her at the café with that guy — who he now knew was Dan Michaels — Quinn had gone a little crazy.

The date had been a mistake. He'd known it as soon as he'd agreed to it. Sandy was someone he'd gone out with a time or two a long time ago, and when he'd run into her that same afternoon and she'd invited him to go for drinks, he'd said yes mainly out of desperation. It had killed him to think of Anna with someone else, but he knew if she was moving on, he had no choice but to move on as well.

But after he had kissed Anna in the ladies' room, Quinn knew he couldn't do it. He'd gone back out to the bar and faked an emergency at the shop and left. Sandy hadn't seemed overly upset and he hadn't heard from her since.

It wasn't until a week later that Aidan fessed up and told him how Anna really wasn't dating Dan and it had been a business meeting. Quinn wanted to kick himself. She had essentially told him the same thing in the bathroom, but he'd been too riled up to listen. Seeing Dan with his arm around her and sitting so close to her in the pub had pretty much pushed every one of his buttons.

And now look where he was.

A quivering mass who was afraid to go into his own bedroom. Anna had obviously had a rough night, and the last thing he wanted to do was upset her even more.

Unfortunately, for the first time in months, he genuinely felt ready to go to sleep. He looked over at his couch and grimaced. It was too small and it wasn't comfortable. He kicked off his shoes and poured himself a glass of juice. He finished it in two great big gulps and then looked toward the bedroom again. He wanted to sleep, and he wanted to hold Anna while he did it.

"Of course you do, you selfish bastard," he cursed himself. "Glad to see you're only thinking of yourself, as usual."

Yeah, he pretty much despised himself right now.

Walking around the house, he locked up and turned off the few lights he'd turned on. It was a little after six in the morning, and he had a feeling Anna was going to sleep until at least noon. He had a second bedroom and Quinn had resigned himself to sleeping in there when he heard Anna call his name. It was soft at first, then a little louder.

Cautiously, he opened the bedroom door

and stepped inside. "You okay?" he whispered.

"What . . . ? How did I get here?"

Quinn sat down on the edge of the bed, not trusting himself to get too close to her. "I just happened to be heading in to the shop early and I found you parked on the side of the road. What happened?"

Slowly, Anna sat up and ran a hand through her hair and Quinn could tell she was still disoriented. "What time is it?"

"It's a little after six."

"We had Bobby's going away party at the pub last night. I stayed afterward, to talk with Steve." She yawned. "I didn't leave until after three. I blew a tire. I tried calling everyone and no one answered."

"Why didn't you call me?" he asked softly.

She gave him a wry look. "I know how to change a tire. It was just a little more . . . challenging when it was pitch-black out."

"So you changed the tire?"

She nodded and yawned. "It took me over an hour. By the time I was done, I was near delirious. I guess that's when you found me."

"I'm glad I did." He was almost shaking with the thought of what would have happened if he hadn't come along at that point. "I'm glad you didn't try to drive home."

404

"Speaking of . . . I really do need to get home. I'm exhausted and . . . and . . . and I shouldn't be here."

"Anna, it's really early and you're exhausted, and to be honest, so am I. I was just going to the guest room to grab a couple hours of sleep."

"But you just said you had been heading to the shop," she reminded him.

He nodded. "I was, but you scared the hell out of me and I haven't been sleeping well, and suddenly I feel like I might actually be able to sleep."

"Oh."

He looked at her, studying her face in the dimly lit room. She was so beautiful. How had he looked at her face for so many years and not realized that?

Anna made no attempt to lie back down.

Quinn made no attempt to get up and leave the room.

He saw her swallow hard and then lick her lips. He wanted to do that for her — lick her lips and then every inch of her. But it was too soon to hope he'd ever be allowed to do that again. He willed her to say something, anything — preferably to ask him to stay — but she just continued to watch him warily.

Resigned, he stood. "Get some sleep. I'll

take you to get your car later. Don't be mad but I had it towed to the shop. You know, just so it wouldn't be sitting there on the road. You need to be safe."

Silently, she nodded.

So did he. "Okay then." Quinn turned to leave the room when Anna whispered his name. He stopped and looked over at her. "Are you okay? Do you need something? I put a glass of water on the nightstand for you."

"Don't go."

If he hadn't been watching her, he wouldn't have been sure she had indeed spoken the words. He sighed her name.

"Please."

And then he was lost to anything and everything but Anna. He pulled his shirt over his head and watched as she slowly stood and peeled her jeans off. He followed her lead, and in seconds, he was down to nothing but his boxer briefs. Anna did that funky little trick where she took her bra off without taking her shirt off. He loved that trick but would have loved seeing her without a shirt too.

Crawling back into the bed, Anna lay back and waited for him. Unsure of how he was going to survive being this close to her and just sleeping, he said a silent prayer and then climbed in beside her.

Without asking, she curled up beside him — her head on his shoulder, her hand over his heart. Which was just as well, because it belonged to her.

The next time Anna opened her eyes, she really believed she was still dreaming. She was in Quinn's bed, in his arms, and everything seemed just right. Sighing happily, she snuggled closer. She loved these dreams. In them, they were always still together and he loved her and had begged her to take him back — after she'd made him grovel for a little while.

Yeah, she loved these dreams.

His arm tightened around her, and if it was possible, that one simple act made her feel a myriad of emotions — safe, protected, cherished. Another sigh. Her thigh was wrapped around his. In her dreams, they were both always naked — mainly because of the hot and steamy sex they always had. But when she shifted her leg, she could feel his boxer briefs. Then she moved again and realized she had on a T-shirt.

Oh crap . . . Everything came crashing back to her. The party. The tire. Quinn. Her mind began to scramble for a way out — a way to excuse her practically begging him to sleep with her without making her look pathetic. Plus, she really wanted to leave just in case one of his new girlfriends decided to drop by. Ugh . . . that would just about kill her.

"I never thought someone's brain could be so loud, Anna, but yours could compete with a freight train," Quinn murmured right before placing a kiss on the top of her head.

She squirmed against him, but Quinn held her firm. "I need to get up."

"No."

She struggled a little harder and cursed a blue streak when he wrapped his other arm around her. "Dammit, Quinn . . . let me up!"

"I don't think so," he said mildly.

With a loud sigh, she ceased moving. "Fine. Happy now?"

"Did you sleep okay?"

Anna wanted to punch him. Like seriously inflict major pain on him. "I guess."

"Mmm . . . good," he said.

They lay there like that until Anna was certain she'd go mad. "You can't keep me here forever, you know. Eventually you'll have to move."

"I'm not so sure. I'm pretty content just like this. I don't have any place to go and no one's gonna call, so . . . really, I'm good."

Yeah, she was gonna punch him hard. "Dammit, Quinn, come on. Maybe you don't have anything to do today, but I do." His grasp instantly loosened, and she took full advantage to put some distance between them and sit up. Frantically, she looked around the room and spotted her jeans and bra, and was about to swing her legs out of the bed when Quinn reached out and put a hand on her arm.

"Don't," he said softly. "Not yet."

Anna looked over at the clock — it was almost one in the afternoon — and groaned. "It's late. I need to get my car." When she met his gaze, she saw the defeated look on his face — it was something she'd never seen before. And suddenly, she didn't feel so good about herself or about how she was just thinking about him. She started to say his name, but he was rolling out of the bed and pulling his jeans on.

"Just give me five minutes and we'll go," he said as he walked out of the room.

That was it? He wasn't going to argue with her or force her to listen to him? She looked around in confusion — as if she were in the middle of a *Twilight Zone* episode. Jumping up from the bed, she stepped over her pile of clothes and walked out of the room after him.

Why she couldn't just be thankful he was being agreeable she couldn't say. But for some reason, his quiet acceptance was more irritating, more insulting than his arguments ever were.

"So that's it?" she called after him. He was standing in the middle of his living room and he turned and looked at her in confusion. "You hold me in a death grip, telling me I can't leave, and then just —"

"Agree and let you leave?" he finished for her, but there was very little emotion in his voice.

"Well . . . yeah." She studied him. He'd lost weight, he needed a haircut, and . . . he bore little resemblance to the man she'd always known.

He shrugged. "What is it you want from me, Anna?" he asked sadly. "When I argue with you, you're pissed. When I playfully disagree with you, you're pissed. And when I give you exactly what you ask for, you're pissed. Baby, I can't seem to win. So if you'll just tell me exactly what it is you want, I'll do it. I'd do anything for you, Anna."

Slowly, she advanced on him, her eyes never leaving his. When she was only inches away, she stopped.

For a minute, Quinn looked hopeful —

like he took it as a good sign she wasn't fighting with him and maybe, just maybe she was coming to him to hold him, hug him, forgive him.

He was wrong.

With everything she had, Anna reared back and punched him in the stomach. His loud *oomph* filled the room as he staggered backward. "What do I want from you?" she cried. "I want to know why it is you can go from being this amazing man one minute to a colossal jackass the next!"

"What? When . . . ?"

"Every day, all the time," she responded sarcastically. "Do you have any idea how many changes I put myself through to be the perfect woman for you, you big jerk?"

"I never asked you to!" he said defensively. "There wasn't anything wrong with you!"

She punched him again — this time in the arm.

Hard enough that her knuckles stung.

"I changed the way I dressed! The way I did my hair! My job! Hell, I even took some stupid classes on automotive repair so we'd have that in common! And you know what? I hated it! All that engine grease and dirt — it was disgusting!"

"You said you enjoyed learning about all that stuff!" he argued.

"Yeah, well . . ." She huffed. "Okay, it was interesting. But I don't want to make a career out of it. And that's not the point! I did so much and made myself crazy to get your attention! But did you even notice? No!"

Quinn quickly stepped back and moved behind one of the living room chairs to put some distance between them. "I didn't know! I never wanted you to change, Anna! You were perfect the way you were!"

"Clearly I wasn't!" she argued and began to walk toward him. She chuckled when he looked around for an escape route. "For years I did everything I could to make you see me — really see me — but you didn't. And then finally — finally! — you did, and I still wasn't enough for you!"

He held up a hand to stop her advance. "That's not true. Anna, I swear. It's not true."

Something in his tone made her stop. She waited for him to continue.

"You know me better than anyone, Anna. You know me better than my own family — you always have. I may come off as being confident and self-centered, but I'm really not. I'm afraid to fail. I've always been afraid to fail. And if I ever think there's a chance of that happening, I bail." He shared

412

with her the conversation he'd had with his father. "And then there was you."

She looked at him quizzically. "Why would we fail?"

He stepped out from behind the chair with a bit of fire in his eyes as he turned the tables and began to advance on her. "Why would we fail? You mean other than the fact that every single person we know pointed out how I didn't deserve you? Like I wasn't good enough to even touch you? Or maybe because no matter what I tried, I was never going to be as considerate and thoughtful toward you as you are to me? And believe me, people had a field day reminding me of that one!"

"Why didn't you tell me? You know, you and I used to tell each other everything. Some would say we shared too much! But as soon as we went from being friends to lovers, you stopped talking to me!"

"I did not!" he denied fiercely. "We talked every day, all damn day!"

"No, we talked about safe stuff — work, what we wanted to eat, or what movie we wanted to watch, the basics — but you never shared with me how much everyone was freaking you out. Not until I pushed. And I never had to do that before."

His shoulders sagged. "When have you

ever known me to admit a weakness?" He waited a moment and before she could answer, he added, "But I never had to with you — because you always knew. You knew and you helped me. Only now . . . now you weren't looking, and I felt like you were judging me for them."

"Me?"

He nodded. "For as long as we've known each other, we talked about everything, and you stopped talking just as much as I did. And when everyone was making those comments about me not being good enough for you, you didn't exactly correct them."

"What was I supposed to say?"

"Oh, I don't know, how about that I *was* good enough? Or maybe that you loved me for who I am and not some stupid image everyone had built up for you?"

He had a point there. She hadn't said a whole lot to defend him. Wait . . . he almost had her again! "So because I wasn't playing cheerleader for you, I deserved to be taken for granted?"

"I'm not perfect, Anna!" he shouted and raked a hand through his hair. He began to pace and let out a growl of frustration. "I'm never going to be perfect! And you know what? I didn't think I would have to be with you! Everywhere we ever went when we were just friends, no one questioned us being together. But suddenly I've got my arm around you or look at you differently, and all of a sudden people are looking at me like I've committed some federal offense by touching you! Do you know how it made me feel?"

Anna opened her mouth to speak, but he stopped her.

"But now? Being without you all this time? I'd gladly take the comments, the looks, the sneers . . . all of it. I'll take it, and hell, I even agree with them. I don't deserve you. I never deserved you. But I need you." His voice cracked. "I love you, Anna. I know I screwed up and I hurt you, but if you could find it in your heart to give me another chance, I promise to spend the rest of my life making it up to you."

"Quinn," she sighed.

"I sent Jake's cars back," he said quickly. "I never should have agreed to work on them. Even though you said it was okay, I should have known you were being selfless — for me. I was so busy paying attention to what I wanted for the business that I let you down. I don't need that kind of fame and attention. Not if I have you."

"Quinn," she said a little more firmly, a smile beginning to form.

"I know I'm begging . . . Hell, I'm groveling. I'm not good at it, and you're probably wishing you could just leave — my truck keys are on the counter. You can take them and go. I won't stop you." He shook his head. "I should have just taken you home earlier. I took away your choices — again. Shit. See? I'm standing here talking about trying not to screw up and I'm even screwing that up!" He closed his eyes and turned away from her. "Really . . . just take the keys and —"

Anna's lips claiming his stopped his words. She had to work a little harder to get him to give in, but once he did, he simply consumed her. Quinn's arms instantly banded around her, pulling her close, and he kissed her until they were both falling to their knees, gasping for air.

"I love you, Anna Hannigan," he said, raining kisses all over her face, her throat. His hands reached down to the hem of her T-shirt and began to wander upward, taking the garment with him. "I love you so damn much."

"I love you too," she sighed, relishing the feel of those work-roughened hands on her skin. She never thought she'd feel them again except in her dreams. "I missed you."

"I missed you too, baby." He sighed and

then groaned when his hands cupped her breasts. "This may not be the right time, but it kind of feels like it is, and I need you, Anna. It's been so long. Please, baby."

Leaning back, Anna pulled her T-shirt over her head and pressed against him. Quinn's chest was still bare and the skin-on-skin contact was glorious. "Yes," she sighed, anxious to feel the rest of him.

She gasped with surprise when he scooped her up in his arms and walked across the room. She was perfectly content right there in the middle of the living room, but the thought of Quinn and a soft mattress was far more exciting.

When he had her sprawled across the bed, he simply stood back and looked at her — like a hungry man eyeing a feast. "You're mine, Anna," he said, his voice a low growl. "You've always been mine, and from this point forward, everyone's going to know it."

No words had ever sounded sweeter.

"Of course, they're not going to know it today because I plan on keeping you right here with me for the rest of the day, all of the night, and probably well into tomorrow." Shucking his jeans and briefs, he joined her on the bed and then froze. "Oh shit . . . wait. You said you had someplace to be." He started to jump up. "Okay . . .

okay. I can wait. We can go and do whatever it is you need to do and come back here later."

The poor man was sweating and trembling, and Anna started to laugh.

"What? What's so funny?"

She rolled her eyes. "I don't have anything to do. Well, I do need to make some calls, but other than that, I'm completely free."

"But you said —"

"Yeah, yeah, yeah . . . I was being a brat and making you suffer a little bit. I was embarrassed about my behavior earlier, how I practically begged you to sleep with me."

"Believe me, you didn't need to beg." And then he crawled back onto the bed and covered her body with his. "So we're good here? No one needs to leave?"

Anna shook her head. "Not for a very long time."

A slow, sexy grin crossed his face. "That's good because the things I have planned are going to take a very long time."

"Quinn?"

"Hmm?"

"Stop talking. You know how I love a man of action," she said with a sexy grin of her own.

And then he spent the rest of the day being exactly the man she wanted.

CHAPTER 13

"I saw your picture in the paper last week," Anna said. It was two in the morning, and they were in bed after just finishing a late-night dinner of leftover Chinese food.

Quinn groaned. "I didn't mind the article, but the picture was corny."

She chuckled. "It certainly wasn't your best photo."

He pulled her in close and kissed her. "That's because you weren't there with me."

"So tell me about these cars."

He sighed and shifted to get comfortable, hating to bring up a sore subject. "Remember the reporter who was in my shop that day?"

Anna nodded.

"Well, when I sent the cars back to Jake, he reached out to me and said he knew a couple of collectors who were looking for a restoration guy like me."

"Quinn, that's great!" She turned her

head to look at him.

He shrugged. "There's more. Basically, the magazine likes to have several restorers they keep on staff, so to speak, and are able to follow their jobs from start to finish. They offered me a position."

"Oh my gosh! That's even better!" She leaned forward and kissed him and then pulled back. "Wait . . . why aren't you more excited about this?"

"Well . . . I don't get to pick the cars. So I could get some really cool cars, and I could get some not-so-cool ones."

Beside him, she groaned. "Dude, all cars can be cool. You need to change your attitude a bit. I mean, you probably won't get to work on any Australian muscle cars — they are considered some of the best in the world — but . . ."

And then he laughed and rolled her beneath him. "God, I love you," he said and then kissed her thoroughly. "You're perfect for me, Anna."

"Yeah, well . . . sometimes you just need a swift kick in the ass."

He chuckled. "I've heard that before — recently, as a matter of fact."

"Whoever said it was extremely wise."

She had no idea how accurate she was. "You're right. I need to have a better attitude. I haven't given them my answer yet, so —"

"Why not?"

Quinn rested his forehead against hers. "Because I would need to make this shop my home base, and all this time we were apart, I was going crazy. It was hell for me to live this close to you and not see you. So I was thinking of going back on the road and doing that whole lifestyle again."

Anna cradled his cheek in her hand. "It was pretty hellish for me too, you know."

Rolling off her, he got comfortable. "Okay, so here's the thing — if I do this, then I'm pretty much staying here. This is where I'm going to be. I never thought I'd stay this long back in the place I grew up, but there it is." He paused. "I don't want us living in two separate houses." He turned his head to look at her. "I want to be where you are, but I want it to be a place that's ours — not your house I move into or my house you move into. Do you think with all your real estate savvy you could find us a place?"

They were words she never thought she'd hear from him.

"I know we never talked about it before," he went on, "but it's something I've been thinking about. Honestly, I thought about it a lot before. I probably should have said something sooner. I used to hate coming home to get a change of clothes or to sleep alone." He stroked her cheek. "I want to be where you are. Always."

"Oh, Quinn," she sighed. "I want that too."

"I want us to find something we can grow into . . . someplace big. With a huge master bedroom, so we can have a king-size bed and one of those big bathtubs, because the thought of being in one of those with you has kind of been a fantasy of mine."

She elbowed him. "Stop. It has not."

He nodded. "Has too. And we'll need a room big enough for a game room — you know, pool table, dartboard, maybe a foosball table or one of those air hockey ones."

"You've really put some thought into this," she said with a laugh.

"Definitely. And we'll need an outdoor kitchen with one of those huge grills because you know how much I love it when you make things on the grill."

She nodded. "Anything else? An indoor basketball court? Olympic-size swimming pool?"

"Nah, I think I hit all the important stuff. And word around town is you are the queen of finding the perfect house for interested buyers. So what do you say? Know of any houses that fit my description, Miss Realtor of the Month? Who am I kidding? You'll end up being Realtor of the Year in no time."

"Um, funny you should mention it because . . . I think I'm giving up that particular career."

He let out a very loud sigh of relief. "Thank God."

Raising her head, she looked at him questioningly. "What? Why do you say that?"

"Baby, I knew it wasn't the right career for you, but I wanted to support you. I knew pretty much from the beginning you weren't happy, and I hated it for you, but after a while, you were making it work, so I kept my mouth shut. Whatever it is you want to do, I'm here for you. I'm sure Steve would give you your old job back, and if it's not enough for you, I'm sure one of my brothers would love to have you working for them. I mean, Aidan's company is growing and he could use someone like you in the office, and with Hugh's resort getting ready to start going up, you know he'd need the help. And —"

"Slow down, slow down," she chuckled. "I don't need your brothers to help me out. I actually got a pretty sweet offer last night." Then she laughed even harder when she felt him stiffen beside her. Playfully, she smacked at his chest. "Oh, don't go getting all freaked out. Steve offered the pub to me."

"Seriously? Anna, that's freaking fabulous! And I think it's the perfect job for you because you love that place!" And then he kissed her again and relaxed beside her.

She told him of Steve's plans and how she felt a little guilty for even considering his offer. "He deserves to make some money off the sale of the business, Quinn. It just feels wrong to let him sign it over to me like that."

"Steve doesn't strike me as the kind of guy who would make an offer like that if he wasn't financially able to do it. He's been single his whole life, with no one to take care of but himself, and the pub has been a very lucrative business. If he's able to offer it to you on those terms and go into business with his buddies someplace tropical, then he must be doing all right."

"I guess," she sighed. "But I still feel weird about it. I just don't know how to counter his offer."

"How soon do you need to give him an answer?"

"He's not in a rush, but still, I feel like I should have something in mind."

"Well, to be fair, you only found out last

night and you've had an eventful twenty-four hours since."

"Eventful, huh?"

"Mmm-hmm," he hummed as his lips began to kiss a trail across her shoulder. "Some might even say adventurous."

She purred when he reached the sweet spot between her neck and shoulder. "Adventurous? Hmm . . . I'm not sure if that really describes this. I mean, we haven't left the bed other than to eat cereal and cold Chinese food."

"Yeah, I probably should buy some food," he murmured and then went back to gently biting her earlobe. "Later though."

"Yes. Much, much later."

"I am so, so sorry."

"I know."

"No, I'm serious. I can't even believe I did it. I'm, like, the worst."

"It's really not a big deal. I think things worked out for the best."

Zoe slouched down in her seat, arms crossed, and pouted. "Dammit, Anna! Would you just yell at me or something? I can't believe I fell asleep on you when you were stranded on the side of the road! I'm a horrible friend!"

Anna shrugged. "I'm not gonna lie to you.

I pretty much wished hateful things on you right after it happened, but, like I said, I think things worked out for the best." Both women turned and looked at the brothers who were standing by the grill in Aidan's backyard, talking.

Once Anna and Quinn had resurfaced from their twenty-four hours in bed, Anna had found that Zoe had left multiple voice mail messages for her, each one desperately begging for forgiveness. Apparently, she had thought Anna was purposely ignoring her calls. It wasn't until Anna finally called her friend back that Zoe had realized Anna had had a good reason for ignoring everyone's calls.

As much as Anna was enjoying reuniting with Quinn and all the ways they had been rediscovering one another, when Zoe extended the invitation to dinner a few days later, Anna had accepted. Luckily, Quinn had readily agreed.

"You must have a guardian angel watching over you, my friend, because it was dangerous for you to be out there by yourself."

"What was I supposed to do? No one would answer their phones, and those who did fell back to sleep," she said with an evil grin.

"Thank you! That's what I needed!" Zoe cried. "Be sure to throw it back at me a few more times. I mean it."

"Oh, stop. I'm fine, the car's fine . . ."

Zoe leveled her with a glare. "By fine I hope you mean Quinn put it out of its misery and got rid of it."

Anna nodded with a big smile. "I have my Honda back and all is right with the world."

"Thank God. Not that I'm saying Bobby did anything wrong, but clearly the dealership must have refused that thing as a trade-in."

"Yeah, I haven't gone there with him yet, but at some point I will."

"Have you talked to him at all? Is he settling in?"

"It's really only been a few days. I talked to him briefly yesterday, but he was dealing with the cable guy and getting all his games and gadgets hooked up, so he was a little distracted."

"Did you tell him about you and Quinn?"

"I did," she said with a nod. "And believe it or not, he was happy. Genuinely happy. He even invited us to come down and spend a weekend with him." She chuckled. "I never thought I'd live to see the day when my brother would be willing — and happy — to spend time with Quinn."

"How does Quinn feel about it? Do you think they finally had it out with one another?"

"Neither of them mentioned anything. I just think Bobby knows I'm happy and he's happy for me. I think his issue with Quinn had a lot to do with the way he didn't return my feelings for all those years."

"Well, duh. We all knew that. You're the only one who seemed to not get the memo."

"Yeah, well, sometimes ignorance is bliss."

"So what's next for you guys? I heard about the restoration gig Quinn got offered. Is he going to take it?"

Anna shared with Zoe all their plans — the restoration work, the pub, and the house.

"That's awesome!" she squealed and then leaned in close. "But don't tell Aidan about it. If he hears about the game room idea, he'll want one too and I just cannot handle the thought of it."

"Oh, come on. It could be fun. You could convert the room over the garage!"

Zoe shook her head. "No way. No one is changing that space. It's the first place Aidan and I . . ." She stopped and cleared her throat. "Never mind. Let's just say that space is not an option."

"Ugh, too much information."

Zoe merely grinned.

Aidan and Quinn walked over. "The steaks are almost ready," Aidan said, kissing Zoe on the top of her head. "What else do we need to do?"

Zoe stood and kissed him back. "I've got everything else ready in the kitchen. All you need to do is bring the steaks in. Anna made potato salad, and I've got a big tossed salad ready and waiting." She walked away and Anna followed. Together, they put everything on the dining room table and soon the four of them were sitting down to eat.

"I talked to Riley yesterday," Aidan said to no one in particular.

"Oh yeah? How is he?" Quinn asked.

"Weird." He took another bite of his steak. "He's moved on from that annoying state of paranoia he's been in and onto some sort of needy, clingy . . . I don't know. All he kept talking about was the importance of family and how great it is how we're all so close. He mentioned us all going away together on vacation — something about how our wedding was so magical because we were all together under one roof."

"Yikes," Quinn said and took a sip of his drink. "That's not weird. That's scary weird."

"Oh, stop," Anna said. "Has it occurred

to either of you that maybe he's just lonely? Maybe being surrounded by a bunch of kiss-asses isn't all it's cracked up to be?"

"Hell no," the brothers said at the same time and then laughed.

"I don't think it's a bad idea," Zoe said. "Maybe we should give it some thought. Instead of going to Australia, we could —"

Aidan immediately cut her off. "Don't even think about it! We have been planning this and planning this and planning this," he repeated for emphasis. "I am not giving that up for anyone — not even my brother!"

"Sheesh, relax," Zoe grumbled. "It was just a suggestion."

"Well, don't go suggesting it to anyone else," Aidan said. "If Riley's got a need for some family time, he's going to have to come to each of us individually. We all have lives and we can't just drop everything to accommodate him."

"I agree," Quinn added. "This is essentially where he'd get to see almost everyone, but with me getting the restoration business off the ground and Anna taking over the pub—"

"Hugh building the resort and Aubrey's advancing pregnancy," Zoe added.

"I've got two subdivisions going up and Zoe's business with Martha is expanding,"

Aidan said.

"Okay, so we've pretty much established how we all lead very busy lives," Anna finally said. "But it doesn't answer the question of why Riley's looking for some family time."

"He mentioned he's having some issues finishing the new CD," Aidan said after a minute. "And he knows he needs to do something about it and needs to start getting some publicity for it."

"He better not think we're going to jump on the PR bandwagon," Quinn said with a laugh. "Can you imagine? Like a Shaughnessy reality series or something?" Then he laughed even harder.

"Oh, good grief," Aidan said in disgust. "No one needs to see that."

"Exactly. Maybe I should give him a call tomorrow and feel him out a bit," Quinn said. "What do you think?"

"I don't know. Maybe."

"Maybe one of you should talk to Owen first," Anna suggested. "You know they're the closest out of all of you. Maybe he'll have a little insight into what's going on with Riley."

Aidan and Quinn looked at one another. "You may be onto something there," Quinn said, winking at her. "I'll do that."

Anna smiled at him.

"So, Australia . . ." Quinn said — officially changing the subject.

Later that night, Anna was curled up against Quinn's side, this time in her bed. "I hate to say it, but I like your bed better. It's much bigger."

"Yeah, but there's something to be said about a smaller bed — you're forced to stay close to me. Where you belong."

She couldn't help but sigh when he said things like that. Knowing him for as long as she had, Anna knew he didn't normally talk so sweet, so mushy, to anyone.

Only her.

That put a smile on her face.

When she remained silent, Quinn said, "I want you to know I'm going to try very hard to be a better man, Anna, someone who's worthy of you."

Raising her head from his shoulder, she looked at him. "Let me tell you something, Quinn Shaughnessy — you're a good man. One of the best men I've ever known. Remember how you once told me I didn't have to change — how I was fine the way I was? Well, I feel the same way about you. There's nothing wrong with either of us. We need to remember that even though our relationship has changed a bit, we're still the same people. We need to talk to each other when something is bothering us."

Quinn chuckled.

"What? What's so funny?"

"The last time I tried telling you something was bothering me, you kind of beat me up."

That had her laughing too. "And how many times in our lives have I done that to you?"

Quinn thought about it for a minute. "A lot."

"Okay, so why would that change? I've always been prone to doing that when you're being a jerk."

"And yet I don't retaliate."

"Maybe not with your hands, but certainly with your attitude," she replied.

"Attitude? Me? I don't know what you're talking about."

That had her laughing even harder. "Quinn, you are the king of attitude."

"But you love me anyway, right?"

Slowly, Anna crawled on top of him until she was straddling him. "Yes."

"Say it," he whispered. "I need to hear you say it."

Reaching out, she skimmed her fingers across his cheek. "I love you, Quinn Shaughnessy. From the very first day when we snuck into my house and stole those chocolate chip cookies and then hid behind the jungle gym, I was hooked."

"You may not believe it, but that day I got hooked on you too. It just took a little longer for me to realize it."

"Twenty-four years, but who's counting," she teased.

One of Quinn's hands came up and curved around her nape. "I'm a slow learner."

"It's okay. You were worth the wait."

"You're not going to have to wait anymore."

She looked at him oddly.

Carefully, he sat up, keeping his hands on Anna's hips to keep her in place. "I had lunch with Aidan a couple of weeks ago, and he asked me where I saw our relationship going. At the time, I was feeling scared and insecure, but it got me thinking. All these years that I was — as everyone has reminded me — serial dating, it was because I couldn't see myself with any of them."

"Quinn —"

"No, no . . . hear me out. Please." He paused. "I couldn't see myself with any woman, and yet whenever I thought about my future, you were there. Always." His hands left her hips and traveled up until he was cupping her face. "You're my past, my present, and my future. You're my life, Anna. I love you."

She sighed and leaned down to kiss him. "I love you too."

"I know I just said I was a slow learner, but it's one of the things I'm working hard to change. Anna Hannigan, will you marry me? Be my best friend, my partner, my wife? Will you stay by my side and kick my ass when I need it, and love me and bake me cookies in the middle of the night?"

She smiled. "That's a pretty specific list you got there."

"Well, the cookie part is negotiable, but not the rest. What do you say, Anna? Will you marry me?"

Tears filled her eyes and emotion clogged her throat. All she could do was nod as her hands went over her heart.

Quinn's thumbs instantly went to work wiping away her tears. "I told you I never wanted to be the reason you cried."

"These are good tears," she finally said. "Really good tears."

He visibly relaxed and let one thumb glide across her bottom lip. "Good or bad, I hate to see you cry, baby."

"I'm afraid you're stuck with this," she

said. "If we get married, you're going to have to deal with the fact that I will cry from time to time."

"*If?* If we get married?" he croaked.

She chuckled and leaned her forehead against his. "I meant when. I'm marrying you, Quinn. You're not getting out of it."

"I don't want to get out of it. You're it for me." His arms banded around her as he twisted until she was sprawled out beneath him. "Forever, Anna."

Yeah . . . she really liked the sound of that.

EPILOGUE

Six months later . . .

"This is how life was meant to be lived."

"You got that right."

"Why don't we live this way?"

"Because we're poor and have to work."

"Oh yeah. I temporarily forgot about that. Thanks for the reality check." Anna stretched out on the chaise lounge by the pool on her belly and simply sighed with happiness.

"It's what I do," Zoe said from her chaise beside her.

Aubrey hummed her approval, rubbing her hand over her very swollen belly. "Although I have a feeling we're going to get caught."

The three women were out in Quinn and Anna's new backyard, sitting around the pool in new lounge chairs. The sun was shining, there was a beautiful breeze, and right then, it was downright heavenly.

"I have to agree with Aubrey," Zoe said.

Anna lifted her head and looked at her. "What makes you think that?"

"We've been out here for almost thirty minutes and we were supposed to be making lunch. It's only a matter of time before one of the guys comes looking for us — and food," Aubrey said. "And to be honest, I am kind of hungry."

"You're always hungry," Zoe reminded her.

"I do feel a little bit guilty about it," Anna said. "Not that you're always hungry, but how I don't have a whole lot here for you to nosh on."

"So maybe we should go and fess up and ask the guys to take a break. We can go into town and grab something to eat," Aubrey suggested.

"Nah. There is so much stuff still on the moving truck. There's no way they're going to even notice we're not around or that lunch isn't ready yet."

The sound of a male clearing his voice had them looking up.

"Uh-oh," Zoe murmured.

It wasn't one Shaughnessy male; it was all of them. Plus one Hannigan.

Anna jumped up from her chaise and stood, almost falling over. "Oh, hey, guys!

How's it going?"

"We're all busting our asses getting the truck unloaded and you're out here sunning yourself?" Bobby snapped. "How the hell is that fair?"

"Okay . . . I know it looks bad, or like we're just slacking off, but —"

"It looks that way because it is that way." Aidan chuckled. He looked at his wife and shook his head. "I'm ashamed of all of you."

"Um, Aubrey," Hugh said, "I don't think it's a good idea for you to be out here in this heat. You should be inside where the air-conditioning is running."

She waved him off. "I'm fine. It was just so relaxing out here, *was* being the operative word."

Quinn stepped forward menacingly, but there was a glint of humor in his eyes as he made his way toward Anna. "We just spent the better part of an hour getting our bedroom set up because you specifically mentioned it was the most important room, and instead of making lunch, you're out here sunning yourself. Do I have that right?"

She took a step backward and knew she was in trouble. "Okay, I'll admit it was a little wrong of me to take an extended break while you're all working so hard. But . . . but . . ."

"An extended break?" Quinn repeated with a grin. "Is that what we're calling it? When did you even have time to unpack your bathing suit?"

Okay, that one will take a little explaining, she thought. "I . . . um . . . I wore it under my clothes so I could cool off if I needed to."

"We'd all like to cool off, but you said we needed to get the truck unloaded first."

"All right, I'm sorry!" she said, a nervous laugh escaping as she noticed she was getting dangerously close to the edge of the pool.

"No, no," he pressed, "you said you needed to cool off . . ."

"Quinn . . . don't you dare," she said, holding her hands out to stop him. "I swear I'll go inside right now and make lunch."

He shook his head. "Not good enough."

Anna shrieked when he lunged at her.

"Wait a minute, wait a minute, wait a minute!" Zoe yelled, coming to her feet. "It's not her fault."

Quinn paused and turned to look at his sister-in-law. "I'm sure you're just trying to buy her some time, but go ahead and humor us. How is this *not* Anna's fault?"

"Zoe," Aidan began a bit hesitantly.

"No, no, no . . . it's okay. First, I ordered

pizza for everyone for lunch, and it should be here soon."

"You did?" Anna asked. "Why didn't you tell me?"

Zoe shrugged. "I got sidetracked."

"Ooo . . . so there's food on the way?" Aubrey asked, slowly coming to her feet with her husband's assistance. "Please tell me one of those pizzas has bacon on it!"

Zoe grimaced. "I cannot wait for you to have that baby because your food cravings are making me queasy!"

Quinn looked between the two women quizzically. "Okay, so you ordered lunch. That still doesn't excuse Anna's hanging out here relaxing — in her bikini, no less — while I'm sweating my ass off!" He tried to sound angry, but he didn't quite pull it off.

"I asked Anna and Aubrey to come out here and sit with me because I needed to talk to them. But then we got all comfortable and talking about the house and I never got to tell them what I needed to."

Anna stepped forward. "Are you all right? Is everything okay?"

Aidan came to stand beside his wife and wrapped his arm around her waist. Zoe looked at him and smiled. "We're having a baby!"

In the blink of an eye, everyone was

around them, offering congratulations and hugs and well wishes.

"When did you find out?" Anna asked, squeezing Zoe's hand.

"I went to my doctor yesterday to confirm. Looks like we conceived him or her while we were on vacation in Sydney!" Zoe looked over at Hugh. "Your resort there was especially romantic and will always hold a special place in our hearts."

Hugh grinned. "That's great! But I hope you won't mind if I don't use that blurb in a travel brochure or anything."

"Shut up," Aidan said, but he was smiling from ear to ear. He looked at everyone. "I told Zoe I didn't want her lifting anything heavy today so that's why she lured the girls out here."

"Not that I could do anything either," Aubrey added and then looked back toward the house. "So . . . do we know exactly when the pizza is going to get here?"

"Oh, for the love of it," Anna said. "Go inside. There's some fruit and crackers in the kitchen." She looked at Hugh. "Go and make sure your wife doesn't pass out from starvation," she teased.

Everyone was talking at once, and a few minutes later, the sound of a car horn beeping quieted them. "I bet that's lunch," Zoe said and led the group out of the yard and into the house. Everyone followed except Anna and Quinn.

She looked at him shyly. "Are you really mad?"

He grabbed one of her hands and pulled her in close before kissing her soundly. "Mad?" He shook his head. "Not really. Although I hate how you're parading around here in this bikini while everyone's here."

She rolled her eyes. "We have been over this before — multiple times! It's not a big deal!"

He shrugged. "To me it is."

Wrapping her arms around him, she pressed up against him. "I'll tell you what, when everyone's gone, I'll parade around all you want, just for you."

A grin slowly crossed his face. "Oh yeah?"

She nodded. "Yeah." Looking over her shoulder to make sure no one was within earshot, she added, "I'll even parade around back here in nothing at all and we can go skinny-dipping."

He groaned. "I'm going to hold you to that," he said and kissed her again.

"Now come on, or all the pizza will be gone." She turned to walk away, but Quinn grabbed her hand.

"Not so fast."

"What? What's the matter?"

Without a word of warning, he tugged her in close, and before she knew it, Quinn had swung her up in his arms and was moving close to the side of the pool.

"Quinn! No! Don't! I said I was sorry!" Then she was flailing in midair before splashing into the icy-cold water. She went under and quickly came up sputtering. Swimming to the side of the pool, she shook her hair out and away from her face. "You are going to pay for that!"

"You'll have to catch me first," he teased, but made no attempt to move.

"I didn't say you'd have to pay right now," she said calmly, climbing from the pool. When she was standing right in front of him, dripping wet, she looked up and smiled.

Quinn's eyes were locked on her glistening body, and he swallowed hard. "We . . . um . . . we should get inside," he said, his voice low and gravelly.

"Mmm . . . we should," she said quietly, closing the distance between them. Her arms went around his shoulders as she plastered her wet body against his. She was just about to kiss him — distract him, actually — before dragging him back into the pool with her, when Bobby shouted from the door.

"We've got an emergency in here!" he yelled.

Anna and Quinn instantly broke apart and dashed for the house. "What is it?" Quinn asked as they stepped inside. "What's going on?"

"Aubrey's water broke!" Zoe said with a huge grin.

Hugh was running from room to room, collecting their things, while Aubrey looked at everyone and smiled. "Sorry to cost you a mover," she said and then winced with pain. "But we really need to be going."

Riley looked over at Bobby. "Come on, Mr. Policeman. We're going to need a designated driver who can get us to the hospital and knows the fastest way to get there."

"Yes, please," Aubrey said with a tight smile. "I don't think Hugh can drive right now. Or at least he shouldn't."

Bobby looked over at Quinn and Anna and smiled apologetically. "Sorry, but duty calls."

"Don't worry about it," Anna said. "Just go. We'll be there as soon as we can!"

Five minutes later, Hugh, Aubrey, Riley, and Bobby were gone. Anna looked around and quickly did the math — Quinn, Aidan,

Ian, Owen, and her dad, plus herself and Zoe were all that were left. Everyone was eating pizza and talking excitedly about how there was soon going to be a new family member joining them.

Anna felt slightly overwhelmed — not about the move, but about life. So much was happening, changing. Quinn looked over, caught her expression, and instantly walked over and wrapped her in his arms.

"You okay?" he whispered.

"For so long, it seemed like nothing ever happened around here. Everything was always the same and I used to almost resent it. And now, in just a short amount of time, everything's changed."

He tucked a finger under her chin and forced her to look at him. "But they're all good changes," he said.

She nodded. "I know. But we have so much going on, and yet I look at Hugh and Aubrey and now Aidan and Zoe and . . . I'm envious."

His eyes went a little wide. "Yeah?"

She nodded. "Yeah." Then she shrugged. "I know we haven't talked a lot about it and we're so busy and we're planning a wedding, but . . . I wouldn't mind doing something small like Aidan and Zoe did and . . . and starting our own family."

Quinn looked around the room and frowned. "I kind of wish we weren't talking about this with our families here."

"Why?"

"Because if we were alone, I'd strip that tiny bikini off you right now and start working on that family," he growled against her ear. "Then I'd book us on the next flight to Vegas and marry you tonight."

She almost swooned at his words. "And I would love every second of it."

"How about we —"

"Okay," Ian called out. "Break time's over. We have a lot to do and I know I'm not the only one who is anxious to get to the hospital and wait for the baby to be born."

"How much is left on the truck?" Anna asked.

"If you hadn't been sunbathing, you'd know that," Quinn teased, and she elbowed him in the ribs. "Ow!"

"We have two rooms of furniture left and about two dozen boxes," Ian said. "Now I don't mean to be rude, but I think we should just get the boxes in their proper rooms and get the furniture unloaded, and we can come back tomorrow and help you get it all in place, if that's all right. I'd really like to run home and shower before going to the hospital. It's not every day a man gets to meet his first grandchild for the first time."

Tears were back in Anna's eyes and Quinn pulled her close before addressing everyone. "Okay, I agree with Dad. If everyone can give us an hour, I think we can empty the truck. If anyone wants to shower here, you're more than welcome to, but I can't guarantee I know where the towels and soap are just yet."

Rather than answer, everyone sprang into action. Anna pulled on her shorts and T-shirt over her bathing suit and joined in. She assigned Zoe to unpacking the master bathroom box just in case anyone took Quinn up on his offer to shower.

In an hour, they were done and people were all filing out the door with the promise to meet up at the hospital. When the last car pulled out of the driveway, Quinn turned to Anna and swung her up into his arms.

"Quinn? What in the world?"

"This is our first home and I am carrying you over the threshold."

"That's what you do when you get married," she said with a laugh.

He shook his head. "Well, I'm changing things up and doing it now." He walked them into the house and kicked the door closed behind him. Carefully he locked the door and continued to carry her up the stairs of their new two-story home and into their bedroom. The room was a mess — the furniture was all in its place but there were no blankets or sheets on the bed and no curtains on the windows.

When he placed her down on the bed and smiled, Anna smiled back. "Wow! That was kind of fun. We may need to make that a thing."

"Don't get used to it. That was a lot of stairs."

"Hey!"

He chuckled. "Just kidding." And then he stretched out beside her. "Welcome home, Anna."

"Welcome home, Quinn," she replied. They lay there in companionable silence for several minutes before Zoe said, "I think we need to get showered and changed and head to the hospital. I know first babies normally take a while, but nothing about Aubrey's pregnancy has been typical. I wouldn't be surprised if everything went really fast."

Rather than moving and getting up, Quinn began to kiss her shoulder, then her neck and her cheek.

"Um . . . this isn't helping us get ready," Anna purred.

"I disagree." His hand trailed up her thigh to the button on her shorts and quickly popped it open.

"Quinn . . . we need . . . We have to —"

His lips claimed hers, effectively cutting off anything she was about to say. When he finally lifted his head, he gazed into her big brown eyes. "I was thinking about what we talked about earlier. I'm not saying we have to run off to Vegas tonight — or at all — but I certainly wouldn't mind getting in a little practice on making a baby before we head to the hospital."

Anna smiled up at him and continued to smile as he stripped off her shorts, shirt, and bikini. His hand rested on her flat belly, and he smiled as she sighed his name.

"This would be a big change," he said softly.

"Quite possibly the biggest one yet."

"Are you sure about this?"

As much as she wanted to accuse him of being a chicken, she suddenly was one too. "Maybe we can talk about it a little bit more after we come back from the hospital. Or after we babysit a couple of times."

Quinn stripped his shirt off and grinned. "I think that sounds perfect." He stood and kicked off his jeans, sneakers, socks, and briefs before joining her back on the bed.

"We should probably let Aidan and Zoe have the spotlight for a little bit longer too."

She nodded. "And when it's our turn, we'll know it is the perfect time."

"You know it."

Even though they knew there was someplace they needed to be, Quinn made love to her slowly, sweetly, perfectly.

And later, as they stood side by side smiling into the nursery to meet their new nephew, Quinn squeezed her hand. "Yeah, I definitely want one of those with you."

"Just one?"

He shook his head. "Hell no. We're going to need our own little league team!"

She rolled her eyes.

"Just think, we can have our own team and challenge all the other teams in the community, and I can train them at home. The yard is big enough for a T-ball stand. How early is too early to start kids on learning how to hit a ball?"

Anna could only chuckle. There was one thing she was certain of — her life with her best friend, the man she loved, was never going to be boring.

And she wouldn't have it any other way.

ABOUT THE AUTHOR

New York Times and *USA Today* bestselling author **Samantha Chase** released her debut novel, *Jordan's Return,* in November 2011. Although she waited until she was in her forties to publish for the first time, writing has been a lifelong passion. Her motivation was her students: teaching creative writing to elementary-age students all the way up through high school and encouraging those students to follow their writing dreams gave Samantha the confidence to take that step as well.

When she's not working on a new story, Samantha spends her time reading contemporary romances, blogging, playing way too many games of Scrabble or solitaire on Facebook, and spending time with her husband of twenty-five years and their two sons in North Carolina.

The employees of Thorndike Press hope you have enjoyed this Large Print book. All our Thorndike, Wheeler, and Kennebec Large Print titles are designed for easy reading, and all our books are made to last. Other Thorndike Press Large Print books are available at your library, through selected bookstores, or directly from us.

For information about titles, please call:
    (800) 223-1244

or visit our Web site at:
    http://gale.cengage.com/thorndike

To share your comments, please write:
    Publisher
    Thorndike Press
    10 Water St., Suite 310
    Waterville, ME 04901